- - - - - - - - -

The

Potency

of

Ungovernable

Impulses

Also by
MALKA OLDER

MALKA OLDER

The

Potency

of

Ungovernable

Impulses

Tor Publishing Group

New York

THE POTENCY OF UNGOVERNABLE IMPULSES

Copyright © 2025 by Malka Older

A Tor Book
Published by Tom Doherty Associates / Tor Publishing Group
120 Broadway
New York, NY 10271

www.torpublishinggroup.com

Tor® is a registered trademark of Macmillan Publishing Group, LLC.

The Library of Congress Cataloging-in-Publication Data
is available upon request.

ISBN 978-1-250-39606-8 (hardcover)
ISBN 978-1-250-39607-5 (ebook)

Our books may be purchased in bulk for promotional, educational, or business use. Please contact your local bookseller or the Macmillan Corporate and Premium Sales Department at 1-800-221-7945, extension 5442, or by email at MacmillanSpecialMarkets@macmillan.com.

First Edition: 2025

Printed in the United States of America

0 9 8 7 6 5 4 3 2 1

For all the good academics

Don't be a comemierda.

- - - - - - - - -

The

Potency

of

Ungovernable

Impulses

Prologue

There were not so many places to lurk in the scholars' residence on Thanma Street. Certainly, to while away some time while waiting out a storm or for a visitor, the place was replete with comfortable options: the library; the game room; the common room, if one could gain access. But furtively keeping an eye on a scholar's accommodations was more difficult, the narrow landings offering little but those austerely closed doors. In principle, Mossa approved of the protection from outside eyes; in practice, she had found herself unable to knock and unwilling to return home and extremely averse to being the object of pitying or curious glances.

Fortunately (or un-; perhaps a complete lack of cover would have goaded her into a more salubrious decision?) there was an access panel that allowed for repairs to the dumbwaiter shaft from the landing. There was always something in people's lives that they wanted to pretend was magic and effortless; hiding those mechanics usually offered hiding places for less desired intrusions as well. Mossa crouched there, the panel door pulled almost shut, and argued with herself until she heard footsteps and pressed her eye to the opening.

A person with an amiable gait toddled up to the door in question. Even expecting it, the knock made Mossa flinch; she closed her eyes before the door opened. She had already recognized

Lessenan, a scholar with rooms on the next floor up, and was unsurprised at her opening sally.

"Hullo, Pleiti! What do you think about a concert tonight?"

Lessenan had a conveniently loud baseline tone; the reply was more of an uncertain murmur. Mossa opened her eyes again, but Lessenan also had a large and inconveniently located back.

"It's the Classical orchestra. They're doing Maalouf in the first section and the Indigo Girls in the second. Come along, do, it's been ages since we've been to a show."

Go ahead, get out, enjoy yourself, Mossa thought, and at the same time, less coherently, hoped that wouldn't happen.

"Well," came the reply, a little clearer this time (that would be Pleiti remembering that Lessenan was hard of hearing). "Well, no, I think I'll stay in tonight."

"Waiting for someone?" Lessenan asked, all twinkly.

"No . . . no. Just, you know . . . busy. And the fog is terrible. Maybe another night?"

"I'll hold you to that!" Lessenan was cheerful, pleasant, in a committed ace relationship, and not inclined to women. Mossa knew she needn't feel the faintest twinge of jealousy, but in her current state it was impossible for her to imagine Pleiti wanting her, or benefitting from her association in any way, and so even Lessenan seemed like a rival. No, not a rival even: simply a better option.

Mossa leaned her forehead against the too-close wall. She should leap from this ridiculous shelf she was huddled on and go to the woman who was obviously waiting for her. Or if she couldn't, really, *really* couldn't, she should send Pleiti some excuse so she would know she was free to attend the theater with whomever she liked.

Instead Mossa stayed in the access cubbyhole for some indeterminate amount of time, her temple against the cool wall of it. She should go in, she should go in, she should free Pleiti entirely or she should go in and love her.

It took so much effort to push open the panel, unfold her legs, and stand up in some posture approximating upright. She looked at the door, imagined Pleiti on the other side, comfortable and happy by the fire.

She should go in.

But instead she turned for the stairs.

Chapter 1

A storm was writhing over Valdegeld, its tendrils churning Giant's ever-present fog and pressing sleet and freezing rain through the atmoshield and onto the august buildings of Valdegeld University and auxiliaries, including my—less august, but evocative and comfortable—lodgings.

I had canceled my last tutorial of the day, knowing the student needed more time to gnaw on their thesis in any case, and had long since been ensconced in my rooms with a blazing fire, a pot of tea, and a plate of scones up from the kitchens. I had spent a few dutiful hours with my work, but as the evening wore on I had decided it was well past time for leisure and switched to a Modern novel instead, a tale of early settlement derring-do and romance, with a railcar heist and a space shuttle rescue that fit the mood of the evening.

I had been rather hoping that Mossa would come for a visit. She had been somewhat, amorphously, absent of late; uncommunicative, or offering excuses that seemed reasonable until considered in bulk. I had been trying for some time not to feel worried about the situation—surely, after all we had been through together, *surely* if something was wrong she would tell me?—and I did not want to miss any opportunity for intimacy with her, so when a friend suggested going for a concert that night I refused, just in case. However, if she were to join me that evening I would have thought she would arrange to arrive before the worst of the storm, and my hopes had dimmed considerably when a knock on my door raised them again.

I opened it with Mossa's name on my lips, only to see instead a narrow wedge of a woman, her coif showing some of the effects of the storm, a dripping raincoat and atmoscarf over her arm and a determined smile on her face. "Hullo, Pleiti," she said, a little hesitantly. "How are pubs?"

Her face was uncertainly familiar, but I couldn't immediately identify it, not when I was expecting to see Mossa's instead. Before I could make too great a fool of myself, Nakalo the porter leaned around her shoulder. "Sorry for bringing her up directly, but as a scholar and she said she knows you from student days . . ."

Bless him, the name popped right into my head. "Petanj! It's been so long. Er, would you like to come in?"

She hesitated. "Not if it's not a good time for you. Or, well, we could meet somewhere else, it's just, there's a small matter . . ."

I tend to be somewhat jealous of my rooms, but I had become slightly more sociable of late, and in any case the unheralded appearance of an acquaintance on such a night had aroused my curiosity. "Not at all, not at all." I mouthed a *thank you* to Nakalo behind her back as I closed the door and ushered her to the fireplace, wondering the while. I knew Petanj, as Nakalo had intimated, from when I had been at Valdegeld the first time, as a student; like me, she had since earned a place as a scholar—even before I had, if I recalled right—but she was in the Modern faculty, less prestigious than my Classical appointment. As the faculties didn't mix very much, and we hadn't been especially close as students, I didn't see her often; indeed, I wasn't sure I'd met her more than once since returning to Valdegeld. For her to appear in my rooms, therefore, particularly on such a tempestuous night, suggested some significant motivation for the visit.

"Thank you," she said, letting me take her raincoat to hang it up. "I know it's unconscionable, my coming here without any warning, but I just don't know where else to turn."

"Oh?" I couldn't imagine in what arena I could be a place for her to turn, but my heart was beating faster nonetheless. "Please tell me what I can do for you. But first—some tea? Something to warm you? It's horrid out."

"It *is*. Tea would be lovely, thank you." There was a brief silence while I put in the order, and it stretched after I had seated myself. At last Petanj swallowed and spoke. "Forgive me again for the intrusion. I . . . well, I have heard that you had a, er, a connexion of some kind with the Investigators . . . ?"

I answered as carelessly as I could. "Oh, you mean Mossa. She's not here tonight, but I'm sure . . . Didn't you know her at school?"

"Not—not very well." I wondered if the tinge of embarrassment was from vaguely disliking Mossa (as many people did) or from liking her too much (as some people surely did as well). "Is that . . . well, what I mean to say is, perhaps you can help."

I hoped my face was bland. "If you're looking for an Investigator—" I hesitated. It would be rude to tell her to go directly to their bureau; unbearable to think that if I sent her to Mossa's place Petanj might see her before I would; presumptuous to the point of risible to suggest I could manage whatever it was instead.

"No! No. I was hoping for you, in fact." I felt my eyebrows rise in disbelief. "That is . . ." She twisted her hands. "When I heard about the things you've done recently, you and Mossa, well—I thought perhaps you could help me. An Investigator . . . well, they might help or they might make it worse, if you understand."

The service bell dinged, and I stood to get the tea, considering what she meant. "It's a . . . a reputational matter?"

"Exactly," Petanj agreed hurriedly. "Exactly that."

Everything seemed much easier suddenly. "Not to worry. Mossa is entirely discreet—" I hesitated again. She *was,* but it also seemed very unlikely that she'd be even distantly piqued by the sorts of petty academic bickering that I imagined we were talking about (*especially,* my undermind whispered, *in her current range of moods*). "And she's much more understanding of, er, academic *nuance* than most. But she is quite busy, of course . . ."

"Yes, I'm sure. And her responsibility will be to the Investigators' Bureau, naturally, and I'm not sure that those official channels would be the wisest approach for this. They might not understand the, the seriousness of it."

"Precisely," I agreed, pleased to have found a potential excuse that wasn't solely reliant on Mossa's personal inclination. "If she's wil—that is, if she has availability to take on an additional case, I can tell her what we've discussed."

"Then you'll listen?" Petanj leaned forward with such a melodramatic mien that I instantly felt guilty.

"I may not be able to help at all, mind. But yes, I'll listen."

"That alone would be an enormous relief." Petanj took a fortifying sip of tea, then leaned back and began her tale. "I am not here for myself really, but for my cousin, Villette."

"I remember you were close," I commented, pouring.

"Yes, more sisters than cousins. We grew up on a small platform and—in short. I don't know if you heard, but a few years ago Villette received an appointment in the Modern faculty at Stortellen." I clicked my fingertips in polite admiration. Our

Classical faculty was far more renowned, but in Modern studies Stortellen was nearly as well-thought-of as Valdegeld. "She was quite pleased, and I was naturally very proud, although we did hope at some point in the future we might find appointments in closer proximity." Stortellen was about as far away as it was possible to get on the network of geo-synchronized rings and platforms that formed humanity's habitat on Giant; the initial logic, of course, being to provide universities within reasonable distance of all platforms.

But it was more than two days of travel between Valdegeld and Stortellen, and that if the connections were good; reasonable that these sisterly cousins might have wished to be closer together. Reasonable even that the distance might engender some worry. I wondered if Villette had disappeared, or if Petanj thought she might have; that seemed like the sort of problem she might have sought Mossa and myself out for, given our recent adventures.

Petanj was silent for a time, her lips pressed neatly together. I leaned forward to refresh her tea, though I didn't have quite enough in the pot to fill her cup all the way, and that seemed to rouse her. She lifted her cup, raised her eyes to mine. "She has come up for the possibility of a donship."

"Enhorabuena," I murmured, with surprise—at her age, it was quite an accolade—but Petanj had barely paused.

"It seemed likely, I thought. Then, last week, she was accused of falsifying data."

My stomach dropped. "In truth?" Mossa did not have much patience for meaningless expostulations, and I quickly gathered myself to say something useful. "Who accused her?"

"It was anonymous, which naturally created much skepticism, and perhaps it will come to nothing, but . . ."

"But of course they had to look into it." I still felt sick, imagining it. And I could see why she wouldn't want to go to the Investigators without a conduit; even those accustomed to working in university platforms would not fully understand the vital threat of your research being undermined; might not understand how devastating a careless investigation could be. All it would take was a thoughtless interview question—*Have you ever seen any suggestions of plagiarism by this person?*—to the wrong person, and an academic career could slip down the rungs of prestigious positions, or all too easily disappear altogether. I grasped for some cheer. "Well, and if the university *is* looking into it"—rather than dismissing her or quietly letting the donship possibility evaporate—"that is a hopeful sign, surely?"

"Yes. Yes, I do hope so. Villette has assured me there's no need to worry, she says it is certain that the evaluation will vindicate her. Of course, she *would* say that—because she herself knows she is innocent of any wrongdoing, you understand, but also because she's awfully trusting, my cousin." Petanj frunced slightly in disapproval. "She attributes to everyone a general good faith comparable to her own, but even more than that she has a confidence which I cannot at all share that institutions— well, the university in particular, but also the committees; the student guild; the Investigators, for that matter; et cetera, et cetera—are all doing their best towards their stated purpose."

This, too, started an uneasy resonance within me. I had been badly quaked by my university's role in the cases I had helped Mossa investigate, the more so because I had not realized I was so trusting of them.

"It *had* occurred to me to request a separate investigation of the accusations, in case the university efforts proved, let us say, insufficient. In truth, I have for some time wanted a confidant for these worries," Petanj admitted. "But I had not made up my mind to take such a step—I *know* Villette will call it unnecessary interference, although she might not mind so much if it's *you*, Pleiti—and if that were all I probably would not be here." She paused long enough that I itched to prompt her; but, again thinking of Mossa, I refrained. At last Petanj spoke again, her eyes fixed on my rug as though she were thinking carefully about each word. "Yesterday I received this letter."

I held out my hand almost without thinking (it was what Mossa would have done) and perused the laminate she handed me. "Troubling," I remarked, starting my first reread. The brief mentioned anonymous missives and malicious chisme, and urged Petanj to arrive as soon as possible *to urge caution on your cousin as only you can*; I was unsure how *caution* would help with these (presumably) foundless accusations. Did she fear some physical harm? That did seem suggested by the reference to *ambiguous alarums,* but perhaps that just meant the chisme. "But sadly lacking in specifics." There was something about the tone of the note—for it was little more than that—that worried me, as though the author intended some double meaning, or perhaps simple insincerity, but I couldn't be certain. It could even, I thought, be intended as either a threat or a cubreculo by the very author of Villette's distress. I peered at the signature: one Wojo K'tuvi, Modernist scholar. The name sounded distantly in my memory—perhaps I had seen it in a citation list in one of my few ventures into reading Modernist scholarship? Rather telling to sign with one's title, I always thought.

"Wojo is . . . particular, of course," Petanj said with a mueca, perhaps noticing my attention to the designation. "But I have gotten to know her better in my visits, and I do not think she would exaggerate such things. This has convinced me that there is a thorough-going effort to discredit my cousin; that even if the"—she lowered her voice, perhaps unconsciously— "*plagiarism* accusations are refuted, the campaign will likely continue—possibly even escalate."

I nodded slowly. I could imagine it all too distinctly: struggling with the obscure and onerous university bureaucracy, far from family and classmates who might support my reputation against slander, with a donship hazing in the balance like a gas-mirage.

"I wish I could trust that Stortellen will support her, but . . . Pleiti, I doubt you follow Modernist scholarship—"

"Very little," I admitted, with the requisite moue.

"Villette's research is . . . very successful, evidently, or they wouldn't be offering her the donship. But she . . . well, she's not very good at playing the loyal scholar, if you know what I mean—values the research itself more than her own prospects, do you see? And the university values it quite a bit more than they value *her*, if you ask me."

Again I made a noise of agreement, for this was passing relatable.

"And at the same time there are always people who are jealous or, well, they disagree with her research choices for one reason or another, as if it were any of their business. And I know Villette is determined that everything is fine, and would tell me not to worry, but . . ." Petanj twisted her hands, then went on with a bit of rue. "Perhaps I *am* worrying overmuch."

"Better than worrying too little," I offered, partly out of sympathy. I, too, was prone to excessive concern, and this scenario was more than enough to unleash it.

"Yes. I would rather be overattentive than regret the opposite. That's why I've decided to go to Stortellen immediately, to check on her—to support her and—and help in any way I can. I would have gone for the donship ceremony anyhap, so this just means leaving a little early. Will you come?"

I stared at her, although surely this was where the whole conversation had been leading. "Er . . . that is, I'm really not sure I can help in this case . . ."

"I realize this is not exactly what you have done in your past investigations," she said in a rush, "and I don't expect you to be an expert investigator, truly, I—I just would like someone on my side, and perhaps your experience will give you some perspective that I lack. If you would join," she added somewhat diffidently, "I could talk to Dean Mars. See about working out an arrangement." One that would mean I was not using my holiday time for this, I supposed. "And of course . . . if Mossa would—that is, if she has time . . . But even if she can't—" She was twisting her hands again, and somehow that decided me. "If you could see your way to join, it would mean so much . . ."

I was invigorated by a sudden sense more of purpose than of obligation, underpinned by the suspicion that working together with Mossa again might make it unnecessary to address her recent reticence. I handed the laminate back to Petanj crisply. "I'm with you. I'll go talk to Mossa tomorrow. When are you leaving?"

"As soon as possible. Perhaps tomorrow night? I'll send you the optimal itineraries." She tapped them over.

"Well then," I said, with more assurance than I felt. "I'll be in touch."

Chapter 2

It wasn't until I was on the brief railcar ride to Sembla (after a rather restless night and a few tasks that took up much of the daylight portion of the diurnal) that I counted up how long it had been since I'd been in the same room with Mossa. Perhaps I hadn't allowed myself to notice before; looked at squarely, it was certainly too long. Terrifying how quickly that gap had sidled into what I had thought of as a positive-trending, reasonably healthy relationship. We both had jobs, we lived on different platforms: we usually saw each other once, maybe twice in a week. Easy enough, then, for a few postponements with reasonable grounds to extend into more than a month of absence.

I tried to think back to the last time we met: Had I done something wrong? Disgusted her somehow? But ponder as I might, I could identify no moment of coolness, no fissure or argument. Perhaps it was nothing, and this distance really was the chance conjunction of mishaps.

Or perhaps it *was* nothing, and that was enough, because it didn't always require *something* happening to fall out of love.

It was full night when I arrived in Sembla, gaslights burnishing the metal of the platform, Ganymede glowing large in the sky. I hoped, as I ascended the ramps to Mossa's apartment, that she was still on this diurnal; her job sometimes required her to switch, but even back in university she had been liable to moods in which she lost track of time and slipped from one schedule to the other without recognizing the décalage.

My emotions floated as I saw the gleam of light from within outlining her door, and I knocked with perhaps more enthusiasm than necessary.

There was no answer, and I knocked again, calling out softly as I did to identify myself.

Silence.

Starting to feel worried—about Mossa's safety, now, as well as about her regard for me—I called out again: "Mossa?" My voice quavered and I started to consider how I could get in if she was hurt.

The lock clicked.

That was the remote key, and so when I pushed the door open I expected to see Mossa, as I had so many times before, standing at her desk in the alcove on the far side of the sala. Instead, she was sprawled on the divan, playing something intricate and quiet on her kinnor.

"Mossa!" I exclaimed, and then immediately modulated my tone, trying to fit the timbre of her music. "Are you well? We've a mystery to investigate."

She turned her eyes from the ceiling towards me without haste, and I had a brief fantastical fear that they would be blotted black, or bleeding, but her gaze seemed usual enough, if heavy-lidded. "Pleiti." Her voice was heavy too; perhaps she had been on the point of sleep when I arrived. I approached the divan, decelerating as I saw the detritus of empty glasses and unorganized laminates around it. And books, piles of books, and no fewer than three teapots on various surfaces, spouts ringed with tannin. She was wearing a silky garment I had seen before, more of a chemise than a robe. It must have had some sensory or talismanic significance for her, because I had noticed she wore it for comfort. (It had a sensory significance for me as well, although I wouldn't have tagged it as *comfort*.)

"Mossa," with more caution this time, "are you well?"

"Well. Well, Pleiti. Well enough."

I peered at her eyes in sudden alarm that my intrusive horror had been a premonition, but no, her pupils seemed normal; if she was altered, it was by her usual addictions: narrative, tea, music. "Come on then," I said, my cheerfulness tinny. "We've been asked for our help with a little matter, off in Stortellen, which should be entertaining—"

"No."

I couldn't think of anything to say but *No?* and Mossa hated meaningless repetition, and I repeated myself meaninglessly so often, maybe she hated me or maybe I was changing myself for her and that was a mistake or maybe I hadn't changed enough or—

"I'm not going to Stortellen." Lower: "I have no help to offer."

I swallowed. "It will be— The problem is an interesting one, actually, I think you would— That is, you remember Petanj? And her cousin Villette?" I held out the laminate I had brought with my notes from the conversation. "They have a spot of difficulty, a *delicate* matter. Surely—"

"No." Mossa felt around for something on the floor without looking, hoisted up three glasses before she found one with liquid in it. "Not. Going."

"You don't want to?" My voice rose plaintively on *want*, irradiate it all, I *knew* I shouldn't be like that, I was falling into the failed patterns of university as though we'd never left them (*had* we left them?). I should try something different, put a slap in my tone instead: *Get up this instant!* But I couldn't, I couldn't order Mossa around, not convincingly.

I put the laminate on the table and dropped into a crouch

beside her instead. "Mossa. I can see you're feeling a bit . . . a bit Jovian . . ." Too tentative, she was already scoffing.

"Pleiti, I am not going to Stortellen. I am not going to *help*. You can go, or you can stay here—though if you do I'd thank you to take yourself to the other room and *leave me alone*—but I am not going anywhere." She closed her eyes and tilted her head back against the curling armrest of the divan. The lamplight flickered on the skin of her throat.

I left.

I could have stayed and argued more. Almost as soon as the door closed behind me I wished I had. But truly, what would be the point? I knew well enough that I would not change her mind.

By the time I reached the station in Sembla (where, tiresomely, I discovered a wait of almost an hour for the next railcar that stopped in Valdegeld), I was wishing I had stayed not to convince her, but just to stay with her. But (I recalled after about twenty minutes of pacing), she had exiled me to the guest room in the event I did stay, and there was no reason to think I could have suaded her from that decision either. How long would it have taken before I cracked the shell of her apathy?—If apathy it was; what if she was feeling disdain or, or repugnance? And meanwhile, Petanj who had asked our help, Villette still subject to whatever vile rumors and perhaps discredit, perhaps worse . . . No.

Still, for the entire slough of my wait on that andén, I could not help but hope for the sudden sound of my name unexpectedly close by, or a silent, sardonic presence beside me. I glanced over and over towards the wide and curlicued arch at the entrance to the station, and I was the last to board my railcar when it finally arrived, standing by the corridor window even when it arrancó, hoping against all expectation to see a slight figure hastening towards us. But Mossa did not come, and before the next daybreak I was on my way towards the farther reaches of Giant without her.

Chapter 3

The railcar rumbled towards Stortellen. It rumbled towards Stortellen for *hours,* while I stared at my reflection in the window, fog-bound and mulling.

I had, with an effort, refrained from making any excuses for Mossa's absence, on the basis that she certainly would not have done so. I did say that I hoped she would join us later, because I did hope that, I did believe it was possible. I had, after all, left my notes in her flat; she might, at some stage, bestir herself to read them, and find herself intrigued, and . . . but that assumed she had refused for lack of interest in the case, and since she had not let me give even the most cursory description of it, that seemed unlikely.

Why had Mossa not wanted to come? Was it me? Was our— surely our *affectionate relationship* (as she had once called it) was not *over*? No, she had not said *I never want to see you again* or *We are done* or any other such thing, and if that was what she wanted she *would* have said so; Mossa was direct as a rail-car, she would have made it clear without hesitation.

I clung to the comfort of that generally uncomfortable character trait.

I blinked and saw my own face reflected in the window. It had gotten dark while I was wandering in thought. And there were still days to go in this confounded journey, and hours even before I could decently retire to sleep. To distract myself, I pulled out and opened a missive from my parents, which had arrived shortly before I left—although its value as distraction was undermined by my awareness of the customary asking-after-Mossa lurking near the salutation. I focused resolutely on the content. In between my bapa's chisme about the residents on their small farming platform, my mama had added a piece of more significant news: they had applied for a permit to build a terrace and farm rice.

I lowered the laminate to look out the window. I knew they had been thinking about cultivating rice, but I hadn't realized how serious they were. Rice was an unusual crop on Giant; it was so water intensive that it had been illegal to farm during the early settlement. At this point it was allowed, but still curbed to avoid excessive cultivation or abuse of the status it had gained from scarcity.

My parents could easily claim a cultural basis for growing it, given that everyone on their platform was at least partially of Southeast Asian descent. I had grown up being told to *finish my rice* long before I had ever seen a grain of it. I knew that made this different from the sorts of Earth-aspiring vanity projects that led to specialized, free-range kopi luwak farms and juniper plantations, but I couldn't avoid a whisper of that same unease I felt whenever I heard of one of those initiatives.

Then again, I was happy enough to take advantage when the result was a foodstuff *I* was particularly fond of. I looked around the car. "Petanj?"

She looked up.

"You're a Modernist scholar. Do you think we're ruining this planet as we ruined Earth?"

She snorted. "You really think Modernist scholars are all the same, don't you? I'm a *musicologist*."

I muttered an apology. I *had* known that, of course, I had even gone to some of her lectures in our student days, but

I had thought she might nonetheless hold an opinion more informed than mine. Or maybe I just wanted reassurance. The settlement on Giant bore in its bones the desperation of those early decades of exiguous planning and management for maintaining our supplies of the most basic necessities. Granted, we had for more than a century been in a situation of cautious sufficiency, even occasional luxury; perhaps it was impossible to avoid a bit of spillage. Perhaps it was even beneficent. After all—

I froze, staring at my face in the window. Why had I not realized? I should have recognized immediately that Mossa was mired in melancholy! In a Jovian melancholy no less, so named because of its pervasiveness during the early days of the settlement. Hardly surprising that people would be depressed: the world had ended, and entirely because of the greed, imaginative failures, smugness, and lassitude of human beings; there was grief, of course, and guilt, and the accumulated uncertainty and terror of the years on space stations, crammed into those unforgiving environments, desperately searching for a more livable way to continue to exist in the universe; and even once it was possible to move onto Giant, the early platforms had been exceedingly bleak.

There was considerable melancholy *during* the end of the world, of course, and even more in the space station years; but those periods were better known for resentment, fear, desperation, as well as outbursts of collective heroism. The apocalypse had been busy and urgent; then there was the elation of having survived, the exhilaration of scientific achievements forging one by one the precarious links to a new place. The space station years had offered very little privacy, which had probably contributed to the general reserve.

The outflow of extreme melancholy once people had arrived

in the relative safety of an artificial surface on a gas giant was, for the most part, unexpected. There was an explosion of deeply depressed literature—most of it highly compressed in form, since no one felt confident about the supply of either paper or gigabytes—expressing guilt, loss, and the growing awareness that the entirety of the foreseeable future would be spent on a planet without a breathable atmosphere, local life forms, or solid land. Indeed, contemporary sociologists—some probably displacing their own depression, others admitting it—blamed the pervasive sorrow on everything from the environmental changes, atmospheric congestion, and diet (lack of rice, certainly) to the distance from the sun.

As time passed and society normalized, scholarship circled back to the idea of a certain level of depression as normal in humans, regardless of what planet they were on or how badly they had fucked up their lived environment, and many of the Classical treatments and approaches were revived to coexist or compete with newer methods. Nonetheless, the idea of a specifically Jovian melancholy stuck. (Although, in a linguistic oddity, *jovial* continued to signify cheerfulness.)

And I should have recognized the signs! Mossa used to get the morbs on occasion in university. She'd disappear—re*comb*inants, just like she had this time—and when I had found her, the symptoms had been the same: immersion in her chosen addictions; lack of appetite; general disaffection; on occasion, extreme rudeness.

Why hadn't it even occurred to me that she was melancholy? I had even said the word to her, *Jovian*; I had just meant it in the more colloquial sense, of feeling a bit down in the moment. Why hadn't I just stopped and thought for long, enough to recognize that she was struggling with something much vaster?

I had a sinking intuition that if I hadn't seen that—hadn't even thought of it as a possibility—maybe I wasn't seeing Mossa properly at all.

I had thought that her melancholy at school had been a youthful effusion, an overspilling of emotions. Somehow, I had let myself assume that she had grown out of it, that she was as contained and controlled as she seemed. Or perhaps I had wanted to believe that being with me somehow accorded her a magical happiness that solved all her problems.

And the moment that proved untrue? I left. At her first insistence. Instead of staying to inquire, to listen, to care for her, I left.

I dropped my face into my palms.

"Is everything all right?"

I looked up at Petanj. I hadn't thought she was paying attention—in truth, I'd all but forgotten she was there. I stretched my mouth, but it pulled into a grimace instead of a smile. "Fine. Just . . ." I finished with a vague gesture for lack of anything better.

"It's a long trip," Petanj said, as if it were agreement.

It *was* a long trip. I had been *looking forward* to the long rail-car ride, or I'd thought I had. It seemed that I had been looking forward to a long ride *with Mossa*.

Petanj didn't look too happy either, come to notice it. Mossa would have noticed immediately, of course, Mossa would . . .

Mossa would tell me to question all my assumptions, to distrust any information that came from a single source.

Presumably Villette would confirm the situation when we arrived, but . . .

I eyed Petanj, who had gone back to her book. Could she have orchestrated this whole adventure? But for what possible purpose? Was she envious of Villette's success, perhaps? But why would she ask me to investigate something she had instigated? Was it a ploy to get me away from Valdegeld? Me *and* Mossa, since she couldn't have known Mossa wouldn't join. Unless . . . could she be responsible for that too?

I shut my eyes and leaned my forehead against the window in an attempt to clear my head without doing something so obvious as yanking at fistfuls of hair. I made myself think back to the Petanj I knew from school. Yes, she could have changed in the interim, but . . . I remembered how easy she had been with Villette, her interactions with Mossa, with myself. I didn't *think* she would betray us, but I didn't have Mossa's genius for character reading and interpretation; I had to recognize that I might be wrong.

I shifted in my seat, wishing it were Mossa sitting across from me.

Well. What would Mossa do if she were here?

"What do you think is really going on?"

Petanj sighed, turning to look at the swirling fog. "I'm not certain. Perhaps it's some ill-meaning stranger, or someone who takes exception to her research, although goodness knows Villette tries to engineer for good." I lost the thread for a few moments there, thinking about *good* in the context of our Classical studies; wondering, morosely, whether what the rector had done could possibly be considered *good* or whether I had done *good* in stopping him. When I listened again Petanj was talking about the tightly netted relationships of, I presumed, Stortellen's Modern faculty. "You know how the faculties can be: the rivalries, the petty jealousy, too close, too intertwined, everything is blown out of proportion. And Villette is very young to be proposed for a donship. I've heard of people trying to sink confirmations in the past." She recounted five or six stories, some of which I was familiar with (although the one about the mistreatment of library resources was indeed shocking), and I nodded and murmured and brooded. Mossa would have no interest in any of this; what was I thinking inviting her along? I should have stayed instead. Stayed and *cared for her,* like a copine should. I could have been curled against her on the divan instead of stuck in this railcar listening to a litany of old gossip. Could I possibly disembark at the next station and reverse course? It would be a ridiculous act, the more so as we were nearly halfway along the arc of our journey, and probably hurtful to Petanj, and yet I longed to do it with an almost physical compulsion.

"... can't help feeling she's in serious danger."

The last word yanked my attention back to Petanj. I blinked at her, hoping my mind could reconstruct what had led up to that—ah yes, the university rivalry seems more plausible, but—

"Why do you think so?"

She shrugged uncomfortably. "I don't know. It seems unlikely, but... Well. Probably it's only her reputation at stake, which is certainly enough to be getting on with. I just... I'm overprotective."

"Or maybe something you observed, perhaps without consciously noticing, on one of your previous visits?"

She did not deny it.

Chapter 4

We alit in the middle of the night, several tedious diurnals later, at the rather lovely station in Stortellen. With my bag under my arm I stepped from the egress and looked around, blinking in the emerald-tinged light from the green-shaded streetlamps. I hadn't been to Stortellen in years, not since a school trip with an eye to prospecting universities when I was fifteen or so. From the station it was a pleasant prospect, with not only trees growing in the dirt furrows lining the avenues, but a few shrubs unfurling from "thimble gardens" planted in pockmarks of the platform. Despite the hour, there were people in the streets, strolling past the lighted windows of shops and restaurants or on their way, in giggling groups, towards some feestje.

This vibrancy should have heartened me, but rather left me more desolate; a prickle of chill isolated me from the appealing visions of companionship and purpose. I should have stayed with Mossa. Arriving had not mitigated the urge to turn around: to walk back into the station and step onto the next railcar going in the opposite direction. Indeed, that impulse was almost irresistible, my brain or my body insisting that everything would go from wrong to worst if I did not. But I had traveled an eighth of a planet away from her. To turn back would be the height of foolishness. The craving to do so was, I told myself, deceptive: not an imperative, but a fantasy.

"Well." While I battled with my impulses, Petanj had been scrutinizing a note in the greenish lamplight; a porter hovered nearby as though they had just handed it to her. "Some of us are gathering for a meal, it seems—Villette knew the arrival time and sent along the invitation. I don't suppose you'd be up for joining?"

"With Villette's friends, you mean?" Truly, I would rather have scrubbed off the travel and stretched in a bed, but I had no doubt what Mossa would have done. "It might be useful. Er . . . any chance of a quick wash first?"

"Oh yes, we can stop at the lodgings on the way." Petanj had managed to get the visitors' apartments on Villette's stair for me; she herself would be staying in her cousin's rooms.

She plopped her bag into a sort of open cart; following suit, I saw that the wheeled conveyance ran along tracks set into the platform, a mini-railcar for baggage or impedimenta. "Useful," I said, nodding at it as she grasped the extendable handle.

"Better than lugging our bags along." She grinned as we started off.

Stortellen University itself was somewhat smaller than sprawling Valdegeld, and the platform roughly the same size, which made the city feel more spacious and at the same time less focused on the university. The streets were broader—to make space for that railed cart? Or was that rather an innovation taking advantage of the space?—and the buildings tended lower. I frunced at it all, itchily longing for Valdegeld's tight-winding alleys, though I had often admired the same effect in Sembla.

Villette's lodgings weren't far. Noting how the streetlamp shadings modulated to teal, then blue, I realized that the colors indicated neighborhoods. A pretty effect, though I wondered how noticeable it was in the daylight. The lodgings lacked, for the most part, the curlicues and kickshaws of Valdegeld architecture, but looked comfortable enough, the storm shutters painted indigo to match the pools of light around the streetlamps. I took only the most cursory glance at the rooms themselves in the banked glow of the hearth (the only observation that stuck was that the bed was wide enough to share easily, had Mossa only joined . . . !), hurrying rather to change my travel-tired kurta and splash water on my face before rejoining Petanj below.

Petanj cleared her throat as we started off. "I, ah, did not tell Villette you were coming." I stared at her, and she raised her hands. "I thought the conceit would be easier to explain in person, and perhaps unwise to commit to a telegram." We had agreed during the railcar ride that we would not tell anyone other than her cousin why I had ventured as far as Stortellen, beyond supporting Villette with the donship.

"Then perhaps meeting her in the midst of a group is not ideal?" I suggested, with some restraint.

Petanj snapped her fingers dismissively. "Villette won't question it. She'll be happy to see you. And this is a good opportunity, in fact, to establish your presence here, so you don't have to keep explaining individually."

I was dubious, but inertia carried me along in her wake, as though I were still on the railcar gliding along its single track.

The neighborhood where we found Villette sparkled as invigoratingly as the one by the station, but rather than the windows of shops and restaurants and sedate promenaders, it glowed with chattering, laughing people, most of them sitting *outside* despite the chill, at tables set on the borders of that wide avenue, catered by pubs and estaminets entirely open to the street. Petanj wove through the cozening crowd and stopped by a long group table outside an establishment proclaiming itself Pecanto.

I realized at that moment that I had been expecting to find

Villette in need: alone, friendless, reviled perhaps, perhaps weepy. I was so prepared to defend and/or comfort her that when I saw her face it took me a moment to recognize it: not because she had changed since I last saw her, nor because, as had been the case with Petanj, I wasn't expecting her, but because she was glowing with quiet conviviality. The peach-tinted lights of that neighborhood illuminated the faces of her tablemates—her friends, or her colleagues, all intent with social engagement: laughing, talking, listening. There were near half-a-twenty of them around the table—yes, Petanj had mentioned a Modernist clique or something of the sort, I really hadn't been attending properly on the train—and they looked, en masse, comfortable and effortless and confident.

In other words, terrifying.

Petanj—struck by the same observation, or with politesse—hovered by the table without interrupting. A young person in a dashingly cut djellaba looked up at her, seemed puzzled, and went back to conversation; another glance, from a notably tall woman, skated over both of us without apparent recognition; then I was almost sure that the woman on the end—who had rather large, beautiful eyes, emphasized by the rainbow-tinged translucency of her atmoscarf—saw Petanj and knew her; but before she could react in any way beyond narrowing those striking eyes, the loudly gregarious woman next to Villette nudged her and directed her gaze towards her cousin. Villette let out a pleased cry and sprang to her feet to embrace Petanj, then greeted me with, as Petanj had foretold, only slightly less enthusiasm (and apparently none of the hesitation I had felt when seeing Petanj after so many years).

There was a sputter of introductions, people standing in turn around the table or nodding from a distance, a flurry of names among which I was only able to retain that the woman sitting beside Villette was Wojo, the person who had written the note. Chairs were dragged over for our benefit, the screech of their metal legs against the metal platform almost covered by the continuing burble of conversation around us and the string septet faintly audible from the end of the street. Throughout I was distracted by something odd about the whole scene, something so fundamental that it took me until we were all seated again to grok: Villette, and Wojo beside her, *were not wearing atmoscarfs.*

Atmoscarfs are not, strictly speaking, necessary for survival in Modern times. The atmoshields around each platform provide necessary levels of oxygen, as well as minimum temperatures. But those basic conditions are far from ideal. Buildings provide additional insulation and oxygenation, and atmoscarfs, in a lesser way, do the same while outdoors. They are often customized for individual needs or preferences. When I was in school we would pass around configuration specifications intended to increase oxygen flow and supposedly improve exam performance; there were vendors in Valdegeld that offered illicit additives to do the same, and I knew tutors who required everyone to remove their scarves before quizzes for that reason. It was common enough to push down atmoscarfs to talk or eat or emphasize a facial expression, but to go entirely without one, outside, passed strange.

Not only that (my brain continued to cogitate slowly as I nodded greetings, made introductions, and settled into the chair pulled over for me), but I was recalling that Villette, in particular, had especial need of filtering. She had some condition, congenital or from early childhood, I could not remember, but her atmoscarfs had always been unfashionably bulky. I could picture her now reaching for her atmoscarf during some long-forgotten seminar or meeting in one of the older buildings at Valdegeld where the filtering was antiquated and poorly maintained, taking a few long gulps before sliding, with unnecessary embarrassment, back into her seat.

And now she was sitting outside without wearing one at all? (I raised a finger absently to include myself in a toddy order.) Had she been cured of her ailment? Or—my brain supplied, aptly but belatedly, the memory of something Petanj had said during that lingering rail journey: "... as you know," (she had been looking out the window, one leg curled below her; I must have been looking at her even as my self-pity outshouted her words) "she works in atmospheric chemistry and engineering..." (*Had* I known and forgotten? I did remember Villette being science-y in university, but with my general lack of interest in such topics I apparently hadn't assigned her further details in my mental files.)

Stars. Had Villette engineered the atmoscarf into obsoleteness?

No wonder someone was trying to discredit her research. She was lucky they weren't trying to kill her.

Chapter 5

"—fortuitous, really," Villette was telling her cousin as I emerged from my ear-pounding shock, "we're in fact celebrating tonight because they've just scheduled the donfense!"

I felt another shock at that, or perhaps more of a thud: with the accusations eradicated and the donship back on, there was no real reason for me to be there. Then again . . .

"Wonderful!" Petanj embraced her cousin again. "When is it set?"

"Uranday week."

A week and a day. My sudden vision of returning immediately to Mossa was damped; there was no way to excuse myself from staying for the celebration, after coming all this way, not easily or kindly. And besides—my disappointment and hopes both replaced by a chill pressentiment—if someone *did* wish to prevent Villette from the promotion at all costs, that left them a limited time to accomplish it.

I was burning to ask Villette—or even Petanj, space my silly reticence about not listening in the railcar—about her invention: its potential, its constraints, why only two of them were using it, whether it had been or would be sold—but there were social niceties occurring, and at the moment most of them were aimed directly at me.

"So you are here for our Villette's donfense?" This came from the woman I had noticed at the end of the table, the one with the soap-bubble atmoscarf, who spoke the word with a

Geldan accent so pronounced—donfen*suh*—that I wasn't sure if she had spent time on our platform, was pretending she had, or was mocking me.

"Truly?" The person in the creamy carmine djellaba at the other end of the table slid forward to join in. Across from me, Wojo's eyes narrowed and darted between myself and Petanj. "You came all the way here from *Valdegeld* just for a donning ceremony?" Valde*geld*.

I resigned myself to not hearing the name of my university pronounced without heavy sardonics until I was back home. "I had been wanting to do some collegiate exchanges here as well," I said, hoping my tone sounded as mild as I wanted it to. "It seemed a good opportunity to support a friend at the same time." I wanted to be talking less about myself and the reasons for my journey. I turned to the soap-bubble woman, who looked the type to be ready to talk about herself at any moment. "What do you study?"

The woman—Evna, her name was—went on at some length about her research in Modern astronomy and its fundamental importance for our lives on Giant and even, *eventually* (that adverb with heavy emphasis) for the effort of returning to Earth. Petanj and Villette were twittering cozily to each other, but I could not make out the words. I tried to ration my sips of the toddy (potent, and quite tasty) but still counted seven before the conversation finally slipped, or was brangled, out of Evna's control. Wojo, looking somewhat annoyed, told us at only barely less length about her research testing Giant's gaseous mixture at different depths, something in which I had not the slightest interest. Filtering out her words, I watched her body language instead, and her expressions, her toothy smiles very visible without an atmoscarf. She displayed the expression of continuous almost-laughter that I had, during various epochs of my life, practiced in my mirror, pasted on to my fantasies, and attempted to disdain. Occasionally, though, I caught her eyes dodging from side to side as she laughed, checking our reactions.

Experimentally, I left my own atmoscarf below my chin between samples of my toddy, trying to look as though I was simply not bothering to pull it up. Perhaps, after all, it was mostly custom. But no; after just a few minutes I could feel the telltale rasp of the air and the onset of the slight headache I associated with being outside unscarved. I pulled it up again and looked around.

Someone farther down the table, perhaps as bored as I was (presumably they all already knew what each other studied?) had fortunately opened up the topic of an apparently unpopular university update. Out of nowhere, I felt a swell of misery. I did not want to be there, at that silly party; I *couldn't* be there; I needed to be with Mossa. She needed me.

Unless she didn't.

She had certainly acted like she didn't. Perhaps the best thing I could do for her was to pursue these investigations, such as they were, such as I could, without her.

Perhaps I should forget about what I could do for Mossa and think about helping Villette; helping Petanj, who had asked me to come, because she did need me.

With that idea in mind I glanced around the table again, wondering if, beneath all the superficial, edged gaiety, one of these scholars hated Villette, hated her enough to ruin her.

Wojo, no longer controlling the conversation, was shifting unsettled in her seat, darting responses in where she could fit them; the person in the djellaba was debating some point with bright-eyed Evna. Watching the colors in her iridescent atmoscarf, I wondered why they hadn't all adopted the new technology. Perhaps Villette had only made a few prototypes? Or maybe there were constraints; perhaps the device was unsuitable for some people. Or maybe it was an aesthetic choice; that atmoscarf certainly brought out Evna's eyes—which, I realized at that moment, were fixed on me. Unable to manage a sincere smile at that point in time, I offered up an insincere one and turned my gaze, reaching for my mug in what I hoped was a casual manner. My toddy was cooling, and I looked around for a warmer. In Valdegeld it was not uncommon to have a raised platform in the middle of an outdoor table for that purpose; here shallow recesses built into the surface functioned as tiny fireplaces. A pretty effect, I could admit; but they were individual, rather than central, and because my chair had been squeezed into a space not designed for it, I didn't have one. Petanj, equally scrunched in, was next to her cousin, and they were sharing one amicably, each with half of their mug over the flames.

"Here," murmured the woman to my right, picking up her mug and nodding at her warmer.

"Oh—thank you," I said, and girded myself for more conversation.

"Prego. I'm Maki Benoz." The scrap of fur on her shoulder raised a languid head—a sloth, I saw.

"Pleiti Weihal, enchanted." I cast about for a way to continue. "What do you study?"

She was a large woman, taller and broader than I, and while she did not hunch, she carried herself with a sort of containment. "I'm an ethnographer."

"Oh?" I said, in a way I would have described as *politely* but which probably contained more than a hint of condescension. "I didn't realize that was a . . . Modern field of study." I associated ethnography with intrepid scholars of the Classical era;

but as I spoke I realized how rude I sounded and hurried on. "What, er, specific areas do you focus on?"

She took a slow sip of her toddy, eyeing me with incredulity, and then apparently decided to move past it. "I study communities on platforms with smaller populations, usually agricultural."

"Oh!" I said, yet again and with another intonation. "I—I grew up on one of those. What, uh, what exactly—"

But before I could figure out whether to be pleased or prickled that she studied people like me—likely incurring more offense in the process—the attention of the table shifted and both I and Benoz looked up to follow it. A rather gangly and tactically tousled man and a similarly rangy woman had ambled up to the table and stood there, waiting for acknowledgment.

"Oh, Hoghly," Villette said, jumping up and sketching a gesture of greeting. "And Vao. I wasn't sure you would make it— sorry, we can bring up another table."

"No need," Hoghly said, though obviously there was. "We can squeeze in."

They couldn't, and while the table was shrieked into place by Petanj and one of the servers I asked Benoz who the newcomers were.

Her expressive mouth flattened. "Villette's coauthor. And his wife, she does something in town, I don't know what. Something with clothing or textiles I think."

Across from me, Villette jumped as an ignition sparked: Wojo leaning across the table to light Hoghly's warmer. "Well then, we're all here," Wojo said, aiming a condemnatory glance at the recently arrived couple. "Shall we dedicate a libation to the successful donfense"—*without* the satirical Geldan accent—"of our sweet Villette? Now that the unpleasantness of those baseless accusations of"—she ducked her voice in a way that made it more conspicuous rather than less—"*plagiarism* are behind us—"

Incoherently protesting voices rose around the table; beside me Benoz coughed loudly, a little too late to cover it; as the clamor faded and Wojo's laughter—shamed? Defiant? Both?—still rang above the table, Villette shifted uneasily. "Wojo . . ."

"We all *know* it's ridiculous, of course," Wojo said, her collarbones leaping to prominence as she leaned forward. "Of course! But Villette, my dear, if we refuse to speak of it, that rather lends it credence, sabes? Far better to show boldly that it doesn't worry you in the least."

Villette looked unhappy, and Petanj leaned around her. "Whether *we* know it's ridiculous doesn't matter in the least, *as* you should well understand," she hissed, the venom in her voice making me think Wojo grated on her as much as she was starting to irritate me. "It's the stain on her reputation we need to manage and I'll thank you not to be shouting about it *in public!*"

Wojo looked taken aback for a blink, and I was fiercely grateful to Petanj.

"No one could think it was anything but a bit of evil-minded gossip," Hoghly drawled, sounding a bit too pleased about it. His wife plucked at the cloth of his sleeve and muttered something to him, presumably that the topic should be dropped. He tugged away impatiently. "Nonsense! It affects me too, y'know!"

His wife—Vao, her name was?—offered an anemic smile around the table. She had a slight slump, which probably passed as charming now but would translate to regrettable posture when she was less winsome.

I was really being awfully judgmental. I diagnosed exhaustion and melancholy, and took another gulp of my toddy, in hopes it would ameliorate at least one of those.

Villette was also slumping, although it looked less characteristic and more dispirited. Petanj, presumably in the interest of changing the subject, was unwinding a long tale of Geldan gossip. Wojo, meantimes, had taken it on herself to introduce the research areas of the other people around the table, and I was yanked back to the conversation with a shock. ". . . and our dear Makila studies how animals evolve here on Giant."

"*Evolve?*" I almost choked on the word, even as my brain, catching up with my unconscious assumptions, remembered reading something about this Modern field.

Makila—the one in the djellaba—smirked, and Wojo looked just as smug, while Benoz tickled the chin of the sloth on her shoulder with what looked like satisfaction. "Most Classics scholars have that sort of reaction. But you can't expect the animals we gestate here to stay *static*, can you?" Makila offered.

No, I thought, *of course we do not; that's why we keep the salvaged genetic material as well.* But it seemed unproductive to start an argument, so I simply nodded with a thoughtful expression as the Modernist waxed froth full about the many Giantesque adaptations observed in the animals living on platforms. I wondered if the sloth resting on the ethnographer's (rather fine) shoulders beside me had *evolved* in any appreciable way—but no, of course not, there was no place where sloths could live wild here, it would have been gestated.

"Imagine, though," Makila said, leaning forward with a wiggle. "Villy here thinks her invention—the nasal filter, you know—could be applied to *birds*."

"I only said *theoretically*," Villette started, with more resignation than annoyance.

I was utterly baffled. "Why on Giant would you do that to

birds?" When I had thought I would like to learn more about the device, this was not what I had in mind.

"So they could fly between platforms!" Wojo seemed to think this mingbai'd everything, and Makila was nodding with some enthusiasm, but I was still lost.

"Why," I could feel my tone slipping from incredulity to outright scorn, and attempted to salvage it, "would you want birds to fly outside of atmoshields?"

"Just imagine, you're sitting in a railcar, staring out at *nothing,* really, at the fog, and then you see a goshawk fly by!"

Again, this was greeted with amused approval by at least half the table. Villette was staring out along the street as though wishing herself elsewhere. I was in the midst of calculating the extreme unlikelihood of a goshawk happening to fly by a railcar window before exhausting itself and punching to a cruel death on a planet with no land. Were they—these Modernist scholars who chose to focus on this planet—so desperate to imagine themselves back on Earth that they wanted to see birds fluttering through the gaseous atmosphere as though it were air?

I opened my mouth, and Petanj caught my eye. *Not worth it.*

"More academically, though," Makila went on, and though I suspected more performance I reluctantly allocated her my attention again, "it *would* be fascinating to see how they would evolve once exposed to the broader environment of Giant. Would they develop navigational capacity, for example?"

I couldn't stop myself. "That would require them living long enough to reproduce, which seems unlikely if they're flying around between platforms."

That started a flurry of explanations: *Well, of course they would train them . . . There would be optimally spaced perches along the rings . . . homing beacons . . .*

I must admit I had always thought of Modernism as . . . well, straightforward. Lacking the subtle analysis required in Classical studies. After all, Modernism was studying what was right there in front of us; it could hardly be the same as teasing out numbers and relationships from sources writing about an obsolete world as if their readers would be familiar with everything they referenced, as if we stepped out every day onto soil. This conversation hadn't entirely changed my mind; there did seem to be more to it than I had suspected, but I wasn't convinced that these Modernists weren't purposely complicating their fields.

I could carve out an exception for Modern ethnography, though. Humans are incomprehensible wherever they are.

- - - - - - - -

Chapter 6

During the rather unsteady return to our lodgings the night before, Petanj had encouraged me to take some intentional indolence (as the youngens say) to recover from travel. I suspected she was giving herself the same prescription, and indeed, though I myself woke up well into the daylight hours of the diurnal, when Petanj opened her door to my knock she was, though dressed, still blinking and lassitudinous.

"Villette got off to the lab early, of course, sarariman that she is."

The comment was affectionate, but I couldn't help responding anyway. "With the donfense less than a week away, I can hardly blame her."

"Yes yes," Petanj responded unabashedly, "she's going to be insufferable until then, not much fun for you, I'm afraid."

"I'm not here for fun," I reminded her. "Shall we go talk to her?" That was the moment to ask Petanj to repeat whatever she had told me about Villette's work during the train ride, but I was still ashamed to admit that I hadn't been attending, and still less wanted to explain why.

As we walked through the foyer of the lodgings, I noticed a curious sort of alcove by the entrance, with four or five youngish, gradudent-looking people idling there, most of them reading, which supported the gradudent hypothesis. I caught Petanj's eye and nodded at them, curious.

"Oh, Stortellen does not pay for full-time porters in the

lodgings here, did you not know? So gradudents tend to hover around to run errands and so on, for a small consideration."

"Hmm, seems inconvenient."

"Yes, well, not everywhere is Valdegeld, as I'm sure you will hear many times during your stay here." Petanj's tales of how Storties managed to backhandedly insult our university kept us occupied on the way to her favored breakfast spot, a small restaurant ("They call them cafés here, Classically, even though coffee isn't any more common than in Valdegeld") on the way to Villette's laboratory, where we ate chapatis with a fry-up of quail eggs and chantarelles.

The lab was architecturally unimpressive, a building in the outdated dome style, distinguished from others around it mainly by its slightly more grandiose size. Just inside the entrance was an anodyne foyer where we were obliged to wait while the skinny man at the reception desk sent a message to Villette and proceeded to cordially ignore us until informed that we were, in fact, expected. He unlocked the door for us with two separate keys, and, I think, expected the messenger—another gradudent, if I have any eye—to escort us directly to the lab, and presumably to maintain our discretion. Petanj clearly knew her from previous visits, addressing her by name.

"Howzit, Kenore," she said chummily, handing over a small packet stamped with the crest of a Geldan candy maker so well-known that just the sight of their marque made my mouth water. "Any joy from the microbes?"

"Still watching and waiting, Prof." Kenore pocketed the sweets with a wink. "And your own work?"

"Oh, well enough, though not as illustrious as my cousin's. I'll let you get back to it, we know the way."

Kenore nodded and trotted off with unnerving confidence as to her place in the world and the external perceptions of it.

I, an inveterate second-guesser of how my appearance might dissonate from my internal feelings, had always envied people like that.

"This way," Petanj told me, leading us to a series of ramps. "The atmospheric studies labs are down in the basement—just in case they blow up, you see, that way they won't take out the atmoshield for the whole platform." She laughed at my expression. "No, that's just a blague they tell here. They have an off-platform site for anything with a risk of explosion."

"Off-platform site?" I repeated, trying to imagine a laboratory completely untethered from Giant's system of rings.

Petanj waved her hand at me. "It's attached to this platform, but removed from it, so as to avoid risk of damage to the residences here or even to the ring. And of course the atmoshield for that area has spark-dampening chemicals and so on, I don't know, I don't think Villette has ever had to use it. The real reason *this* lab is under the platform is so they can easily access the atmosphere—there are airlock rooms with various different filters."

"Fascinating," I muttered as we rounded the final curve and came to the doors of the laboratory, also locked. Petanj ran her hand over a button, and a moment later the doors cracked and Villette's face appeared in the gap.

"Ah, there you are."

The space she led us into was large, though the walls tapered downwards—apparently the building was not a dome construction after all but a sphere, only set lower than most such buildings, with close to half of it below platform level instead of only a sliver. There were dividers of varying heights—some complete to the ceiling, some only partial—around the space, and I suspected it could be reconfigured based on the number of scholars and the work they were doing. Villette's area was against one of the curving walls, with two separate half-size doors in it—to the airlock rooms, presumably—and three separate counters with different equipment ranged upon them: engineering, measurement, and chemistry from the look of them.

"Pleiti." Villette reached out to embrace me. "It's good to see you! I'm sorry about last night. I should have stopped them from teasing you so. They can't resist picking at Valdegeld when they get the chance, I'm afraid, but they really are sympa, you'll see. And I really am glad you came. Err . . . *did* you really come all this way just for my donship ceremony?"

"I asked her to come," Petanj said as I hesitated. "She can help us—look into who is causing these problems in a way we can't."

Villette looked at me with incomprehension. I supposed news of my recent exploits had not extended so far as Stortellen; certainly an advantage if I wanted to be sneaky. She turned back to her cousin. "But Petanj, the problem is over!" Or she was bemused not by me, but by the idea of needing help. "The donfense is scheduled, and *as you said last night,* the fewer people are aware of it the better! Not you, Pleiti," she added hastily, turning to me in contrition. "I know you will be perfectly discreet. But to look into it as though it were more than a bit of malicious gossip gives it credence! I will already have to put up with questions and snide remarks at the donfense; I don't want this to follow me further! A scholar's reputation—"

"A scholar's reputation is their greatest treasure," Petanj began in a singsong voice, "and once tarnished, can never be recovered," Villette joined in nasally on the second half, and the cousins smirked at each other at what was clearly a shared memory from their platform school, but Petanj did not back down. "Do you really think this is over?"

For an eyeblink Villette looked uncertain and afraid, then she rallied her incredulity. "Why shouldn't it be? The donship—"

"Come *on*, cuz!" Petanj lowered her voice further. "These accusations weren't the only attempt to discredit your work, n'esp?"

"Perhaps," I interjected, hoping to crack the ice-rime of tension a bit, "we could discuss it somewhere a bit more private?"

Villette's expression had gone stubborn, but I fancied that moment of uncertainty had revealed the real fear she was covering, and she nodded before too long. "We can go into the airlock room," she said, leading the way to a door in the curving wall and running her fingers over the color panel in some prespecified manner to unlock it. I couldn't repress a shudder while ducking in, although I comforted myself with the reminder that this space surely had every possible alert in case of malfunction.

Villette, at any rate, looked entirely at home even in the rather harsh lighting—electric, rather than gas, which probably made sense given the nature of the experiments that might take place there. She leaned against the wall and gestured at Petanj, who silently handed her the laminate she had shown me. Villette frunced her brow as she clocked the signature at the top, and as she read she grew more and more serious. When she put it down we were both waiting.

"Wojo is metida, she always has been, Petanj, you know that." She said it distractedly, an automatic response perhaps.

"Do you know what she's referring to?" I asked. "These other incidents?"

"The chisme? I don't know!" She threw her hands up. "Nobody would mention it directly to me anyway!"

"What about the *ambiguous alarums* she mentions? Has there been anything that put you in harm's way?"

"I don't know! No! Well . . ." She paused, and Petanj glared. "I did have a bout of gastro, and I thought—but I'm sure it was just chance, something had gone off."

"What did you think?" I asked, as sharply as I could. Villette evidently did not want to imagine anyone's culpability; she was trying to minimize rather than aggrandize every threat; if she had suspicions, if she brought it up even, I had to think she had foundation for doing so.

Indeed, she fidgeted before answering. "It was just because— well, it was after we'd been out in a group, like last night, and we had dinner communal-style, all taking servings from the same serving bowls, but I was the only one to get sick. And, er, it was the night before a rather important presentation." She offered us a rote smile. "I got through it, but it wasn't pleasant."

"What presentation?" Petanj asked. "Would someone have benefitted by taking your place if you had cried cancel?"

"No, no, not at all. It was one of the preliminaries for the donfense, in fact. If I had canceled, we would have had to postpone, and it would have been awkward and annoying, but hardly a serious problem, and certainly not an opportunity for anyone else. And in any case it does happen, sometimes, doesn't it, that one person is simply more susceptible to whatever the irritant is, and has a reaction when no one else does?"

"Naturally it happens," I agreed. Petanj was giving me a Look that said *We should be impressing the gravity of this on her, not downplaying it!* but I needed Villette soothed enough to cooperate. "For the sake of . . . completeness, however, caution, can you remember who was present on that occasion? Was it the same group that we met last night?"

"Um. More or less." Villette's eyes unfocused in memory. "Benoz wasn't there. Hoghly was there, but not Vao. I think Haxi was there. Otherwise I think it was as last night, but I may not be recalling exactly." I had fortunately brought a bloc, and scribbled down the names as unobtrusively as I could.

"What about these anonymous letters?" Petanj asked, poking at the note.

"Oh . . . well . . . those, I haven't had one in some time."

"They were disturbing, though?" I asked.

"Rather." Villette made a face. "But to connect them with this foolish accusation . . . I don't quite see . . ."

"Maybe you can tell me more about the plagiarism claims," I suggested. "I know they've been discredited, but even so."

"Not just discredited, they were ridiculous from the beginning!" Villette visibly bit down on the sudden flare of exasperation. "Sorry. It's perfectly reasonable for you to ask. Pues. It was the classic: saying that I got the idea from someone else. Which is normally very hard to disprove, because of course multiple people can have the idea at the same time, and the path of inspiration is difficult to trace, and so on." She had started to pace the small area, which unfortunately drew my attention to a delineated panel with buttons on it which I realized, with a pulse of cold sweat, must be the outside door of the airlock. "In this case, though, there is a very clear reason why I was thinking along these lines"—she gestured in the general area of her respiratory system—"and in any case I keep extensive notes, almost diary level, about thoughts and ideas as well as every step in the experimentation and construction process. So, as I *told* you," that was pointed at Petanj, "I was fairly confident."

"Where are those notes now?" Petanj asked.

"With the committee investigating the accusations, of course. *And* I made copies before I gave them the originals, yes."

I winced at the amount of work that must have required. She was not so naive as to ignore some precautions, at least. "Who were you supposed to have stolen the idea from?"

"They wouldn't tell me." Villette shrugged. "Since the accusation was anonymous, it could have been someone trying to cause issues for both me and the other person—assuming there even was a specific person named."

I wondered if I could get the university to show me the accusation. If only Mossa had come, with her official status and her knowledge and procedure. On that thought, my energy swept out of me like a railcar leaving a platform bereft. I made an effort. "And you worked together with Hoghly on that?"

"On the nasal filter? No." Villette sighed, and went back to leaning against the wall. "That's a different project, looking at atmoshield efficiency and condensation capture and—well, you don't want the technical details. Basically, the university— the dean—asked me to work with him. It seemed to make sense—his work is on condensation, precipitation, and so on, but we . . . haven't suited."

"The university was trying to use you to get some decent work out of him, since he doesn't do much but preen on his own," Petanj put in acerbically.

"Maybe." Villette was staring at the wall. "It's true that he's . . . not very proactive. I have also thought . . . it's possible that they were hoping he'd . . . rein me in a little, perhaps."

"Why would they want that?" I asked.

"My mentor—the one the university assigned when I started here—hated the nasal filter project. Thought it was too . . . too individualistic. We stopped working together over it. And then, when it started to look like it would be successful . . . well, there was a lot of interest, from producers and so on. I think it made the university nervous."

"What will you— How does it work, by the way?"

Villette raised a sardonic eyebrow. "Again, I'm assuming you don't want the technical details." She delicately flipped a lentil-sized contraption from her nostril. "One on each side. Can be easily removed indoors but I usually leave them in."

"Ye-s," I said, trying to control my shudder. "Er . . . What are you planning to do with it?"

Villette turned away to reinsert it; my disgust must have shown more than I had hoped. "What I have always said I would do."

"Which is?"

"Make it public," Villette said, as if it were obvious.

"What?"

She turned, eyeing me with surprise. "Make the design public. *Naturally* I'm going to make it public. What did you think I was going to do, sell it?" Petanj smirked in the background. "This would have made such a difference to me when I was younger—it makes such a difference now! I'm not going to deprive anyone of that." She looked to her cousin, then back at me. "You think this is about the nasal filter?"

"I don't know. It does seem," I added cautiously, "like at least one possible lightning attractor. But I really don't have enough information to draw conclusions from yet." I considered. "Do *you* have any idea who might be doing this?"

"No!" It was a much more forceful response than I had expected. "No, I imagine it's someone . . . someone far away, in another department or university, who just . . ."

"Villy . . ." Petanj started, her voice surprisingly gentle, but Villette broke away from her outstretched hand.

"I know, I know you think it's someone who knows me, maybe even someone who was at that party last night, but *why*? Why would any of them want to hurt me? I haven't argued with any of them, or done anything to them. We're *friends*. No."

I was aware, through my Classical reading if nothing else, of the theory that excessive denial suggested the opposite, and

I wondered if Villette did know, or suspect, who the perpetrator was. However, although I could feel Petanj tense beside me with what was probably a combination of sympathy and the urge to browbeat, I couldn't see that pushing her on the point would be effective at that moment. Or, at least, I could feel that my own tolerance for emotional upheaval, already attenuated by the separation from Mossa, was close to its limit. I needed some time alone, ideally with engrossing textual matter.

And so I shrugged. "As I said, it's too early for me to speculate. Perhaps I can see those anonymous notes, at least. You did keep them?"

"Yes, they're all in my files. In my office, not here." Villette sounded almost as weary as I felt.

"If you could show us the way—or, Petanj, you know where the office is? Formidable. Then we can let you get back to work here."

Subdued, Villette opened the door back into the lab, which had emptied out for the midday meal. I followed Petanj through with some relief and, thinking to lighten the mood with trivial matters, turned back to ask Villette how often she worked in that terrifying place only to see her jump and slap at her nose. "Villette?"

She raised her other hand to the other side of her nose, patted at it, then met my gaze with a wild, disbelieving countenance. "We need to go."

"Dafuq?" I asked, wondering what I had missed.

"We need to go, now! Petanj, you need to get out of here!" She pushed us in the direction of the door, half running already and urging us faster. "Yalla, out!"

We careened across the broad, eerily empty lab space. "What is going on? What are you doing?" Petanj yelled. I wondered if everyone had left because of whatever had alarmed Villette, expected at every moment the slam of depressurization or perhaps some explosion, but even the panic felt far away; I was feeling a little zeroG from the adrenaline and shock of it. At last we were out, and Villette slammed the lab door behind us. "Go! Follow the exit signs!" she yelled, but Petanj realized soon, before I did, that she wasn't with us.

"Villette! Come on!"

"I'll be right behind you." She had turned back to the lab doors, but Petanj ran back to her and grabbed her arm.

"What is going on?"

"I just need to check something, I'm better protected than you are, go!"

"Your nose is bleeding," I said dreamily from where I was leaning against the wall. Villette raised her hands to the dark liquid dripping from her nostrils, and that's when the gas leak siren started wailing.

Chapter 7

Gas leaks were, for obvious reasons, not terribly uncommon on Giant. By the same token, there were numerous safety measures in place. The evacuation routes were clearly marked, and the egressing crowd orderly, even Villette, who had given up on whatever she was going back for.

"Was it your notes? Some data?" Petanj hissed at her as we traversed the corridors at a fast walk. "What was it that you thought was important enough to risk your life for?"

"No." Villette was still dabbing at her nose. "I wanted to see why the sirens hadn't gone off in the lab."

Petanj and I both stopped short, and were immediately goaded into motion again by a condemnatory grumble of voices behind us.

"You're right," Petanj said thoughtfully. "That's odd."

"How did *you* know?" I asked. The corridor ahead of us lightened, I felt the chill of outside, and all of us sped up just a little.

"I built an alert into the nostril filter. I thought it made sense for completeness somehow, even though it hardly seemed worth the trouble." Every building on Giant had sirens, usually redundant ones, not to mention the platform-operated alarms and dedicated repair teams; gas leak fatalities for a given year were usually in the single or low double digits.

"That's why your nose was bleeding!" I was pleased, as we

stepped out of the building, that my brain had recovered well enough to work that out.

Villette nodded, looking a little avergonzada. "I hadn't fully considered the consequences of a vibrating alert. I'll have to figure out a way to modify that . . ."

"But Villette!" Petanj's brain was well ahead of mine. She even remembered to keep her voice low. "If you felt it as soon as we came out of the airlock, and the sirens in the corridors worked perfectly well, that means it started in your lab!"

Villette's expression told me she had already thought of that. Of course she had. I had pulled my atmoscarf up automatically when we left the building, but I pulled it down now and took a breath of the biting, brackish air without it, hoping to clear my head faster. "That's not so unlikely," Villette was saying. "Many of us in that lab work with various concentrations of the atmosphere, and accidents do happen."

"Yes, but the sirens—" Petanj started, and Villette, who had been scanning the small knots of scientists, gradudents, and auxiliaries standing around in the street outside of the exit, touched her arm.

"Look, there's the envirolabs director! I have to go tell ta about this!"

She hared off, dodging through the crowd. Petanj's lips were pressed together; she pulled up her atmoscarf and started after her cousin. I followed, glancing at the crowd around me. Some people had evidently left their atmoscarfs on a peg somewhere when they abandoned the building; I saw shirt collars pulled up and arms held across faces, and some people, less susceptible perhaps, ignoring the situation altogether. My throat was already stinging, however, and I tugged mine up again as we approached Villette, deep in earnest conversation with a narrow person with protective goggles pushed up on ta's forehead and an atmoscarf that looked like it was probably rated for hazardous materials. Above it, ta's eyebrows were lowered in concern, and we arrived in time to hear ta say, "Didn't you register some gas experiments recently?"

Villette blinked. "Oh—that was, that was a few weeks ago . . ." She went blank with time-calculation for a moment. I wished I could wipe the dried blood off her face.

"I don't remember anyone else requesting since . . . definitely not in your lab. Which output were you using for the gas?"

"The one at my lab counter—there was no one else around, and it was only a quick check." She touched a finger to her nose, probably thinking that if she had run a longer test she would have caught the nosebleed bug. "But I reset the sirens, *of course* I reset the sirens—"

"Look, it happens," the lab director said. "Let me go tell the patch team in case they haven't pinpointed the leak yet." Ta tapped Villette gently on the shoulder as ta edged past her towards the building.

Petanj stepped up to take ta's spot, putting her arm around her cousin's shoulders as she stared after the director.

"Villette," I said hesitantly. How did Mossa *do* this? "Can you tell us—"

Villette shook herself. "No—I mean, yes, of course, I'll tell you whatever you need, but right now I need to—" She gestured in the direction the director had gone, or perhaps at the laboratory building in general; looking that way, I caught a glimpse of the gradudent from earlier, Kenore, handing out the generic sort of atmoscarfs that every large institution kept on hand for situations like these. "I need to help. And explain. And then get back to work." She ran her fingers into her shortish hair. "I will see you both tonight? I'm sorry, but—" Another meaningless gesture.

"Of course," I said. If I couldn't be as astute as Mossa would have been, at least I could be more soothing. "We'll talk later."

"I cannot like it, Petanj." After watching Villette's decided departure we had wandered away from the building in a more desultory way, and the crowd had thinned to the point where we could speak of it without being indiscreet. "This is significantly more worrisome than how you presented it."

"It's more worrisome than I knew. The gas leak *could* have been a chance occurrence." Petanj sounded as doubtful as I felt. "But it does seem awfully unlikely, what with everything else going on."

"Petanj, if someone is really trying to injure her . . ." I wished again Mossa had joined me, but this time with more anxiety than yearning: she at least had a whip-lasso, a knife, a readiness for violence. "I know nothing about bodyguarding. Perhaps," reluctantly, "it would be best to go to the Investigators."

Petanj paced in silence for a moment. "Do you know someone at the bureau here? Or do you think Mossa might?"

"I can send her a telegram to ask." I tried not to show how uncertain I was that she would answer.

"Because without knowing, or at least knowing of, someone reasonable there . . . I doubt they'll take it seriously, Pleiti. They won't understand how important the anonymous accusations are, and without that there's nothing to make anyone think that the gas leak—or the indigestion, or anything else—was other than an accident."

"Surely they'll investigate if we ask them to."

"Yes, I'm sure they will—if they're not busy with something they consider more important—but will they really believe us that this is dangerous?" I considered that glumly as the street lights around us modulated from purple to violet. "They won't understand," Petanj went on, tugging at her knot of hair. "And they'll talk about it, and joke about it, and the consequence is everyone knows Villette's been accused of"—she lowered her voice; we were well out of the crowd, but there were still students and scholars frequenting the streets around us— "academic dishonesty!"

"She's been exonerated," I said, but I knew it was weak; suspicion would linger. "Anyway, does it really matter in her case? Her device works, obviously."

"Yes," Petanj bit out, "but she doesn't *want* to go make repeats of this device for some firm! She wants to give it away and keep researching new ideas!" She stopped and turned to me. "Pleiti, how do you think the university feels about Villette giving away the results of her research?" I winced, remembering a nasty squabble over university-gestated technology in our previous case, and Petanj didn't wait for any further answer. "They might support Villette for a while, reward her with a donship, because obviously she's a genius. But now they know that all they're going to get from her is what her presence adds to their reputation. If she becomes too tiresome, too much trouble— Pleiti, you realize that all they have to do is find that there *was* plagiarism, and then they can decide what happens with the device?"

"Surely..." I started, appalled, and then had to stop, because I couldn't think of any argument against that succession of events that I was sure of.

Petanj started walking again. "And even if they don't outright take her ideas, if they kick her out, what do you think happens? That saying about a scholar's reputation—we laugh at how seriously they used to take it at school, but it's still true.

You know as well as I do how easy it would be for her to be ostracized from the acadème. She wouldn't find a job anywhere."

We were gloomily silent.

"At least," I said, trying to be hopeful, "we don't have to worry about the atmoscarf firms."

"Hmm?" Petanj raised an eyebrow at me.

"She's not selling it," I explained, "so the trouble isn't coming from some rival firm . . ." I trailed off as Petanj shook her head.

"Ah, Classicists," she said. "So naive."

I sullened, which was perhaps an overreaction given her teasing tone, but the needling from the night before had left me feeling bruised.

"Sorry," Petanj amended immediately, putting her hand to my elbow. "But you must see: if she's making it public, that threatens *all* the producers of atmoscarfs—maybe of atmosfilters too."

"Yes," I said slowly. "I do see. Discrediting her research would make sense then. But if she's already using the prototype herself . . ."

"And some of her friends."

"Then at some point that's not enough, which might explain the possible attack on the lab." I shook my head. "Too many possibilities. Perhaps looking at those anonymous notes will help." I could not muster much optimism.

"Chht!" Petanj put a hand on my arm. "Look, there's Wojo." There she was indeed, lounging atmoscarf-free on a bench swing outside of a teashop of some sort. "Come on. I want to know exactly what she was thinking with this letter she sent me."

Wojo looked up as we approached, a (probably well-practiced) smile quirking into something considerably less congenial as she recognized us. "I'm glad you were smart enough to pay attention to my letter," she said to Petanj without intermediate words. "But what is she doing here?"

I suspect I recoiled slightly at her rudeness, but Petanj seemed unaffected and even unsurprised. "Of course I'm here, Wojo. I would have come for the donfense regardless. I brought Pleiti precisely *because* of your missive."

"Oh?" Wojo glanced at me suspiciously, but didn't seem to think it worth including me in the conversation. "Why?"

Petanj inhaled with exasperation, about to speak. I knew that strategically it was better if people did not expect me to be investigating, but it was the horror of hearing my recent adventures extolled, to a stranger, *while I was standing right there,* that drove me to intervene. "Did you really think she was going to be able to protect her cousin solita? Twenty hours a diurnal?"

Wojo jerked and scowled, perhaps because I jumped into the conversation slightly too fast or slightly too loud, or possibly because she didn't want me to speak at all. "I could have helped," she said.

"You have your own work," Petanj said pointedly.

"Who do *you* think is the threat?" I wanted to get somewhere beyond all this silly sparring. *Obviously* the academic community here—the Modernists, at least, I amended—had tangled and dramatic interrelationships, fine. I didn't care. "Who wants to hurt Villette?"

Wojo threw her hands in the air. "If I knew, I would have done something about it!" I could not help wondering whether she meant "something" like *going to the Investigators* or "something" like *a quick shove off the platform.* "Her old tutor resents her, Hoghly is a useless bit of platform oxidation and resents her *more,* her entire department probably envies her, maybe her whole faculty."

"Except you, of course," Petanj put in with a smoothness approaching snide.

Wojo ignored her. "The university wants her not to sell her devices unless that involves them snagging part of it, and they hate that she's not-selling but also not-keeping-it-solely-for-the-greater-glory-thereof."

"Devices?"

She ignored me too. "I have not been privy to her meetings with atmoscarf firms, but I can't imagine any of them are happy. And she doesn't care! Worse, I don't think she's even noticed! She thinks she can just do her ridiculously good research quietly and then give it away and everyone will be happy, just like her!" She turned back to Petanj, jabbing at her accusingly with a forefinger. "Talk to Villette! She *trusts* you! Make her see sense and use some caution!"

Petanj left a long pause. "I'll see what I can do," she said, frost-edged, and stalked away. "Let's get something to eat," she growled, as I caught pace with her. "Alarums and excursions make me hungry."

It was not until we had both made decent headway into our pajeons that Petanj seemed to relax. "Sorry," she said, into the long silence between us. "Wojo gets on my nerves sometimes."

I snorted at that. "Glad to hear I'm not the only one. But, Petanj . . ." I leaned closer, although the place was almost empty. "Why is Villette refusing to admit to the danger? I understand the resistance to believing something so unusual and awful is happening"—I had certainly felt that discomfort myself—"but this seems . . ." It seemed like something more than that. And Villette had acted with commendable grip during the gas leak.

Mossa would already have a working theory for exactly what was going on. Without her brilliance and experience, her character-calibrated brain, I could only ask.

Petanj expelled a heavy sigh. "Wojo's not wrong, you know, or not entirely. Villette . . . she's the sweetest, she's a panda-de-dios, she is, and she means every moment of it, not like me, I'm always ready to bite, but she—I don't know, even while she wants to be nice to everyone she's also so focused on her research, and just so *good* at it, and people hate it and she doesn't know how to deal with it."

"I can understand that," I said encouragingly, hoping to imply *But that's not all, is it?*

She picked at what was left of her winter cabbage and fennel triple-piquant pannekoek. "The thing is . . . even being so kind, she's never really had an easy time making friends. She's always been very research-oriented, very earnest, and of course we're both very debris." I jerked my hand involuntarily, as though to revoke that less-than-complimentary argot, and Petanj waved my objections away. "It's true—our platform is tiny, and far from anyplace more cosmopolitan, of course people notice. And I don't mind anymore," she added, so fiercely that I could not quite believe it. "But for Villette . . . This group that she's found here . . . I always wanted to feel relieved about it, even if I didn't like some of them that much individually. At least she had people to hang out with who shared some of her interests, or respected her interests, I suppose. It's meant a lot to her. Of course she doesn't want to believe that one of them hates her enough to hurt her—and to do it by undermining exactly that passion for research she thought they shared." She looked at me helplessly and I nodded as sympathetically as I could.

"It's still possible it's someone with an interest in atmo-scarfs, or maybe the university." I grimaced myself, thinking the latter might not be much better. "And in any case, let's see if we can convince her to take more precautions," I added, in an effort to sound encouraging.

We were en route to Villette's lodgings when I noticed a courier post on the other side of the road. Telling Petanj I'd just be a moment I crossed over (tripping only slightly on the rail down the middle of the road), and found a telegraph form on the counter. It did not take me long (I had been composing telegrams to Mossa in the nether reaches of my mind all day, in several different genres) to scribble a message:

SORRY SHOULD HAVE STAYED CAN'T GET BACK NOW STOP THREAT HERE SEEMS WEIGHTY STOP STAKES HIGH STOP DO YOU KNOW ANY COLLEAGUES HERE STOP NEED ADVICE ASSISTANCE ~~STOP WISH I WAS THERE OR YOU WERE HERE~~

After crossing out the last nine words heavily enough that there could be no mistake, I made my way to the desk. "Is the line open to Sembla?"

The operator checked the flaring citrous and carmine gas-bulbs of his switchboard. "There's a break on the line between Cynkar and Vruz, and another on the other routing just before Prupal; we're trying alternatives. But at least one of those should be fixed in a diurnal or two anywise."

They always said they would be fixed in a diurnal or two, and sometimes it was true. I decided to write out a letter to send at the same time, to be on the safe side, and after copying and somewhat expanding on my telegram, I handed them both over and rejoined Petanj outside.

Chapter 8

I was still caught in the spiral of wondering whether Mossa would accept, read, answer, or care about the telegram when we arrived at Villette's lodgings, and perhaps that was why, as we walked through the foyer, my gaze caught on the gradudents' nook. My mood leapt suddenly, the breath jerking from my throat. Those shoulders, that slight espalde—my unrested and eager brain leapt to a recognition and immediately began calculating how Mossa might possibly have arrived within this timeframe—

The person I was watching so fervently turned to speak to their colleague in that moment, and the (subjectively unharmonious) line of their profile disabused my foolish notion. Of course, *of course* it was not Mossa, just my desperate imagination tracing her over anyone remotely like her. I turned away and followed Petanj up the stairs, but the sense of unease stuck. "Petanj," I said, as we stepped out onto our floor, "those gradudents who work as porters. With such an ad hoc system, might that not be a simple way for an evildoer to gain access to your rooms, or at least the hall?"

"Betul," Petanj agreed. "I hadn't even thought about it—I mean, I tease her about it every time I come, but I hadn't thought about the safety of— Villy, what's wrong?"

She had opened the door to the rooms they were sharing quickly enough for us to see Villette startle at the sound of it. She was curled on the low divan, her hands in a mutual clutch. "Sorry," she said, "sorry, I just—the lab director wouldn't listen and then . . . I got back and *this* was on the floor, pushed under the door." She uncreased her hands and held out the laminate she had been gripping between them.

THEY'LL NEVER BELIEVE YOU

The words were hotpen-scrawled so viciously that the laminate was stabbed through at the point of the first *V.* Villette was shaking, and I needed to hear what she had to say about her afternoon at the lab, but first—

"I'll be back! I just have to—" I gestured at random and pushed back out through the door, ran down the stairs, and arrived panting at the gradudent niche only to find that the one who wasn't Mossa was gone.

That didn't matter, of course; they *weren't* Mossa, so there was no reason to talk to them particularly. And yet, as each of the remaining three gradudents replied in turn that no, they had not delivered any notes to the second story that diurnal, no notes under doors anywhere in the building, in fact, that failure seemed less important than the disillusion of not encountering that person who looked a little like Mossa, from a distance.

Finally, unable to stop myself, I asked about any others who had been working there that day. The gradudents looked at one another. "Pindu just left," one of them volunteered. "Off to get dinner for the gent in room N53, he's partial to the tlayuda spot near the smaller station. And, whatstaname, Sassania was here earlier—ta has a tutorial now. But neither of them delivered any notes under doors, not in this building."

"We'd have known," another agreed. "We all talk about the jobs, and anyway no one was away for that amount of time, like. But anyone could have walked in from another building, gone to whatever room—" I hadn't wanted to mention the room number, to prevent any more chisme attaching to Villette's name, and this gradudent apparently resented the lack of confidence—"and left the note. We're convenience, you know, not guards."

I thanked them, and hesitantly—for I was not sure of the proper practice—offered a pourboire that was readily accepted.

As I glumped up the stairs, facing my silliness at having rushed out on the cousins and my complete inability to accomplish anything whatsoever on this investigation, the urge to simply get on a railcar and go to Mossa returned. I was doing no good here, and if I was with Mossa . . . well, I might not do any good there, either, but at least I wouldn't be constantly concertina'd inside by this awful, inescapable longing; the crumbling conviction that I had made a terrible error in leaving and must, at all costs, undo it. I opened the door to Villette's rooms primed to announce my departure or dissolve into tears or both, and both cousins looked up at me immediately with expressions from eager to apologetic.

"Did you find anything?"

"I'm sorry I was so short with you earlier, Pleiti. I can't tell you how much I appreciate you being here."

Not without regret, I took my cue. "No," I told Petanj, "I asked the gradudents downstairs, but they say they didn't deliver it, or see who did. And please don't think of it," I said to Villette. "It's a difficult situation." The less dwelled on, the better. "What happened at the lab?"

"Oh . . . it . . . I suppose it wasn't so bad. There was no real harm done, and the director said so, but ta wouldn't believe that it wasn't me who left the sirens off, and—well, it could have been an awful lot of harm done, couldn't it?"

"Tell me," I said, because if I had to stay, I was going to do my levelest to help, "who knew that you had that alert on your"—what had she called it?—"your device?"

"Almost no one. It has only been in place a few weeks. And of course I do not talk much about the specifics of my work, but then, it was hardly a secret either." No, if she was going to give it away anyway I supposed it wasn't. Villette closed her eyes to think. "Hoghly, certainly, and possibly I mentioned it to Wojo or one of the others when we were chatting about our work. Would that—would that absolve them?"

"I don't know. I don't know whether they wanted to kill you or scare you."

Villette's expression crumpled at that. "Oh. But, sabes, I had to get approval for the testing. No one was around when I did it, but anyone could have seen my request and guessed about it." She paused, running a hand along the seam of a cushion. "I suppose it's *better* if they weren't really trying to hurt me?"

I gestured ambivalence. I wanted to be reassuring, but.

Petanj said it for me. "The use of a gas leak as a scare tactic does not fill me with confidence." She looked at her cousin's expression and huffed with frustration. "I'll make some more tea." She headed to the cupboards; Villette didn't even seem to hear her.

"What about these gradudents?" I asked. "These sometime-porters or what have you."

Villette blinked at me. "Here in the lodgings, you mean? What about them?"

I explained, and she frunced. "I hadn't thought of that. I'm so used to them. And we get to know them, mostly . . . I mean, they do shift around, but most of them just pick a place and stick to it, so . . ."

"So you know their names, and what they study?" I pressed.

"Some of them," Villette said vaguely.

"Por ejemplo, you'd notice if someone came with a delivery or something and you'd never seen them before?"

"I would," Villette replied, "but I wouldn't think anything of it."

"Pues from now on you should!" Petanj interjected. She shook a pot at her cousin. "Is this doni-doni one-cup teapot the only one you have?" Her syntax had shifted into the argot of their small home platform, and I wondered if it was unconscious or an attempt to be comforting.

"What are you doing? Just ring! That's for when I'm up late and don't want to put no one to the trouble."

"Do those pseudo-porters bring the food as well?" I asked, suddenly alarmed.

A flicker of a smile on Villette's face. "No, we do get kitchen staff. Anything to grignoter with the tea?"

We declined. *"Have* you seen any unusual faces around?"

Villette considered, then shrugged with an embarrassed smile. "I really don't know. I only see the gradudent gaggle when I'm entering or leaving, of course, and I do try to nod but it's not like I take attendance."

"No reason why you should," I said, betraying both my own feelings and Mossa, who would certainly have told her to do so, "but you really ought to take some precautions."

"Like what?" Villette did not sound amenable, and indeed we spent the duration of the teapot failing to convince her to various measures. Have someone accompany her to her lab? Ridiculous and impracticable. Alert the Investigators? *They* were hardly going to provide protection to a nervous scholar who had not truly—fine, not verifiably—been attacked. Take additional care, be wary of strangers? She always did, she wasn't a fool. Had anyone threatened her before? No, not really, at least, no one who *meant* it, of course people would say things.

"I'll look through your correspondence first thing tomorrow, to see if I can learn anything from those anonymous notes."

Villette agreed, but with a mueca. "You don't mind if I don't accompany you? After today's disruption I'm even further behind in the lab."

I assured her it was fine—indeed, if I had to go through her private communications, even with her permission, I'd as soon not do it to her face.

I took my leave, trying not to show how dispirited I felt, and dithered for a moment in the corridor after the door closed behind me. I should go to my room—I had given the cousins that impression with full intention that I would. I certainly needed the rest, and putting a few hours into my research wouldn't be amiss either. In truth, a solitary dinner in front of my current matrix sounded wonderful. And yet.

I glanced at the gradudent nook on my way out; the person who had reminded me of Mossa was back, in conversation with another of the ad hoc porters, but the sight no longer gave me that heart-thump of recognition, and I looked away quickly; a telegram to the real Mossa took precedence over making awkward conversation with someone who vaguely resembled her. As I emerged into the night, a peal of changes wafted through the atmosphere, a slightly clangy but melodious rendition of the first ten notes of 桜坂. Somewhere in this town they had a decent set of carillons.

I havered again over a phrasing that would sound urgent but not hapless, that would encourage concern but not disdain, and eventually settled on the deeply unsatisfying: LODGINGS UNSAFE IMPOSSIBLE TO SECURE. I had to stop myself from writing more, writing another extensive annex letter with every detail of the visit so far. She might hate that I was writing to her, might be tossing aside the flimsies in disgust for all I knew, but the act of sending was the closest I could get to her at that moment, and I could not completely steel myself against that minimal relief. Besides which, the more I learned, the more intractable the problem of keeping Villette safe and her reputation pristine seemed; writing to Mossa at least offered the illusion that I might get some help with it.

Chapter 9

The next morning—Neptday, it was, the donfense was in just under a week—Villette took me to her office. It was a tiny space in a clutch of tiny spaces; but then, as Villette said apologetically while she moved a stack of books so as to offer me a seat, she rarely used it. "I'm always in the lab when I can be, but you know," looking vaguely around, "it's convenient to have another space, I suppose." She pointed me to her correspondence files, invited me to make myself free of them, grasped at a few more pleasantries, and looked very relieved as she fled back to the lab.

She had told me, with a faint air of embarrassment that I hadn't quite understood at the time, that the anonymous notes could be found at the very back of the files. I had to fossick around to find them pushed into an unmarked envelope and shoved as far away as possible; she had known it was better not to get rid of them, but she had hated having them all the same, and the contrast with her careful nonchalance told me how much the missives had bothered her.

It was with an attitude of extreme prejudice, therefore, that I started reading, and first impressions did not improve my mood. The letters were heavily fretted with bold characters and screamers; the writer had strong words for the quality of Villette's work and, particularly, it seemed, some of her more theoretical arguments to do with the variability of Giant's gases in the upper reaches of its atmosphere. I didn't completely follow, and I couldn't be certain whether that was my lack of expertise or a problem with the writer: Was this a true, if abstruse, academic disagreement, or the ravings of an obsessive without any real foundation? I flipped to the next letter, and read it carefully: Villette had, it seemed, not made the requested retraction— hardly a surprise—and the language was even more incensed. The pattern continued through three more letters. There were no explicit threats, and the language never quite crossed the line into obscenity, but the anger and sense of righteousness were clear. This, indeed, could be someone willing to risk their own reputation to harm Villette's; moreover, the anonymity was suggestive, aligning as it did with the modus of the accusations of falsification.

A second set of anonymous notes was a little different: clearly some time later, and the matter entirely distinct. I was puzzled at first what had inspired them, and wondered if I might need to read Villette's pubs to grasp the context—time-consuming, but I preferred to avoid asking her—but a line about *wasting resources on cosplaying Earth* made me think they were about the nasal filter, and when I read through them again with that interpretation in mind, it seemed to klopt perfectly. I scrutinized the notes to see if they were from the same person, but the first set was printed and the second hotpenned, and so messily that I suspected the handwriting was disguised in any case. Two anonymous reviewers was certainly not unprecedented in the academic context; on balance, though, I felt the language and tone was similar enough to suggest they were by the same easily angered person.

But where did that leave us? I replaced the notes thoughtfully. Were the early ones evidence of an initial irritant that led to a continued, and increasingly uncontrolled, grudge against Villette? It occurred to me that Wojo worked on something to

do with atmospheric conditions—but then, that would probably also be true of Villette's coauthor, and certainly her tutor.
I decided, rather reluctantly, that a glance through the rest of
her correspondence might be utile. But first, tea.

I stood up, stretched my dorsal, and stepped out to prowl the
surrounding area. I found the hob a few corners away, above a
cupboard of snacks with a cheerfully lettered laminate inviting
people to eat what they would from there and keep anything for
personal use in their own carrels. Whistling softly—the tune I
had heard the night before from the carillon—I deposited the
omiyage I had brought from Valdegeld, a bag of caramels sur-
tidos from a provisioner I hoped they had heard of here, and
selected a small bowl of crushed dried berries to accompany
my tea. When the water was ready I filled Villette's small pot
and took it back to her office with the berries.

I couldn't be sure which of the few mugs on Villette's shelf
was her preferred and which were for visitors, so I was a bit
hesitant in tipping up the one I chose, on the end of the row;
that meant I had a chance to slam it down on its rim again before the horrid scrabbling creature inside was able to escape or
pinch me with its claws.

I found myself against the wall on the other side of the
room, breathing hard. My first impulse was to leave the office,
the building, and perhaps the platform, and it cost me a few
moments of careful breathing and gradually more hinged consideration before I could get to my second thought, which was
that there must be someone who could assist with this. One of
the gradudents who seemed to infest this university, waiting
for spare jobs? Or a facilities maintainer, perhaps? But my curiosity reasserted itself. I had barely any impression of the or-
ganism lurking under the cup, beyond a blurred impression of

pincers and jointed legs; at least a minimal description would be helpful for whatever actions I pursued next, and I did not want to risk losing the evidence, should any assistance prove overly stringent.

Struggling against revulsion, I edged towards the cup. If I flipped it over, would the animalito be able to climb up the steep sides? I decided not to risk it. Grabbing some books from Villette's many bibliopiles, I constructed a wall—permeable or climbable, I was sure, but I hoped not immediately—around the cup. Reaching in gingerly to clasp the base of the over-turned mug, I yanked it upward.

The bestiole was a little larger than my thumb, and spry enough to spring immediately forth and make for the metal wall. I waited only long enough to commit its morphology to memory before slamming the cup back over it, so I did not find out whether it could climb, but even that short time left me shaken enough that I had to spend another five minutes in the farthest corner before I could venture forth to see where it might have come from.

Because how long could a—reptile? Insect? I had forgotten most of the Classical zoology I had learned in school—stay genki when trapped in that small a space with no food or water? Perhaps a long time. Perhaps it moved so quickly because it was hungry. But it seemed more likely for it to have been planted fairly recently.

There had been no one in the common kitchen area when I went to heat the water—had someone from the lab slipped it under the cup then? While I was leaving them *treats*? Was the possible venom from that highly suspicious pointy part meant for me, rather than Villette?—and the space was still uninhabited when I reemerged. I forayed down one of the nearby corridors. The first office was empty, but when I knocked on the second door, I heard a drawled *biaaahhhnvenu* and opened it to find someone I knew sitting behind the desk.

"Needs?" Hoghly had looked up but, apparently not recognizing me, returned his attention immediately to the book he was perusing.

"Ah," I said. "I'm using Villette's office, and one of her cups is broken. I was wondering if anyone had been in there earlier."

He looked at me again, this time with more interest but less comprehension. It was hard to blame him; it didn't make much sense, although I had hoped for a reaction from anyone who might be able to imagine a reason for the cup breaking, and a possibly dangerous bicho loose in the office. Hoghly, however, showed no such concern. "I don't know, I've been working in here with the door closed. You'll have to account to her yourself."

I muttered something acquiescent and closed the door gently. Although the three subsequent offices were also occupied, none of the scholars therein could tell me whether anyone unusual had been in the building. I returned to Villette's carrel reluctantly. I wanted to leave altogether, but the conversation with Hoghly had made me curious, and with a baleful look at the cup, I dug back into her correspondence.

For someone who hated to be in the office, Villette was at least neat in her organizing, and I found the letters from her co-researcher without any difficulty. It was amazing how quickly a person's character shone through the casually penned word, I thought: I could almost hear the querulous tone of Hoghly's voice, fresh in my mind as it was, as I picked through his complaints, petty accusations, and whinging about not getting enough share of the credit. Reading with an academic eye as well as that of an Investigator (and, inescapably, that of Villette's friend), I was rather of the opinion he was getting too much credit rather than too little. He was also, I noted, capable of disparaging a suggestion in one letter and presenting it as his own idea in the next. I could easily imagine him attempting to falsely discredit Villette's work; trying to scare her with a critter under a cup also seemed perfectly in character. The only questionable aspect to it was that any academic scandal about her could so easily tarnish him by association, and it was hard to imagine him accepting such a slight even to harm someone else.

Flipping through the larger files, I next found letters from Villette's former tutor Professor Vertri. His notes were fewer and shorter but did not inspire much more confidence. He had for a while sent her references to papers she might find useful, but those had diminished over time, presumably as his august brain became occupied with newer students and their concerns. Or perhaps as relations had become strained? In one short missive from nearly a Classical year earlier he had referred to a prior conversation: *I hope you have rethought your position, remain disappointed that you were so resistant to my counsel.* I supposed that related to the disagreement over the nose thingy that Villette had mentioned. More recently, he had sent congratulations for the donship nomination, but so briefly as to be almost insulting. At the end of that note he had added with a hotpen *I hope you use this position for the GREATER good!*

Comemierda.

By then I had nearly reached the time of my next engagement, and could leave without feeling like I was running away, but first, with some guilt, I checked for missives under Wojo's name. I did not find anything from her in the files. Either any laminates she had written were kept with personal matters, or were considered unimportant and reconfigured, or perhaps they never corresponded at all, and their friendship was based on drinking or dancing or dining together.

I did find a cache of letters from atmoscarf producers, but most of them were limited to initial queries that Villette had presumably sent negative responses to. One of them had continued to a second entreaty, which I read carefully, but while expansive in its promises to her, should she agree to share her technology with them, it could not be in any way construed as threatening. Still, perhaps they had decided to move from words immediately to actions, and I noted the name of the firm, Philtre, and the location of their representative on Stortellen.

I hesitated before leaving, then found a block on which I hotpenned CAUTION: DO NOT USE. I propped it in front of the mugs, in case Villette should return before I managed to warn her in person. Then I left with alacrity. For the first time since arriving in Stortellen I was looking forward to something.

Chapter 10

I was not fabricating when I told those insupportable Modernists (How *could* Villette tolerate them?) that I had collegiate exchanges planned during my visit to Stortellen. After Petanj's consultation in my rooms, before even my visit to Mossa's, I had sent telegrams to several Stortellen scholars that I had previously met or corresponded with, or whose work I had admired. (And a good thing I did do it before going to Mossa's; had I waited until after that dispiriting encounter I might not have had the energy to write at all.)

An answering telegram had found me at the lodgings, arranging a lunch meeting with a group of Classicists, which I quite approved as a casual way of discussing our work and deciding which of us might profitably pursue more intensive collaboration. It would be, I thought, something of a relief. Surely none of the Classicists could have reason to discredit Villette! Besides which, time with Petanj and Villette was a wearing reminder that Mossa was not with me, and I could not replace her acumen; but she would not have joined this interval, and I hoped to forget her absence for a while.

My correspondent, a scholar of Classical forestry named Starshka Usuf, had suggested I meet her at her office, but she was waiting outside the entrance, one of the rail-bound containers already queued beside her.

"I thought we might go for a picnic," she said, after we had exchanged greetings. "Yes, it's cold," she added, noting my dubious expression, "but we have rugs which should keep us warm enough, and it's a worthwhile experience for a visitor." Glancing at the bin, which held not only a tight bundle of blankets but also a substantial hamper, I agreed readily enough. "Truth be told," Starshka went on as we started off, the bin gliding beside us under a push from her free hand, "we do it often enough even when there are no visitors, for it's a pleasant place, and a reminder of why we study as we do . . . Ah, Gilrad! Akash!!" She greeted the other scholars as we collected them, and soon we were a group of half a dozen.

Along the stroll I fell into conversation with a chemist named Haxi who was particularly focused on the composition of Earth's pre-industrial atmosphere, and was so deeply interested that I nearly walked into the person in front of me when we came to the park.

"We have to carry the baggage ourselves from here," Starshka told me; the rail track ended at the edge of the park, which was entirely laid with soil and growing plants. I gamely took one end of the hamper, and it was only as we lifted it out and I let my gaze rise that I realized where we were.

I should have guessed, of course; it is well known that the highest point in all the platforms is a constructed hill in a park on Stortellen. But it hadn't occurred to me, and even if it had, I don't think I would have been prepared for the sight of that slope rising before us.

"It can't be entirely soil," I said foolishly.

"Of course not." Starshka's smile was habitual, I thought, but pleasing nonetheless. "There's a substructure of asteroid metal, so it's not quite authentic, but as an approximation of topography . . ."

"It's spectacular," I said, quite honestly, and then set myself to the climb. Some of our group—by then we numbered a decenne or so—were climbing straight up the slope, but Starshka directed her bicycle chair towards a smoothed, narrow, metal-clad path that wound up the side of the hill, and I followed with a few of the others. For all the stairs I regularly ascend to my rooms in Valdegeld, which I rely on (perhaps overmuch) to keep my muscles active, I found the curve of the hill an un-familiar challenge, and I was panting by the time we reached the top.

"An extraordinary prospect," I said once I caught my breath. The rugs were spread, looking out at the sunset-gilded, gridded streets of the town and university, a nitid island surrounded by distant curling fog. We were not so *very* far up—certainly not *much* higher than the roof of Villette's lodgings, say—but the effect of standing on the top of a mound of dirt was entirely different than that of a building, somehow.

"It isn't the Preservation Institute." Akash shrugged. "We're all quite envious that you're so close to that, if I may say so. But this is a pleasant spot, as well as useful for some types of studies."

"It is indeed," I hastened to agree.

It was quite chilly—when I looked up, the apex of the at-moshield looked barely out of reach, and indeed the few trees on the top of the hill were stunted, their higher branch-ends brittle from brushing against the cold—but there were hot-water bot-tles packed along with numerous travel rugs, and lanterns to hang from the tree branches and set around our blankets, and we were soon quite cozy and sharing out the delicacies from the two hampers (one rigorously free of nut products).

I won't go into the details of the conversation but to say that it showed academia to advantage: a collection of people trained in rigorous methods, with diverse interests, sharing their knowledge in a conversation that was wide-ranging and agile. At one point we were distracted when someone found a small insect in the dirt—living there! Endemic!—and Akash offered everything ta could remember about it, caveating that ta was a biologist but not an entomologist; Yustia pulled out a small magnifier and passed it around; then a cultural historian whose name I didn't catch added a nursery rhyme and a superstition.

I took advantage of the moment when most people were trying out the nursery rhyme verses to angle a low-voiced conversation with Akash. "If I may presume on your expertise . . ." Ta offered a minimal bow in acceptance. "I saw a Classical beastie recently," I told him, sketching in the dirt with a stylus, "and I couldn't quite remember the name."

Ta examined my diagram, waving me off when I apologized for the lack of skill. "No, no, it's quite recognizable, if you're sure about these claws—"

"Very sure," I confirmed with a shiver.

"And the curve of the tail? Yes, it's clearly a scorpion." The word sent an atavistic chill through me, and I shuddered again, then tried to masque it with frivolous commentary. "You must think me an awful buffer for not recognizing it."

"Not really." Akash laughed. "To be honest, I think the only reason I know about it is because I had an adolescent hyperfixation on Classical constellations."

"Oh yes, there was one of those, wasn't there? Err . . . do I remember rightly that scorpions can be dangerous? To humans I mean. It was quite small." I held out my thumb in illustration.

"Not my area, really. But as I recall there were varieties with more and less venom, so it would depend."

"Do you have a population of them here?" There were quite a few small adaptable animals that had been successfully introduced, at least for a few generations at a time, to the protected environment and resources of various platforms on Giant. Roaches were fairly common, and pigeons, and while most cats one might meet came from gestation, there were documented breeding populations on some platforms.

"Not that I've ever heard, although I'm not fully up on that. I can check for you."

I could have checked myself—most platforms, and certainly any with a university, kept a published record of their fauna— but I had hoped for the offer in order to ask for something else. "If I show you the specimen, do you think you'd be able to tell me more about the specific species?" I wanted very badly to know whether these incidents were meant only to scare or intended to cause physical harm.

"You have it here? I'd love to see it, of course. I don't think I'd be able to tell you much more without additional research, but truly, I'd be happy to do it." I nodded agreement, then let myself be swept back into the primary orbit of the conversation.

All in all, I enjoyed myself thoroughly, and as we reached that stage of repleteness that always makes discussion slow, and Starshka began pouring out a third—fourth?—round of tea from the thermoses, I wondered why such sparkling discussions weren't more common. Was the spontaneity, or at least the introduction of an outsider, in this case myself, necessary? Or perhaps here at Stortellen they *did* enjoy such tertulias frequently, and Valdegeld was simply too hidebound?

Even as I hosted that thought, Gilrad leaned back on his elbows and sighed. "I don't know when I've enjoyed a salon so much. Pleiti, my dear, you must visit more often."

I laughed and said something deprecating. Gilrad was leaning against Akash, who had clasped ta's hand lightly around his ankle, and their easy closeness was distracting me with pangs of heartsprain.

"Do tell us all about Valdegeld, while you're here," Gilrad went on lazily. "What's the gossip that doesn't get into the published papers?"

I had, in principle, no particular objection to a bit of gossip about people who were far away and unlikely to be harmed by it, and I was mentally reviewing the latest nano-scandals, cross-referencing *most amusing* with *least likely to intersect with this group*, when Akash jumped in.

"Oooh, tell us about that rector of yours. What really happened?"

It was like a shock of ice water, so unexpected I couldn't respond for a moment, and in that moment everyone else jumped in.

"Is it true that the species list was completely incoherent?"

"*I* heard that the species sampler was a rumor and he went by himself to prove that humans could survive there before subjecting any other species to the ordeal."

"Didn't work then, did it?"

"Did the university know about it?"

"Know about it? They say the university *sent* him!"

"Will they be sending a follow-up?"

I tried to smile. "We don't really know much," I began, "but—well, I don't *think* the university knew about it or condoned it." Now that it had been suggested, it felt horrifyingly plausible, but I pushed that away to cry about when I wasn't in public. "And as far as I know"—I hadn't personally seen them, even if I had seen the rocket—"he did take samples."

There was a little silence. Either my tone or the substance seemed to have flattened their fizzy gossip glee.

"What is it you're here for, actually?" asked Alpecy, a Classical musicologist. "Surely not just to enliven our luncheon."

"A donship ceremony, wasn't it?" Starshka asked, as I sputtered through another demurral. "Of a Modernist?"

"Yes, Villette Diatoub. She and her cousin were classmates of mine during our studies."

"Oh yes, the one who works on atmoscarfs and atmoshields and suchlike," Haxi said, quite animatedly. "We've consulted each other on a few things, you know. Her work is quite impressive. We've spoken about possibly collaborating on a project."

"Well, it would have to be impressive, wouldn't it? To hit donship so young," Akash put in.

I was still recovering from how casually Haxi, a Classicist, mentioned collaborating with a Modernist. We valued the idea of such transverse projects in Valdegeld, of course, there were many initiatives designed to promote them, but they never quite happened, or at least not without much fanfare.

"*You* know her," Haxi went on, prodding another of the group. "*And* her cousin, the one who comes to visit a lot, you remember they joined us for the festival last year?"

"Oh yes." The scholar frowned. "Isn't she the one that Evna is so unhinged about?" *Evna.* My mind flicked up the memory of a soap-bubble atmoscarf and vivid eyes. She hadn't seemed any more unhinged than the rest of them.

"Evna? What, that astronomer? Ooh, I can't abide her. The *worst* kind of Modernist, completely *me-me-me.*" Evidence of at least some anti-Modernist feeling there, although considering the amount of self-involved palaver I had heard from that clique over drinks, perhaps it was no more than the uncoated truth.

"*Except* when she is talking about Villette's work, which she *will* go on about. All techno-babble to me, to be honest."

"Wait, wasn't her advisor that creep Vertri?"

"Yes, he's a bit of a suvver." Alpecy noticed my confusion about the term. "Do you not say that in Valdegeld? From the Classical, darling. S-U-V?"

"Rather after my era," I told her. I had in fact heard the term but I wanted to be sure precisely what they meant by it here.

"Selfish prat," Gilrad translated succinctly. "And he is really."

I considered if I should try to direct the conversation, but was too afraid to interrupt the flow.

"Villette's nice enough," someone else put in. (I tried to gauge whether there was an implied *for a Modernist* after that statement; the Classicists here seemed so open-minded, it was throwing off my social acumen.) "But I can't understand why she's always going about with that awful chemist, what's her name, Wojo? She's mega rude."

I almost broke my listening-only rule to agree vociferously with that assessment, but stopped myself through the expedient of stuffing most of a rather good spicy cinnamon bun into my mouth.

"I can't understand why she's still coauthoring with Hoghly Katak."

"*Is* she? Ugh I had to work with him once on a procedural committee, the *most* useless."

"Pleiti, dear, you've told us about your research in general, and very fascinating it is too, but is there anything in particular you're working on now?" That was from Zan, a sturdy, grey-haired individual, very friendly and unassuming; it was with a shock that I had realized earlier, due to a chance remark, that she was the chaplain of the Classics faculty. I responded to her with a mix of relief and regret, trying to etch all the chismes in my memory as I expanded on my latest data source. Zan drew Starshka back into the conversation, and we found that the site of the novel I was currently analyzing overlapped with one of the forests she studied.

It was a worthwhile conversation, almost bringing me back to the intellectual euphoria I had felt earlier. Classical studies began with things like game registers and hunting accounts: the records that humans kept about what they cultivated, and extracted, from their surroundings. These records, though somewhat useful, were far from sufficient; it soon became clear that knowing how many, say, venison you wanted in a given forest was not enough, not if you were starting essentially from scorched earth without so much as the forest itself to build on. How many trees, of what species, would you need to shelter that venison? How many shrubs and wildflowers for them to eat? How many birds and insects to pollinate those for the next season? Earthworms would be critical, obviously, but what was the correct ratio? And predators, there would need to be predators (in addition to humans), wouldn't there? Starshka studied the trees of old-growth forests specifically, and the ecosystems they engendered, most of it sourced from academic and professional forestry work; we had a very fruitful discussion about the interstices between her data and mine that we agreed might lead to a paper.

By that time the sun was set, the moons emerging to gleam down on us. Gilrad rose with a yawn, explained that he was on the "offset diurnal" and over-late for bed, and tugged Akash down the hill with him. The party broke up shortly after. Between the ideas for collaboration and consideration of possible suspects, I was a little distracted. I noticed that Zan followed when I accompanied Starshka down the path, but I didn't suspect a motive to it until she said quietly, "I had a note from your Dean Mars." I started, and she held up a comforting hand. "Ta commended you to me, and mentioning that your errand here might be a bit more than, errhrm, support for your friend, ta asked I provide any support possible." It should have occurred to me that the more erai university officials would have networks of correspondence across the universities much as we did. "I'm afraid I don't know much of relevance to your friend's circumstances. I have heard her mentioned as a brilliant scholar, and that she produced work of immediate application, but not much else." That was good news, at least. "But I did want to take the opportunity to offer a word of warning. Use caution with the dean of the Modernist faculty. Though I say it as shouldn't, he's rather worried about their position still, very eager for the Moderns to get prestige, and less cuidadoso of his students and scholars than I would like."

"I appreciate the warning," I said, "very much; and if I may say so I'm surprised you speak so freely."

"Well, I'm a practivist." *Ah.* Practivism held as one of its explicit principles that loyalty to a mundane organization—a university, a library, a presiding committee, or even the practivist movement itself—should never be allowed to override its values. That would make it seem strange indeed that the sect was ever engaged by such organizations, but they were known to be extremely habile at balancing among the many different spiritual paths on Giant, the multifarious Classical and Modern branches of various religions and philosophies. Besides, most organizations liked to believe that conflicts between loyalty and values would arise only rarely, if ever. "In any case, I thought it important to let you know not to rely on the Modernist faculty for disinterested support from a position of authority."

We had reached the bottom of the hill, and with that somewhat worrying thought we said our farewells before starting off through the colorfully lit streets.

Chapter 11

Despite the warning from the chaplain, I made my solitary way through the streets in a buoyant mood. Along with ideas for several promising research collaborations, the group had given me a far better picture of the micro-biome around Villette, the individuals who might have personal grudges against her. I contemplated how I might go about narrowing down the list. Perhaps discreet investigations into their recent movements? Were Mossa on the case, she would doubtless be looking at their personalities, their patterns of behavior. I wasn't as confident in my assessments thereof, but maybe direct interviews would tell me enough about what they were like to have an idea of who would be so mean-spirited? And perhaps the scorpion would yield further clues.

That reminded me that I had a goal in mind. I had been walking at hazard, enjoying the intoxication of being alone and unaccounted for on a platform I barely knew. No platform is truly large enough to become *lost* in the sense used by Classical texts: walk in a straight line and sooner or later you will reach an edge. During the day or on bright nights you can usually catch enough refraction off the curve of the atmoshield to get a sense for how close you are to that edge, even if buildings block most of the view. Thinking of the (possibly) dangerous surprise waiting in Villette's office, however, I shifted from the seductive spontaneity of walking unknown streets in the middle of the night to the enjoyment of deciphering my route. I passed an alley of semi-enclosed food stalls, making me wonder whether Villette's invention would lead to more outdoor eating, and followed it towards the university; then, navigating by the distinctive turrets of a music hall I had previously noted and the sign for a small bookmonger specializing in Classical tomes that I had hoped to spend some time in during my visit, I found myself within recognition distance of the building containing Villette's office.

I took the ramp up to her level on express speed. I had given some thought as to how I might safely transport the noxious creature to Akash, and so I went immediately to the common area and poked about (with some caution) in the drawers until I found the store of metal envelopes every university office is sure to have for the convenience of scholars posting laminates or books to colleagues, journals, or libraries. Getting the critter inside might be ticklish, but I was determined, and lifted the cup with the envelope at the ready—only to find the space beneath it empty.

I jumped back with almost as much startlement as when I first saw the multi-legged horror, and looked around wildly, in case it might have escaped to somewhere else in the carrel, like just by my toes, or over my shoulder. Then I clocked that the warning sign I had left was also gone. Slowly, nape prickling, I stepped out of the room, but the common space was as empty as it had been when I arrived.

The Stortellen night seemed ominous rather than adventurous when I left the building again, shaken. I peered at every shadow, for the culprit must have been watching me, surely, if they had so neatly removed the evidence during my absence.

Although perhaps I had myself to blame for that more than any imaginary supercompetence on the part of the perpetrator; I had been at the picnic for *hours*. What would Mossa say? Even one of her scoldings seemed appealing, if only because she would then tell me what to do next.

I was so busy composing a message to her detailing the latest occurrences that I forgot my vigilance, and was rather startled when I heard a hail from the other side of the lane. I did not at first recognize the person who approached me—I had, it seemed, fixated too much on the fashionable atmoscarf, which had been exchanged for a somewhat staider mauve-tinted one, but the eyes tipped me off just before she reintroduced herself. "Pima, Evna Pima, but do call me Evna."

I murmured my own name and a similar assurance, though I did think it was a *little* premature to be moving to a first-name basis. I eyed her with curiosity, remembering what the Classicists had said about her. And was it possible that I was catching her on her way back from recovering the scorpion? But I was already some cuadras away from the building, and it was hardly surprising to meet her in the environs of the university.

Fortunately for my snooping agenda, Evna seemed inclined to chat. "Tell me," she said, with an attentive stare that showed her large eyes to advantage, "how are you finding Stortellen?"

"Oh, very fine indeed," I said, casting about for something specific to praise. "Er . . . oh yes, I've just come from your hill, quite admirable."

Something flickered over her face, and I wondered if I was about to hear more auto-deprecation about how it couldn't match up to Valdegeld, but instead she smiled. "Yes, I'm on my way there myself, in fact." She indicated the sizable case slung over her shoulder. "I like to do a bit of artisanal astronomy when I can."

I had forgotten that was her field. "What a perfect spot for it," I enthused, both hoping to keep her talking and legitimately charmed by the idea of a telescope on a hill, just as in the further flung days of the Classical era.

"Indeed. You should join me sometime." She glanced up at me through her eyelashes. "I suppose you and Villette are very close? For you to have come all this way, I mean."

"Oh, well . . ." I tried, with some self-consciousness, to knit an explanation that sounded reasonable while having nothing to do with my actual reason. "We know each other since university days, and of course it's difficult over such a distance—" Because Petanj *had* visited over the same distance, and since everyone seemed aware of that, they would be equally aware that I never had.

"I quite understand," Evna said, running a hand through her short hair. I had initially read that hairstyle as the sort of practical convenience a hardworking scholar might affect, but as the strands fell neatly from that practiced movement I began to think there was some calculation related to appearance behind that decision as well. "So trying, the distance. How wonderful that you were able to come now, for her triumph."

"Mmm. And you must be very close with her as well? I must say," attempting to rescue the clumsiness of that conversational volley, "I quite admire the knittedness of your friend group."

"Oh, well. We Modernists must stick together, you know." She batted her eyelashes, and I admitted myself entirely at a loss. The volume of interactions with strangers at the picnic, however pleasant, seemed to have exhausted my social capacity for the moment, because I couldn't at all manage this conversation.

I cast about for a way to end it. "I'm off to see Villette now, as it happens!" Was I overdoing the bonnefemmie? "Enjoy your stargazing!"

"And you, enjoy your evening."

I nodded and walked on with a determined stride until I was out of sight, and then dropped back into a flâneur's stroll, wending my way gradually towards the lodgings. I wanted more time without thinking or interacting; I was also hoping that an oblique route might lead me to stumble across another courier post, to distribute my obsessive messaging across multiple outlets. Unfortunately I did not find one, and reoriented my path to the one I had used (twice) the day before. I was too weary to calculate the perfect message, and composed instead a brief summary suggesting danger and threats and a lack of clues. I had, in university days, been a dab hand at askew art (that being a linguistic corruption of the Classical name, which made much more sense, given that the art is not notably aslant), and I hoped that Mossa remembered enough to decipher the rather abbreviated sketch of a scorpion I composed out of standard characters.

Then I hurried back to the lodgings. I could feel a gelid edge to the air, a sharpening of the wind against my nape: inclement weather loomed.

Chapter 12

I found Petanj lounging in Villette's rooms, drinking tea and reading a Classical novel. "Oh, you're back," she said, sitting up immediately. "Did you find anything?"

"Rather more than I hoped. But I'll tell you both. How was your day?"

"Pues," Petanj began, and then Villette emerged from the interior hallway in a robe, hair damp.

"Pleiti! How are you? Shall we order dinner?" Despite her bright words, I thought Villette looked a little worn, although perhaps it was simply the stress of the approaching donfense. As we awaited our order of yassa quails the cousins chatted inconsequentially, but once the food arrived I started telling them my tale. When I recounted my discovery of the scorpion, Petanj sat up with a brief and pungent oath; when I described the animal, Villette stood and walked to the bookshelf. I'd been worried about upsetting her, but she seemed more thoughtful than frightened, and returned shortly with a book: an illustrated children's guide to Classical animals. "Yes, that's it," I said, examining with distaste the picture she showed us. "More or less. But I believe there were several varieties."

"It says it lived in the desert," Villette reported. "So possibly it could have survived in the cup for some time without food or water?"

"It could just as easily have been inserted while I was there,"

I countered. "I was in the kitchen boiling the water, I didn't rush and wasn't particularly paying attention, someone could easily have slipped it into the carrel while my back was turned."

They both looked to me, startled. "You think someone was trying to hurt *you*?" Petanj asked. "You just got here!"

"Pleiti." Villette put her hand on my arm, uneasy. "Please don't put yourself to any risk, not on my account."

"We don't even know whether it was venomous," I pointed out. "Or, at least, whether it had enough venom to harm a human."

"It's also possible someone ordered it for an experiment, perhaps, or . . ." Villette trailed off. "It seems an odd choice for a mascota, but I'm sure there are people who could feel tender to such a bicho. I wonder if there's a way I could ask around to see if someone is missing a, er . . ."

Petanj snorted, then raised her hands as Villette looked at her. "I can easily imagine, cuz, someone choosing to have a pincered, stinging beast as a pet. I can even imagine them bringing it to the office and it getting free. But to get trapped under your mug, it would need assistance for that."

That silenced Villette momentarily, then she rallied. "But you didn't see anyone around?"

I dragged my eyes away from the menacing shape in the book, explaining how I saw Hoghly, as well as several other scholars in their offices, and that there could easily have been others around as well. I glossed over the picnic with the Classicists, mentioning the chaplain's warning as lightly as I could; Petanj scowled, Villette merely looked glum. The cousins gasped in rather charming unison when I revealed the disappearance of the scorpion. I finished with a summary of my conversation with Evna, although I wasn't at all sure whether it had been important. "It felt a bit odd to me at the time," I explained, "but that may have been me. I think there were too many exclamation points in my email," I said wryly, using a Classical idiom.

"She didn't say anything sinister like *How was the tea to-day,* did she?" Petanj agreed. "We can't assume that she *would,* of course, but merely encountering her near the university is hardly a point of suspicion."

"By the way," I said, making a vain attempt at casual, "that gradudent—the one who escorted us to the lab yesterday?"

"Kenore."

"Yes. Does she often help out with the portering here?"

Villette frowned. "I've seen her around the building a few times, but she may have been delivering something. I don't know if I've ever seen her waiting for commissions here. Why?"

"I saw her downstairs, and I was wondering if it was usual." The person who was not Mossa—whom I should stop thinking about in those terms, since they surely had more important and notable characteristics—had not been in the alcove when I arrived, but I had noted Kenore there instead.

Petanj sighed. "I can't say I feel *enormously* comforted by any of this, Pleiti."

"I can't say I do, either," I responded, detaching the second leg of my quail with some vigor. "I cannot emphasize enough, Petanj, that none of this is my expertise, and I would be far happier if you would take it to the Investigators."

"The Investigators don't provide protection, either," Petanj pointed out.

"I'm not going to the Investigators," Villette put in flatly. "I've seen them scoffing at *academics* and our *drama* often enough since I've been here. Pleiti, I do so appreciate you being here, and your support makes me feel"—she wrapped her arms around herself—"really, so much better. But I know it's not your profession, and I don't expect you to know what to do."

"It's true, Pleiti," Petanj said. "Neither of us holds you responsible, and I'm sorry if I made it sound like I did. Er, speaking of people who might know what to do, any word from Mossa?"

"No reply yet. It's possible she's traveling on an investigation." I sounded as though I were apologetic about her not answering for good reason, instead of being apologetic for misleading them about the fact that she probably was not able to work at all. I hated it. "But, although again, it is not my expertise, I have accompanied her on two investigations recently, and perhaps we can at least make a start?"

The cousins agreed with rather more enthusiasm than I myself could muster, and once we had cleared away the dishes I took some leaves of laminate from a bloc and set about constructing a very improvised version of her storyboard cards. "The first step," I said as I hotpenned names onto them, "is to learn more about our main suspects." I showed them Hoghly's name, and they nodded.

"I don't *really* think he'd do anything to hurt his own reputation," Villette said doubtfully.

"I just don't think he has the initiative for it," Petanj put in.

"I can't disagree," I said, thinking of his correspondence, "but there may be factors we're not aware of." I stuck the card on the wall, and added another for Villette's former tutor Vertri.

"Oh, surely not," Villette objected.

Petanj said nothing, but from her expression I rather thought she was on my side of that one.

"Just people we want to learn more about," I trilled. Truly I was feeling less sure about this—the attempt in general, the method in particular, the idea of replacing Mossa in any way at all, whether my actions had any utility whatsoever—but at least the cousins were listening. Perhaps this would convince Villette to use a little more caution in allocating her trust. "And on that note, what about Evna?"

Villette scoffed. "Just because she happened to be near the university when you were quite understandably upset about the disappearing scorpion—"

"I did hear some gossip that she has a fixation of some kind with you or, err, your work?"

Villette considered. "I don't *think* so? Of course we've chatted about work, but we're not in the same field, and I've never found her particularly pressed about mine. Maybe they misunderstood?"

Petanj patted her hand. "Just people we want to learn more about," she repeated, and nodded at me to put the card up.

Given that reaction I decided for the moment to keep my suspicions of Wojo and the gradudent Kenore to myself, as they were even more tenuous. "Bien," I said. "What about the university?" Petanj was nodding. Villette opened her mouth, probably to protest again, and then closed it. "If there is some, ah, plot within the university to discredit your work, who do you think would be the proximal agent of it?"

"I just . . . I don't see why they would have to go to so much trouble, when they could have simply *not offered me the donship*. But . . . I will say that the dean of Moderns has never liked me."

From the look on Petanj's expressive face, I gathered this was an understatement; in any case, it meshed neatly with what the Classics chaplain had told me. "Excel—that is, quite. I will have to find an opportunity of speaking with him. Now, what about these atmoscarf firms?"

Villette didn't like that idea either, naturally, but she preferred it to thinking ill of her friends or employer, so she gave me the names and local directions of the representatives she'd had the most dealings with.

Wishing I could drop my false heartiness, but unable to do so, I thanked them both and retired to listen to the incipient storm and plan my strategy for the following days.

Chapter 13

After breakfast the next morning I looked out at the worsening weather, braced myself mentally, swathed myself in my thickest atmoscarf, and set off towards the university.

I had decided to start with Villette's former tutor of the tepid congratulations and dubious ethics; aside from the university and the atmoscarf firms, he was the only one of the known suspects I had not yet met in person, and I was curious. I stopped on the way to check for replies to my telegram, but there were none. I imagined the flimsies lying forlorn just inside Mossa's door, ignored and disdained; or maybe she had read them but lacked the energy to respond. Or, perhaps, she was furious with me, or too appalled by my pathetic attempts at detecting or my even more pathetic claims on her attention to bother.

I did receive enough missives to be sure that the post was correctly functioning. There was a telegram from Dean Mars, asking me to keep ta informed as to my plans. I also received a long letter from a scholar in Zaohui that I was collaborating with on an attempt to combine literary with visual media. Neither improved my mood.

I fought my way through the increasing tempest to the excessively Modern building, draped with overhung porticos, where Grelle Vertri claimed offices, and had almost reached his door before I realized I hadn't worked out my approach. Honesty? Or dissemblance?

I half hoped he would be too busy to see me without an appointment, leaving me time to consider, but he stuck a maned head from the door and waved me in, igniting a hitherto unsuspected talent for improvisation.

"So sorry not to have cabled ahead," I began, in response to his query. "I'm a Classical scholar, you see, from the mid-southern reaches," a way of implying *Valdegeld* without saying *Valdegeld,* "and I'm here to"—inspiration arrived with such perfect timing that I barely even feared the gap before I skipped over it—"solicit recommendations for a new honor, the"—was I really going to say this? Oh stars, I was—"the Spandal Prize for excellence in"—*in comemierdería,* I almost said—"in, ah, inter-faculty intersections. After our late rector, do you know." I paused there with someone else's smile ingratiating on my lips to assess the effect. It almost didn't matter, I noted, what I had said: his eyes had widened at *honor* and illuminated at *prize* and he was already radiating bonhomie and a not-quite-effortless charm.

"Of course, what an excellent initiative," he boomed, and took some time to chiacchierare about how he had always appreciated the importance of intersections and what a wonderful idea to use status to perpetuate the name of a dead man, how very novel (he didn't phrase it that way). I had, to my surprise, rather enjoyed the game of invention, but I couldn't feel the same about listening to his nattering, so I took the opportunity to observe the man and his office.

He braided his beard in the asymmetrical fashion that had probably seemed very dashing three or four decades earlier and now looked fusty, disreputable in all the wrong ways, a few narrow plaits trickling from one edge of his mustache; his desk was an interesting specimen of salvaged metal—satellite, perhaps? Certainly its origins included a story he would want to tell if given half a chance—and it was topped with a laminate sheet allowing for notes to be jotted with a hotpen, a gesture of invention and vitality, but the markings on it were old, suggesting rather that he hadn't bothered to reface it in some time. Behind him was an oddity: what looked like an actual photograph, or very good replica, of him. Another artifact that it would be better not to bring into the conversation, I judged, if I wanted any further chance to speak myself.

On that point, I took advantage of a brief pause for breath in his elocutions. "Any scholars you have guided that you might recommend for our consideration? We're particularly looking for"—I grasped; apparently my invention was functioning faster than my memory—"projects aiming for the greater good."

He frunced slightly—whether because that phrase struck an unwieldy note for him or simply because I was asking him to suggest *other* people for the prize, and eventually rattled off a few scholars, arriving reluctantly at Villette only at the end.

"She has been well fêted by the university," he harrumphed, "and I will admit she conducted some excellently rigorous work under my tutelage; but sadly since gaining her scholar's scarf she has narrowed her thinking."

I tilted my head, both projecting and feeling baffled. "In what way?"

"Now she builds *devices*"—he used air-brackets to show his scorn—"and only for very niche purposes. Oh, her latest," he went on, seeing the continued incomprehension on my face, "is for those people for whom atmoscarfs do not provide enough assistance. Yes, yes"—again reading my expression, which I was no longer able to disguise—"worthy enough, I'm sure, but it's a tiny fraction of the population. She could better put her talents, such as they are, to something that would benefit *all* of us."

I am not, despite Mossa's example and recent attempts at encouragement, prone to violence, but I was ready to stab him for that *such as they are*. And for *tiny fraction*. And for the use of *all of us* when he clearly meant himself.

"Besides which," he went on, with a posture adjustment that suggested he was making himself comfortable for a practiced bout of pontificating, "I cannot but think that there is a very unsavory element of Earth cosplay in this fixation on going around without atmoscarfs. Nothing wrong with Classical research—I could have been a Classical scholar, you know—but if one is a Modernist, one should focus on the reality of Modern life rather than trying to pretend we're still on Earth."

I wasn't sure which was more ridiculous: his simultaneous criticism that Villette was not doing enough to help people deal with Modern conditions and that in addressing those conditions, she was trying to make it too much like Classical life; or that he would criticize anyone for *cosplaying* Earth when he prominently displayed a replica photo of himself smiling with a dense forest behind him! Then I suddenly understood what I was seeing: it wasn't a *replica* photo; it was a photo, and *he* was the replica—a repeat genome, or regenerate as such people were known.

The efforts to safeguard and reanimate Earth species had led to great advancements in genetic capacity, and it would have been too much to hope that no one would decide to gestate humans using the DNA of supposed "geniuses" from the Classical era. Such endeavors were occasionally the choice of individuals wanting to start a family, but most of them were sponsored by organizations claiming that genomes "proven" for intelligence were needed to solve the myriad problems of early settlement and Earth reanimation. (Even in those cases they needed to find a person to carry the child; the progress in genetics had not been matched by commensurate research and investment in gestational technology. Since most of those organizations, like most of the genomes they wished to propagate, were overwhelmingly cis male, this sometimes stymied the projects.) While none of these unfortunate regenerates had lived up to their supposed intellectual or entrepreneurial promise, many of them had managed to live reasonably decent lives; nonetheless, human rights groups had suaded the committees to outlaw the practice some fifty Classical years earlier. I was somewhat surprised to see that Vertri made his origins so obvious.

I realized that he had stopped talking and was looking at me expectantly. "I will keep her in mind," I said, scratching out the dagger I had doodled on my bloc. "I understand you no longer work with her? It must be very frustrating."

He growled for a while at that, about the ingratitude of tutees and the Modern mores; I believe the phrase *taught her everything she knows* escaped from his mouth, but in truth my attention wandered, because having worked through my outrage I had realized why his earlier phrase about cosplaying Earth seemed significant to me: it echoed one of the anonymous letters I had read! I tried to think of the exact phrase. Was he repeating something he had heard from someone else? That did seem typical of what I assessed to be an unoriginal mind. Or was he the author of the missives himself?

He was still talking, but I found the game was no longer fun, and I wanted only to leave. I barely waited for a pause before breaking in. "Thank you so much for your time. I will keep all those scholars in mind—and your erai self of course!"

He preened and chuckled and made insincere self-deprecatory noises, and while he was so engaged I paused my trajectory to the door as though on a sudden doubt. "By the way, were you here two diurnals ago? I tried to find you, but perhaps I was misdirected."

"Two . . . diurnals . . . ago . . ." It took him a long moment to pull his mind back from dreams of future glory to the mundanity of the day before, and when he did respond his heartiness sounded hollow. "Oh? What of the clock?"

"Around midday." The scorpion might have been secreted under that cup at almost any time; the gas leak seemed a better foil for alibis that might rid me of some of my inconveniently numerous suspects.

"Hrmm. Ha. Two diurnals ago, midday . . ." He scoped an agenda bloc in a way that he probably thought was surreptitious. "Oh yes, I had a meeting at the laboratories, a new project I'm working on with a colleague, *speaking* of inter-faculty intersections . . ."

I endured his rambling, nodding at more or less appropriate intervals, and removed myself from the office as quickly as I could.

Chapter 14

It was already nearly sunset when I emerged, although it would have been hard to know from the sky, which was uniformly tormentous. I felt the need for sustenance before tackling anything more, and tramped through the wet to the pajeon shop only to find it closed. Fulminating, I settled for a bowl of scrambled eggs, enlivened by fennel seeds and curry leaves, at what was obviously a student haunt.

I could not rule out Vertri. Even without his presence at the labs during the gas leak—and that was the most tenuous of clues, given how many other people had also been there or had access—that interview had given me shivers of repulsion. (Was that what Mossa felt when she evaluated characters to determine the steps of her storyboards?) He clearly bore an animus against Villette, and I could readily see him pursuing that resentment with utter disregard for inconvenience or even harm to others.

Although I wondered if he truly would not feel that accusations of academic impropriety against Villette would reflect on him, as her former tutor? It seemed a risky strategy for someone so caught up in status.

The rain had tapered, temporarily I was sure, into a grizzle when I emerged, but the wind was still twisting along the street, ruffling clothing and rattling chairs and tables unwisely left outdoors. I scrunched my face into the precipitation, weighing my next move. The courier's office tugged at my consciousness like an addiction, even though I knew it would offer no succor—the time was too short, even if the morning's message had slipped down the line and been delivered immediately to her door, even if she had roused herself immediately from the divan, read it, penned the reply without hesitation, taken it to the Sembla office herself—I realized my steps were already wending towards the couriers, and veered abruptly towards Villette's offices. The place still held a residual horror for me, but I wanted to speak with Hoghly Katak. The more I thought about our brief encounter the day before, the less satisfied I felt.

Hoghly was not, in fact, behind his desk, nor in the library building I tried next. I almost went to his laboratory, but on a tip from the savvy gradudent providing assistance in the library I ran him to ground in the scholars' lounge—rather more comfortable than the equivalent in his and Villette's office building, I noted. Hoghly had folded his lanky limbs into a cushioned hammock and dipped into a bowl of fried sprats while reading a book that might, I suppose, possibly have been related to his research.

I waited courteously for him to look up until he didn't, and then I leaned in and waited until he blinked away from his text to start babbling cheerfully. "Oh—hello! It *is* you. We met the other evening, with Wojo, you know, and Villette?" Would he remember me from the office the day before? He certainly hadn't seemed to pay me any mind, and at the moment he looked entirely blank. At least the font of my invention was still gushing strong. "I'm over from Valdegeld, and I've read some of your papers, so when I saw you there I just thought I'd say hello."

It took Hoghly a few minutes to disengage from his book and fully grasp that someone was trying to start a conversation with him, but the adulatory tone was as incantatory for him as it had been for Vertri, and before long he had agreed that I might prepare him a cup of tea. At least, I thought, checking the kettle carefully for arthropods before I filled it, I felt less cranky about the weather, the danger, and Mossa's lack of communication while I was being someone else.

As we sipped our tea Hoghly complained contentedly to me about all sorts of irritants. It was not difficult to work him around to Villette's upcoming honor: "Really *I* should be getting a donship too, then, isn't it? I'm working with Diatoub, aren't I?"

As I had nothing pleasing to say to him, having read their correspondence and thus feeling quite certain that Villette's part was the more rigorous and interesting, her efforts greater, I kept my mouth shut, though smiling.

As so often, that worked better than a series of questions to keep him talking. "The only reason the university is giving it to her is because they like the"—he made the hashtag sign with his fingers—"narrative. They can say she built something she *needed,* that it will *help people,* and that makes it sound like your irradiated Classical nonsense, so they like that, whereas my research is far more abstract and theoretical."

I wondered if it was true. Certainly, Classical scholarship was often held up as *serving a purpose,* while Modernism was seen as abstruse and disconnected or, in its more practical forms, self-indulgently adding amenities to this temporary settlement rather than atoning for our ancestors' misdeeds and preparing Earth for return. It was possible that Stortellen University, better known for its Modern faculty, might look for ways to give such research more consequence. Still, I was quite convinced that Villette's scholarship was more worthy of accolades than Hoghly's, so perhaps there was no more to it than that.

"I heard"—I leaned forward to indicate secrecy, but not too close; there were limits to how deeply I would inhabit my persona—"that there were some unfortunate allegations about the research?"

Hoghly waved dismissively. "All Villette's stuff. I wasn't involved in that project at all."

My cheeks hurt from smiling, or maybe from lying. "But you must know her very well after working with her for so long..."

For the first time, he showed an emotion other than complacency and self-regard. "I *had* to work with her, get it? The dean insisted, and then I agreed to work with her so she would collaborate on *my* next proposal." He snorted. "See how that turned out, scandal everywhere, and now she wants to give the tech—she's pissed off a lot of people, let me tell you. But anyhow, *all* we do is exchange data and drafts. Sure, maybe a meal now and then, but really we've got nothing in common. I don't know what she might or might not have done. I'm just trying to do some research."

"You must be very busy," I said admiringly. "Are you in the laboratory often?"

"Oh, almost every day," he said, but shiftily, leading me to suspect the *almost* was pulling more than its weight.

"I thought I might have seen you there the day before yesterday?"

"Yes, yes, er ... the day before ... yes, I stopped by. Not that it did me much good, that irradiated gas leak took all afternoon to get dealt with. Mess of people waiting around outside."

"Quite the crush," I agreed, as though it had been a fête, and began angling for an exit. "Perhaps I'll see you at the lab tomorrow."

When I escaped, not without hearing a few more useless

grumbles from him, the dark sky was spitting rain at an almost horizontal angle. I careened towards the lodgings as quickly as I could, wanting only a hot bath and a warm hearth, but found myself running aground in the shelter of the courier post all the same. I hesitated there for a moment, in the dimness of a low room whose skylights were doing it no favor in that weather. There was no need to write. There was no reason to write. Moreover, I did not want to put anything indiscreet into a telegram that could potentially be read or copied at every repeater along the line. I wanted to leave it, to go straight home. And yet, I could not resist. I found my way to one of the nooked escritoires and hotpenned a quick letter, sealed it, and posted it before I could stop myself. Then I dashed back out into the intemperie.

It should have been a relatively forthright traverse to the lodgings, but I somehow managed to choose the wrong angle at a quintuple intersection. I had only gotten myself turned back onto the correct approach and was muttering angrily at the wind, the precipitation, the darkness, the miserable purveyor of libel responsible for my being there, Mossa, and myself, when a figure hurrying past in the opposite direction stopped suddenly. "You again!"

The voice was so acidulous that I (foolishly distracted as I was) assumed it had nothing to do with me, and was startled when my elbow was suddenly caught by gloved fingers. I looked up, perturbed, into a renewed burst of icy rain and Wojo's furious face. "Ah," I said, struggling to reorient myself. "Publish much?" I had meant to interview Wojo as well, I reminded myself, and somewhat reluctantly I cast about to see if there were any likely teahouses nearby.

"*Publish much*," she mocked. "Why are you here?"

"What?" There did not seem to be any public establishments nearby, and I turned back to her, brushing the rainwater from the fraction of my visage not protected by my atmoscarf. "For Villette, of course. Er, Wojo, perhaps we could get dinner, get to know each other a bit better . . ."

Wojo snarled. "You don't even recognize me, do you?"

"Uh . . ."

She held her arm across the lower part of her face. "Is it the lack of atmoscarf that's confusing you?"

Was she, possibly, resentful of Villette for making atmoscarfs unnecessary? But then why would she go on wearing the device? It didn't make sense to me (perhaps Mossa would have understood), and I still had no concrete memory of meeting Wojo—could it have been a colloquium? Something with both Classical and Modern scholars . . . No, I had no idea—but at least I had gotten my surprise under control. "Maybe you could remind me?"

With a hiss she dropped her arm, whirled, and stalked away, disappearing into the grizzle-haze. I stared after her, imagining a laminate with her name on it tacked to the top of my suspects board, and then set off again into the night.

Chapter 15

The tempest rose through the night, and I was reveillé'd far earlier than strictly necessary by the ululating of the wind about my rooms. I lay in the narrow bed for a while, listening to the arhythmic cascade of congealed precipitation against the windows; when the solitude began to press in a little too hard, making me think of gas leaks and silenced alarms, I rose and dressed. Going outside did not appeal; my shunted-aside research, on the other hand, was itching at me for attention. I decided to explore the common areas of the lodgings in search of a place to work.

One of the enduring lessons of humanity's time on spaceships and on the cramped early platforms is the attention to the opposing yet complementary urges towards solitude and companionship. It became a deeply held principle of Modern architecture that residences and workplaces should include both: private space large enough to live or work in, common space that was available but not unavoidable. This was expanded to include various modalities of common space: quiet areas where one might expect not to be unreasonably bothered by the company; convivial spaces where gregariousness was preferred; purposeful spaces, such as game rooms and canteens; less directed spaces open to serendipity and reinterpretation; and everything on the spectrums in between.

This approach had become somewhat less uniform on the more populous and diversified platforms, where it was assumed that one could easily find public spaces of various amusing and accommodating types outside of one's lodgings or office edifices, but it was still surprising to find a lodgings house with only one (albeit large) common room. Somewhat shocked, I strolled around it familiarizing myself with its (unimpressive) supply of books and games and (somewhat more up to standard) array of comfortable seating and lounging areas. I had felt that I wanted to be quietly in company, and as there were only a few other people in the common room at that early hour it should have served well enough, but filtered by my disillusionment with the facilities I found it unsatisfactory.

In part from dissatisfaction, in part hoping that maybe I'd overlooked something, I turned to the noticeboard by the entrance to the common room. If the space was underwhelming, they did seem to be putting it to intensive use: I read about a time change for silent communal reading, a narrative summary of the previous night's role-playing adventure, and—not in the lodgings but at some university hall—an upcoming Modern history lecture, part of a series. That reminded me of my reflections on meeting Villette's Modernist clique. Certainly Modern history, while not as challengingly distant as Classical, still required rigorous methods and was valuable as a field. Curious as to the full schedule, I went to lift the messily scrawled laminate that partially covered the listings, and stiffened, my hand jerking to a stop before it reanimated to yank the offending note off the board.

It was Villette's name that had jumped out at me from the cacography, and while the handwriting was bad—disguised?—it was not so abstruse that I could not quickly decipher the repeated accusations of falsehood and academic malpractice verging all the way to plagiarism, collaboration abuse—*really!*—and again that bit about trying to be Earth, although in this case it was phrased as *phantoming* rather than *cosplaying*. Appalled, I glanced around, then pressed the laminate into a pocket and walked quickly away from the board. How long had it been there? How many people had seen it?

I stopped suddenly and turned to make my way towards the entrance, where, I remembered, there was another message board. Hotpenning rather than printing at least meant that reproduction would not be instant, but even so—I broke into an awkward jog, slowing as I passed the pseudo-porters' nook to avoid drawing attention, and scanned the board. This time I didn't bother to read the full scrawl, removing it—casually, people were more attent in the foyer—and waiting until I was alone in my room again to peruse it. Not an exact duplicate— the wording was different—but the same import.

A lot of anger, to burn two such screeds without losing vituperative energy.

I paced for a few moments, wondering what to do, and fighting the impulse to make immediately for the courier's office and apprise, or attempt to apprise, Mossa. Annoyed, I shook my head and went to look for Petanj instead.

I hesitated again outside the cousins' rooms: it was still quite early. But then, the roaring storm should have woken anyone up; besides which, Villette at least struck me as a congenitally early riser. At the thought of Villette, my hand clenched involuntarily on the laminates in my pocket. Was it really necessary to show those to her? Tell her, perhaps; but did she need to read something so upsetting? I decided to keep them on the qt but consult with Petanj as soon as I could get her alone.

Villette indeed opened the door to my knock already neatly dressed, and invited me to join them at a table where tea and youtiaou and bowls of doujiang were already set out; Petanj was sitting on the divan, blinking and still half-wreathed in blankets.

"How are you?" I asked, accepting a cup of lukewarm tea to keep me in orbit while Villette rang for a fresh pot.

"Fine," Villette said with a touch of defiance. "No attacks in the last day, either on my person or on my academic virtue."

I think I flinched a little, and I opened my mouth; but Petanj caught my gaze with a warning look. I don't know what she expected me to say, but I swallowed it anyway and managed to cheer the mood considerably by summarizing for them my interviews the day before. Petanj was spitting with laughter at my imitations of my own improvisations, but Villette's smile was reluctant. "I really wouldn't expect . . ." she began, then shook her head. "Bien, I knew that Vertri was unhappy with my research, but I've explained to him again and again that it's important. Important to me, yes, but also important."

"He's never going to care, because he's a self-centered prof-bro," Petanj commented, in a tone probably meant to be reassuring.

"Let him not care then! But there's no reason for him to be angry about it, let alone angry enough to . . . It's not *his* work, and I'm not *his* tutee anymore." Petanj and I valiantly refrained from comment. "And Hoghly . . ." Villette sighed. "Everyone knows he won't do the work. The university asked me to collaborate with him, because they thought I had the capacity to balance his, err, lacks—"

A minor and indecipherable explosion from Petanj, followed by some angry muttering about the university.

"Anyway," Villette continued, "he really has no reason to hate me, either."

"And when has needing a reason ever stopped anyone?" Petanj demanded.

"The other person I wanted to talk to is Evna, after that strange conversation the other night."

"You said maybe *you* were the strange part of it."

"Maybe," I admitted. "But nonetheless. At the very least maybe she can give me some more ideas or context. Also, perhaps, Wojo?"

"Wojo?" Villette laughed. "Look, Evna, maybe, but there's no way Wojo would do something like—" She gestured the general horribleness.

I glanced at Petanj, but she was studiously looking elsewhere. I wanted to ask about the way Wojo had accosted me the night before but decided to wait. "What about—Hoghly's wife. What was her name? Dao?"

"Vao?" Villette wrinkled her nose. "I barely know her, why on Giant would she do all this?"

"She could be jealous of you?"

"She's not a scholar!"

"Of your closeness with her husband."

Villette recoiled. "Eww!"

"Yes, I understand, but she might not know—or believe—that you feel that way."

"I suppose, but honestly, I rarely see *him* in person. I just . . ." She shook her head. "She could be completely irrational about it, but I haven't seen any evidence of it."

"I heard some rumor that they were multi-, last time I was here," Petanj put in diffidently. "Don't know if it's true or if he just fucks around a lot."

"In which case there's no reason she'd pick me to be angry at."

"Bien, unlikely," I agreed, although internally I reserved it under *still possible*. Meanwhile I was not going to give up on my one reluctantly approved suspect. "Err, I don't know where to find Evna."

"You could go to her office, but I doubt she would fall for that stuff you pulled with the others."

Petanj nodded. "Unlike Hoghly, she'll probably remember you from the other night."

"Oh but you know where she will be?" Villette grinned at me. "At the karaoke slam tonight."

"That's right! You should come with us."

I am certain my face froze in a mueca of startled horror, because the cousins observed me with identical smirks.

"It'll be fun!"

"I'll be singing!" Villette preened in a way that she would never have allowed herself to do about her research. "You have to come cheer me on!"

"You have to come support Valdegeld by cheering *me* on," Petanj interceded. "And perhaps throwing in a few verses yourself?"

That only intensified my panic. I changed the topic. "Villette, those anonymous letters. Do you have any idea who might have sent them?"

It took her a moment to remember what I was talking about—honestly, if I had received such mail, I thought I would be haunted by it, but perhaps Villette was better regulated than I. "Oh, those? It's been a while . . . but no, I never did figure out who sent them."

"Perhaps we could look into it further," I said, a little doubtfully. Investigator offices might have some ways of tracing laminates. Would they be able to match it to the ones I had found on the message boards? Or— "I suppose the university could analyze the composition of the plastics." I doubted it would do much good; there were certain presses known for having a particular type of supply, but most were quite variegated, and in any case it was most likely that it had simply been remolded from some utterly inoffensive printing.

"No need," Villette said, with something of a sardonic expression. "I'm not completely lacking in sense, you know, I did examine them. There's a config mark on the back, but it's from one of the busiest print shops in town." I wondered if the switch to hotpenning meant the aggressor was learning—assuming, of course, that the board posts came from the same source. Villette went on, dismissive. "Yes, they're a bit disturbing, but then they stopped coming and . . . nothing happened." *Until now,* I managed not to say.

"Anyone else you can think of that I might talk to?" I couldn't help a glance over my shoulder at her window. The hail was rattling against it like a shekere. "I suppose I'll try to search out Wojo and Evna then."

"I'm sure they won't be about in this storm." Petanj shook her fingertips dismissively. "Even Villette isn't going out."

Villette swatted at her without heat. "It's true, Pleiti, I'm not going to the lab today. It's a writing day."

The phrase *writing day* called to me seductively, yet I hesitated.

"So you don't have to worry about her safety," Petanj said. "You should get some of your work done, or relax maybe! And then you can take up the chase again at the karaoke."

"You can't *talk* to someone at a karaoke slam," I complained, but I was weakening.

"You won't *interview* them there. You'll just meet them casually and then you can make a plan to meet them later."

"And perhaps," Villette said thoughtfully, "in the karaoke atmosphere a person might be less rigorous about hiding their resentment."

I met Petanj's eyes, surprised that she would admit the possibility at all. That moment of synchronicity reminded me that I wanted to talk to Petanj alone. "Er, if we are doing this karaoke thing," I put in, "perhaps we should talk about duets."

There was some excessive raucousness from the cousins at that, but I did eventually get Petanj back to my rooms.

"So, what shall we sing?" She was rubbing her hands with glee. "You won't insist on it being Classical, will you?"

"Petanj," I said, exasperated, "you must have heard me sing at some point!" She stopped to think, and I shook my head. "If you had, you wouldn't be begging me to do it again. There will be no duet." I handed her the laminates. "I wanted to talk to you because of these."

She scanned them, sitting down heavily on a cushion partway through. I pushed the order button for tea. "Where did you find these?" Petanj asked.

"On the message boards." She flinched. "I was down very early this morning," I said, waving at the besieged windows by way of explanation, "so it's possible it was just put up and no one else saw it. But if it was up on two boards . . ."

"It might be up on more." Petanj stared bleakly while I retrieved the tea.

"It's hotpenned, so it would be a lot of work to do very many of them. But you would know better than I where to look."

"Yes," Petanj said with sudden energy. "Yes, I can go do the rounds. Although—" She glanced at the timepiece, then at the windows, then nodded decisively. "I'll search up Kenore and see if she can help."

"Kenore?" I said doubtfully. "Are you sure we can trust her?"

"Ugh, I suppose we have to think about that." But then she shook her head. "No, Kenore's a good ring. And I want to check everywhere possible."

"I could help."

"You don't know the university, and besides, you do have your own work, which I dragged you away from. You're a beast, Pleiti, really, for doing all this"—I tried not to glow too visibly—"but leave this to us for now. And thank you for telling me."

"Er," I said, before she could dash off to be useful. "I didn't want to show these to Villette—"

"No!" Petanj agreed, horrified. "They'd make her feel terrible! With the donfense coming up . . . I know it's mostly a formality, but she does not need to be doubting herself."

"But she needs to know about them. She *does*, Petanj. At the moment she's in utter denial, and it's not safe."

"Yes. Yes, you're right. I'll find a way to tell her." She sighed, clearly feeling the impossibility of giving it adequate gravity without doing harm. "But first I have to see if I can find any more. I'll see you this afternoon."

I spent some minutes after she left grasping for some brilliant bit of investigating I could and should do. It didn't feel right to *take time off* (even if that meant *do my own research*). Mossa certainly didn't. But then, it had become abundantly clear, if it wasn't already, that I was not Mossa.

So I snailed into my cushions and spent some hours with the matrix I was working on. The novel I was cataloguing was one of the sentimental sort in which a narrator, apparently supposed to be an appealing sensitive soul, comments how being in the city was not *living* but merely *existing*. It was an opinion that usefully led to many glowing descriptions of the flora of the countryside, thereby furthering my research, but which was obviously not very congenial to a Modern reader. Surely (I thought grumpily) our evidently ungovernable passions—Mossa's despair, my yearning, the hatred or jealousy or bitterness that propelled these attacks on Villette—were proof that we still *lived*, despite our lack of arboreal idylls in which to do so?

Deciding that I was too annoyed to be productively employed on that book any longer, I ordered a gentle soup, then passed several rather more pleasurable hours on the collaborative article while the freezing rain pounded the window and the fire whooshed gently in the hearth. I was in a much better mood when Petanj returned, soaked and congelada, and suggested we meet in the saunas, to which I agreed with an enthusiasm that was not misplaced: they were especially welcome as it was the most distressing day of my menses (which might account for some of my crankiness) but in any case an impressive facility that nearly appeased my distress at the lack of other common areas.

Petanj's day had been far less soothing. "We found five other posts," she told me grimly, once we had ensconced ourselves in one of the smaller sauna rooms where we could not be overheard. "I dare to think that might be all of them, at least for the moment. Kenore and her mates will keep an eye out, but we can hardly patrol every message board constantly."

"We have to find out who's doing this," I agreed; and so, when we had finished our bake, and despite the dread with which I anticipated the karaoke slam, I hydrated well and dressed for it with a steady determination.

I was still a little beforehand for when we had said we would depart, so rather than fidgeting song lyrics in my room I decided to quickly check the message boards again. Nothing adverse by the common room, nothing hotpenned at the entrance board. Relaxing slightly, I was glancing through the litter of various university notices and neighborhood alerts when printed words leaped out at me:

LIFE SPROUTS ON EARTH

- - - - - - - -

Chapter 16

I was still standing there, staring at the board, when Petanj and Villette, decked in finery, swept me up in their wake and along into the storm while the words of the posting unspooled over and over in my mind. Yes, I had read the whole text; there was a part of my brain that understood that the giantshaking ti-tle implied an immense leap from the slight data of three tiny plants identified by probe as not only new, but matching one of the species primed in the rector's rocket. I knew that they might yet falter and fail; that the poisoned air, water, and soil of that planet might be taking their slow toll in unimagined ways; that the other genetic material in the payload might not take root, leaving those plants to wither in isolation; that even if the whole hypothetical ecosystem planned by that egotist grew, it might not prove sustainable. It might fizzle out in weeks; it might, yet, delay the possibility of resettlement by generations.

In that moment, in the depths of my mind, it did not matter. This was the largest, most daring step ever taken in the project of resettling Earth, and I had done everything I could to stop it.

Insensate, I followed Villette and Petanj through the ráfa-gas of rain and then into warmth again, a tight-packed multi-salon karaoke boîte. The cousins caught immediately on the hook of the song playing when we walked in, singing along. They must not have seen the news. They signed all three of us up for the main room, then rushed off to see if they could find an empty nook to sing in while waiting; I drifted behind, listening. The music was loud but not enough so to discourage chatter; indeed, most of the people in the crowded room were talking. *Earth*, I heard, and whipped my head around to find out what they were saying about it, but the place was too crowded, steamy with bodies and ceiling heating coils. It was not pleasant, I couldn't understand how all these people found it pleasant, and yet they must, for there they were. Most of the karaoke songs were Modern—I do like *some* Modern music, but at that moment it all sounded thumpy and sour. I made my way to the bar, ordered a spiked beer. There were baskets of qat on the bar and I took a handful and stuffed it in my mouth, slid it to my cheek. I wasn't sure why I was there. I couldn't sing, I didn't know anyone, I was certainly no worth as a bodyguard.

And yet I couldn't leave. A song came on that I did know, and I sang along absently. I wandered the rooms, had another drink. The music had turned plaintive: lost love, lost planet, lost meaning. It did seem I should at least tell Villette or Petanj before I left, but I couldn't find them. I found the toilets, availed myself of them, stared in the mirror for a while. I thought I felt someone else's eyes on me and whirled, but there was no one, only the door vibrating from the music. Or because someone had just left? I went back into the noise, fetched up against the bar again and ordered some tequila, drank it, and wandered on.

I thought I heard someone say *growing*, but again I couldn't catch the thread of the conversation. Maybe they had said *going*. But the specimens were growing. Really, how could anyone think of anything else? A chorus thumped, everyone was singing, I was too, and then it passed into unintelligible verse and released me. Why was I there? It was too soon to know, of course: they might die out, the corrupted environment might be too much for them, or the balance of the ecosystem might be so far out of kilter that they wouldn't even last long enough to fash up our plans. Or maybe they would survive. It was my fault, either way.

I groaned aloud and wended back to the bar for another shot or three. The report hadn't said *where* the species had been spotted. Had the rector been able to aim at all, or had the rocket crashed out of control? Was it a relatively isolated spot, an island like the ecosystems I studied, or some kind of mountain plateau or peninsula or something? That would be so much easier to track. The image of Earth spun in my mind, so far away and so familiar (why wasn't I there?), and I imagined outcomes from different landing sites, different species, perhaps it wouldn't matter, perhaps it meant everything, perhaps we could go—

I walked into someone—I seemed to have had my eyes closed—and liquid splashed over me. I stumbled back, began to apologize, and was met with raucous laughter.

"It's our Classicist!" It was Wojo, leering and loud. "I suppose this isn't your scene, is it? Valdegeld parties are probably all champagne and rocket launches." She leaned in close. "What are you really here for? You've never shown up before, never shown you cared for Villette until she was up for a *donship*. You—"

I barely heard any of that; the phrase *rocket launches* had sent me into a spiral of fury and despair. "What do you know about it anyway?" I might have been thinking of whoever it was at the picnic who thought Valdegeld had *sent* the rector; regardless, I screamed it in her face and the non sequitur probably mattered much less than the agave-laden spittle.

That scream had not, somehow, attenuated my pain, and I was still yelling, I think something about how she only looked at what was right in front of her, which was meant to be a dig at Modernists but in retrospect could have been interpreted in any number of ways, if she even heard it; she was screaming at me too at that point, saying I was only there to gloat, that I was a snob and a fool. She said something very rude about Valdegeld, I countered with the vilest thing I could think of about Stortellen. I remember thinking bitterly (and, I am almost entirely sure, inaccurately) that if Mossa were there she wouldn't have stood for any of this, and then, I regret to recount, I was the one who pushed first.

That is, I regret it now; but when I probe the gallimaufry of blurred memories from that night I can still feel the potency of the ungovernable impulse that demanded I place my palms on her bony shoulders, the elation of pouring my strength into the shove, of feeling her weight and solidity shocked backwards by my hand.

Unsurprisingly, our shouting match had drawn an audience, and my unconsidered epithets about Stortellen had been heard and noted; once the limn of physical altercation had been breached there were plenty of people ready to leap to Wojo's defense, or the defense of their university's honor, or in any case to attack me and one another. I was pushed, then there was a blinding impact, then another hit either intentional or through the tangle of proximity, and I nearly lost my footing. Even through my haze I felt the utter terror of being crushed in that mindless mass, and I struggled towards balance, thrusting fiercely against the heaving crowd around me; but the people managing the boîte—or some canny volunteers, I had no way of knowing—knew their business, and in short order the knot of combatants, never pausing their melee, was expelled, in gulps, through the chokepoint of the entranceway.

I tumbled onto the beaten metal of the platform, taking deep quaffs of the harsh air. My atmoscarf was still hanging in the cloak closet; I laughed ruefully, or maybe sobbed, at the thought of how useful Villette's invention would be for me at that moment. Or maybe not, maybe it would have been knocked loose, and my nose would hurt even worse—I patted tentatively at it, and at my face and ribs. A cluster of strugglers beside me continued to fight, but the cold seemed to have cleared my head somewhat, and I felt no desire to leap back in. On the other hand I couldn't seem to get myself off the ground, either. I sat there while the world spun, and then a face appeared close to mine.

"Prof? Prof, are you well?"

I blinked, trying to clear the fog from my eyes, but it didn't seem to help much. "Kenore? What are you doing here?" I giggled at how funny it was that I should remember the gradudent's name but be surprised that she was at a university party, and then heard how drunk I sounded and stopped.

"Well, well, how the Geldans are fallen." That was another voice, like an oiled spike. I didn't recognize it, and my vision was in that curiously limited state of extreme inebriation. I heard Kenore reply, rather sharply, "Now, Scholar, none of that. Not your affair." Then she bent over me again. "We should get you home, Prof. Come on, I'll help you now." I felt a thread of unease—what if she was my enemy, taking advantage of my vulnerable state?—but I could barely formulate the thought. Kenore got me to my feet with a steady arm, and I tried to take a swaying step away but she had a grip on my elbow. "This way, Prof."

Chapter 17

I woke up feeling extraordinarily awful. I hadn't suffered such a resaca in years, but the utter dryness and roil of nausea were familiar from my student days. The bruises, less so. I eased myself out of bed—my own bed, though I could not remember arriving there—with many pauses for deep steady breaths and made it to the toilet without catastrophe. I spent some time there, testing the resolution of my stomach, drinking water in measured gulps, laving my face and neck, and examining the rather impressive coloration mottling the skin over and around my left eye.

I bamboled back to the bedroom and hesitated: lying down to recover seemed quietly sensible, but I felt some responsibility to check on Villette. I couldn't remember—had I seen her after we arrived at the karaoke boîte? I had some vague notion of hearing her sing, but didn't feel certain of it. What if something had happened to her while I was . . . while I had incapacitated myself? My stomach lurched again with anticipatory guilt. Surely she was fine, Petanj had been with her. But in that crush, anything could have happened—a quick knife, for example; and on the thought I saw again the stabbed corpse I had discovered a few months earlier, and nearly lost my tentative accord with the nausea.

Confirming Villette's state would ease my mind, and surely it would only take a moment—just down the hall and a quick knock—the cousins were far too kind to keep me talking in my state—and then I could crawl back under the blankets—or perhaps I could make it as far as the sauna? I slowly stood from where I had crouched rapidly, head down, after remembering the cadaver—best not think of that again—leaned my way to the door—I could manage this, and I was dressed enough to go just to Villette's room, surely—but no sooner had I opened my door than a person—one of those ad hoc porters—sprang up from the opposite wall of the corridor and approached—it was the one who had reminded me of Mossa—they ducked under my arm—my reactions were understandably slow—and stood in the room waiting as I turned back in, letting the door swing closed behind me.

"Mossa?" I spoke slowly, still not quite able to credit it.

"Pleiti." Yes, it was her voice, if unusually low; her voice, her eyes, even though the rest of her face was different. "You're injured. Can I . . . might I . . . help?"

I stared at her inanely. "How . . . how are you here?" Perhaps it was a dream, I thought, moderating my balance on a sway: the world certainly felt surreal.

"Pleiti." It sounded almost like a sob, or the word preparatory to a sob, but she went on speaking. "Your face . . ." *My* face? She was talking about *my* face when she looked like someone entirely different?

She was muttering some imprecation under her breath, then reprised with more of her usual energy. "Are you injured elsewhere?"

"How are you here?" I couldn't raise my voice, both out of consideration to my delicate constitutional balance and because I was ronca, throat raw as though I had yelled for hours—had I?—but I was going to keep asking until I got answers.

"I've been here, Pleiti. Disguised, as you see."

I closed my eyes. I had seen, I had *seen her,* and I hadn't believed it. "Disguised."

"Yes, to keep the malefactor at ease and investigate freely."
She sounded disgustingly pleased with herself. "A very useful
appro—"

"How long?"

"Hmm? How long what?"

"You've been here how long?"

"Please, Pleiti, you are injured, sit at least."

"How long?" Somehow I filled my rasp with enough intensity to get through even to her.

She stopped, stood very still. She wasn't quite looking at me.
"I arrived shortly before you did."

Something broke: I heard it crack, or maybe just felt the violent shock of it. "You've been here the whole time. I needed
you, I was *worried* about you, and you were right there the
whole time? Ignoring me?" I gasped for air. "You were right
there, *pretending to be someone else* so *I* wouldn't recognize
you. While I did your job. Badly." I had to gulp again, I could
not seem to get my breath in for the sobs trying to get out.
"And you want to help *now*?" I shook my head violently, and
then had to sit down on the floor again.

"Pleiti, please." Mossa was crouched in front of me, not quite
touching, when I was able to look up again. "You—you should
not be so concerned, you were not at all doing badly, in fact you
did quite well. I thought in particular that your approach—"

If I had not been feeling so entirely wretched, I would have
screamed. "How do you know?"

"You wrote me—"

"How did you get my letter?"

She blinked at me. "I had everything diverted to me here,
of course."

"Of course. Of course you did."

"Pleiti? Naturally I wished for news of you, I—"

"Mossa. What of all your secrecy? The postmaster and the telegraph operator and the messengers did not care if you were here. Yet you let them know it. *I* was the only one in this entire irradiated platform who cared where you were, who was *aching* to see you and desperate for your advice and insight and companionship, and *you hid yourself from me?*"

I had to stop for a great swig of air between sobs.

"Pleiti, Pleiti." The odd thing was, Mossa was weeping too, although far more quietly. "You were so— You really wanted my assistance?"

I choked on my fury until I could get the words out again. "Blast your *assistance!* Recombinants, Mossa, I wanted *you!* I missed you! I was worried about you! I—" I realized that this was becoming tiresomely repetitive, and only opening me to more hurt. I dropped my arm from where it gesticulated and turned my head away.

"Pleiti, please. Dearest. I . . . I was so . . . so deep in melancholy, I could not even imagine that you were so eager for my presence. I felt that I could only be a weight upon you, with my constant sadness—"

"Mossa," I said, turning back with some heat, "I can respect and empathize with your melancholy—it's honestly incredible that we don't all succumb, given the state of things—and *at the same time* be furious with the way you act towards me!"

"I am trying to tell you, Pleiti, I wasn't acting *towards* you, I was just . . ." She sketched a brief, futile gesture. "Just, just, surviving I suppose."

The bleakness of it caught me for a moment, but just a moment, because she went on.

"Pleiti, we need to see about your injuries, Kenore told me—"

"*Kenore?* What does— Of course."

126

A brief silence. "Er, well, Kenore has been providing me small services of surveillance and—"

"You suborned Kenore?"

"Suborned? I merely asked her to support my efforts in helping one of her preferred scholars. A bit irregular, perhaps, but—"

"*Everyone* knew you were here except me, didn't they?" Humiliation layered on anger.

"Of course not, Pleiti, and may I say that your letters, far more than Kenore's efforts—"

"No, you may not say." My throat was pulsing with ache and restrained emotion. "Get out."

"I promise, Pleiti, my intention was never—"

"Your intention."

"I—yes, that is—"

"Mossa, do you remember when I visited your rooms, to tell you about this case? When you threw me out, told me you had no interest? Only to, apparently, follow me almost immediately! What was your *intention* then?"

A long silence while the room orbited elliptically around me.

"Pleiti, yes, I should . . . I misspoke, that is, when I said intention, the truth is . . ." Her voice was still low; not, I thought viciously, out of any regard for my aching head, but because she was ashamed, as well she should be. "I couldn't. I couldn't . . . at the time, you see, I just couldn't face it. And then when I was here, well, it became only more difficult, and . . . I am sorry. I am so sorry. I—I couldn't—"

"Couldn't tell me you were here?" I spat out. "Couldn't trust me enough to let me in on this ridiculous charade? Couldn't but let me be laughed at for a fool, couldn't but laugh at me yourself, watching me try to do your job when you weren't able to—" I doubled over again, but it was too much: my battered sides aching, I somehow propelled myself to the toilet in time to cast up everything that I had so carefully negotiated my stomach into keeping when I woke up.

I took the time in between retches to yell "Get out!" and though I didn't hear the door, when I was able to return to the bedroom, panting and hollowed, the room was empty.

I checked every possible hiding place to be sure, and only then started the bath.

Chapter 18

I cried a great deal in the bath, but that's the marvelous thing about truly indulgent quantities of hot water in enclosed spaces: the crying and the recovery from the crying were almost simultaneous. My tears flowed directly into the bathwater and my eyelids swelled and were gently moistened by the steam and subsided somewhat. I won't say I looked entirely fresh when I emerged, but I certainly felt much better.

I did think about going back to bed, I even looked at it with a certain degree of yearn, but it was no use. I could tell my brain was already awake, and resisting that would lead to nothing good. Instead, I opened the door, ready once again to—do what, I wasn't sure, but something beyond hiding in my room.

Mossa was still there. I had, if I'm completely honest, at least half expected that. She might be inventive in finding new and unexpected ways to be unbelievably obtuse, but she was also exceedingly cabecidura once she finally hit on what she'd so brilliantly missed. She sat against the wall, in such a way, I now noted, that she would be inconspicuous from either end of the corridor, partially blocked on one side by a dumbwaiter protrusion and on the other by a bend. She raised her head more slowly this time, but I was careful not to look at her disguised face. "May I come in?" She still spoke softly, so no one could overhear, and I had the powerful urge to yell, or ring for a real pseudo-porter, or otherwise break her ridiculous cover, just to see what would happen next.

"Pleiti. I am sorry. I did not intend—" She hissed in annoyance at herself. "It was not—it was my failure. Not a deliberate choice to hurt you. Please, please, let me tell you."

I gusted a soupire and stepped back from the door. After a moment, she passed inside.

"Please believe me," Mossa said, the door barely closed behind us. "I did not mean to hurt you, or laugh at you."

"You deceived me." My voice sounded stiff and distant, even from me. "You lied, and you—you left me out. Excluded me."

"Yes." Her voice was muffled, and when I finally looked at her, I saw that she had covered her face with her hands. "Yes. I did not mean to, please understand, Pleiti, I wasn't thinking about you at all." I bit down on a hard, hurt retort. "I wasn't trying to deceive you or exclude you, Pleiti. I was trying to hide myself."

I inhaled. "Hide yourself from me."

A twist of her hands. "Yes, if you will, from you. But really from everyone. From myself." A gulping breath. "Pleiti, you saw how I was . . . when you came to Sembla. I was . . . in no fit state."

"I tried," I broke in. "Mossa, I have been furious at myself since I arrived here, that I didn't—try harder to get you to move, or maybe stay with you. I almost turned around the moment I arrived here, but—"

"But that would have been foolish. And I have enough foolishness for both of us." It was hard to tell, with the prostheses she was wearing on her face, but from her voice I thought perhaps she was crying again. "Pleiti, love, you couldn't have moved me that night. And if you had stayed . . . well, I can't be certain, but I think it likely I would have found a way to make you regret it."

"No," I said, and she gave me a withered fraction of a smile.

"I would have tried. Not wanting to, please understand, not

wanting to hurt you so much as hurt myself, not wanting—" She twitched it away, impatient. "But what you said—yes, I remembered, and I thought about it all night, and, well. I couldn't let you come into danger without me."

"I didn't think there was any danger at the time."

"No. But I did. Or maybe I just—didn't want you to be so far. But I thought of the danger to you, and that let me move, let me get here even before you did, for I used the Investigators' railcar—"

"For this?" I wondered how she had justified that requisition, but she ignored the interruption.

"—but even when I was here I couldn't . . . I couldn't bear to let you see me. I couldn't imagine you *wanted* to see me, after my contemptible behavior in my flat that night—"

"It wasn't contemptible, don't say that."

"Pleiti, dearest, it quite literally inspires contempt in people. Most people would, right now, look at me contemptuously; it is, by definition, contemptible."

"Most people!" I said, with unforced contempt. "Mossa, most people are not you. They do not know, cannot *imagine*, what you are feeling. They cannot judge how you bear it. And if they would find it contemptible," I added as she brushed that away, "then I'm sure they hold their own melancholy in contempt as well, and hide it."

She was silent for a moment. "You do not need to defend me simply because I am miserable with myself."

"I'm not defending you! The way you behave in your own rooms, where I intruded unexpected and uninvited—"

"You are always invited, Pleiti, you know that."

"—Unexpected, then, regardless, the way you behave in your own space is not contemptible, I don't defend you by saying that. But what you did in coming here without telling me—" I threw my arms out, searching for words. "It was a vile thing to do, Mossa. Thoroughly human."

"I am well aware, Pleiti." Humble was such an unusual tone for her, it was hard for me to trust in it even if she was sincere. "I think I knew it even at the time, though I tried to convince myself that there were good reasons. I did worry about the danger, I thought that maybe I could protect you—and Villette, I suppose—from a distance, without . . . without having to be *me* . . . Yes, I suppose I thought if I pretended diligently enough, I could *be* someone else, not just hide from myself, but—well, I suppose it was just another form of hiding. And then, you know—this is less disinterested, but, historically, that is to say, in my experience, sometimes if I can manage to *start* investigating, it helps me find a way back from, from . . ."

"Mossa." I waited until she looked up, and then realized I did not know what to say. Especially to that unknown face. "Can you take that off?"

She grimaced. "Not easily. But I will start the process, if you will order something to eat. You need to nourish yourself."

I hesitated, not wanting to give her license to care for me yet, but she was not wrong. Solid food still seemed inadvisable, but I put in an order for a pot of tea and some consommé.

"Dumplings," Mossa advised from the bathroom, where the sound of running water alternated with that of vigorous toweling. "They're very good here, and you need something substantial."

I clenched my jaw against a resurgence of bile, either from the thought of food or from her casual reassumption of her advice-giving role in my life, and ordered the blasted dumplings.

Chapter 19

Though I would have hated to admit it to Mossa, the tea did me good. Seeing her face, instead of the complicated masque of putty and cosmetics, also helped to platform me, to reduce the surreality of the moment. When she emerged from the bathroom with an envelope of damp cloth in her hand, I let her hold it to my swollen eye for a few moments before shaking her off to take control of it myself.

"Are you hurt anywhere else?"

"Bruises," I said briefly. It didn't hurt too much to breathe, so I didn't think my rib was cracked.

"I wouldn't expect Petanj or Villette to let you come back here if you needed the clinic," she fussed, "but if they missed something . . ."

I had only the vaguest memories of how I had returned to the lodgings; I wasn't sure that either Petanj or Villette had been involved. "No, nothing." If all the vomiting and crying hadn't made me feel drastically worse, there probably weren't any injuries precarious enough to cause further damage if jostled.

Mossa delicately ladled broth and a few dumplings into a bowl and placed it in front of me before serving herself. "Well." I felt her hesitate, as though she might plunge back into the painful apologies, her painful sense of herself, and then instead she took up her usual detachment. "Pleiti, I don't want to pretend that this is complete, or that . . . or that you have forgiven me, for example, but I do think we should speak urgently about the case." I bit back something scathing about the scorn she had exhibited, back in her rooms, for what she now called *the case,* and swirled my spoon in my bowl instead. "I say this, again, not to distract from, mm, important emotional matters, but because I do believe there to be significant danger, to Villette and possibly to you as well."

I frowned. "We have pretty much accepted that Villette's in danger, but me?" It was unfair, how easy it felt, slipping into the familiarity of discussing a case with Mossa. "And besides, the latest incidents—which I assume you know about? Yes?" I sighed at the assent of her raised eyebrows. "Of course. The slander on the message boards is again focused on her academic work. There doesn't seem to be escalation towards the physical."

"If those sorts of gambits were successful, perhaps they would satisfy the antagonist, but so far they have not been, and to be honest I'm not convinced they would be enough. You expressed"—she coughed delicately—"in one of your thorough missives, that you thought the danger was heightened until the donfense; at this point I'm rather inclined to believe it would only worsen if that challenge were successfully completed."

"So you don't think it's about suppressing her research?" I asked skeptically.

"Her research already exists, in both published and practical form," Mossa pointed out. "This—what did she call it? Nostril filter?—in particular, while it certainly threatens some powerful actors, is apparently already known and functioning. Should Villette be discredited as an academic, she could still produce and donate her device, though it might hamper uptake a little. If someone wanted to stop that item specifically, they could achieve that threat more efficiently by focusing on the outcome—the device and how well it works—

rather than the very academic preoccupation with the methods used to get there."

"Certainly these attacks are a very academic way to hurt someone."

Mossa's eyes gleamed in that familiar way in her again familiar face. "Quite so. But that doesn't mean that they are solely to stop her from achieving an academic goal. Indeed, I think *hurting someone,* academically or otherwise, is the main point."

"Rather than personal gain," I said slowly. "That's a bit grim, isn't it?"

"Grim or not, it is useful. I believe the attacks are about Villette specifically. We are therefore looking for a person who hates her. Why, I do not know—she always seemed harmless enough in school, but perhaps she has changed. And in any case, the rationale does not need to be, so to speak, rational."

I rolled my eyes, then winced: I had forgotten the massive shiner. I reproached myself for letting Wojo, that fop, catch me with a fist to the face; but then, had it been Wojo? She had certainly pushed me, but the punch? I frowned, trying to remember faces from that crowd anonymized by darkness and drink and drug, tried to put together a sequence that might well have been a dream.

As if reading my mind (and *how dare she?*), Mossa asked with sudden urgency, "And what happened last night, exactly? I heard from Kenore that you were injured, but—"

"From *Kenore*?" That spurred a memory. "Oh yes, was it—was it she who helped me home?" Another thought occurred to me, based on the gradudent's recent ubiquity. "Mossa, are you sure we can trust her?"

"Not positive, of course," Mossa responded, "but I have spent some time speaking with her and I believe her regard for Villette is sincere. Nonetheless, I will keep caution close. But Pleiti, speaking of caution, were you attacked last night? Was Villette?"

"I don't know about Villette," I gruñed, "I was just going to check on her when you intruded on me." Mossa hissed through her teeth. Plungered with guilt, and some obscure jealousy of basically everyone, I spat out, "Maybe you should have been protecting her, if you're so worried!"

"But Pleiti, so I have been doing," Mossa said, with every evidence of being innocently startled by my outburst. "Why do you think I have been staying here, as a dogsbody, but to keep watch on her, even despite the added risk of being recogni—" She broke off, visibly remembering that we were in the middle of a conflict partly instigated by her going to such lengths not to be recognized by me.

Several long seconds into the resulting silence, there was a brisk but gentle set of tocs on the door. I touched the button to release the catch, ignoring Mossa's glare, and Petanj thrust her head in.

"Ah, Pleiti, you're up. How's the head? We didn't— Stars and gradients, what happened to you?" She came all the way into the room. "Are you all right? Surely— Oh, hullo, Mossa, you've arrived at last, chévere."

Bless her and her utter lack of obsession with Mossa. "Good morning, Petanj. I was just meaning to check on you and Villette. All is well?"

"Yes, indeed, aside from the drought behind my eyeballs. Villette was wiser, but then she better be, with the donfense on Uranday."

My gaze slid towards Mossa.

"Did Villette go to her lab today, then?" Mossa asked—not so much as a proper greeting for Petanj, I noted with bitter critique.

"Not at all, she's swotting in her rooms. Might go later, though I did remind her it's Earthday."

Mossa fell into motion. "If that is the case, I should—" She stopped as suddenly. "Er—that is, Pleiti, our—er—conversation, perhaps we could continue it, at some more apropos moment."

"Of course, Mossa," I said with as little gravity as I could manage, but surely some of my weariness seeped through. "Go. Protecc."

She did not hesitate, and Petanj and I stood not quite looking at each other. Petanj spoke first. "None of my affair, Pleiti, and it doesn't need to be, but if you would like to talk . . ."

Immediately I did. "Sauna again, Petanj? I could use a restorative hour or two."

Chapter 20

I barely made it into the small sauna room, its bamboo slats reassuringly worn and homey, before giving in to helpless weeping. Petanj sat beside me, rubbing my shoulder and back and occasionally hugging me to her side or refilling my water flask.

The sobs tore at my throat and pained my ribs, so it really wasn't so very long before I quieted. Petanj handed me a wet cloth and started in. "Like that, is it?"

"Petanj," I said, as solemnly as I could manage through the residual hiccups, "she's been here *the whole time.*"

"What?"

"In. Disguise."

"What?" Petanj took only a moment to identify the most salient element of this. "And *she didn't tell you*?"

From that point, my mood improved substantially. Petanj was in hearty agreement with my anger, indeed furious on my behalf, and we had a very enjoyable time gasping to each other in sympathetic appall as I revealed to her each new layer of perfidy. By the time we left the sauna not only were my aches somewhat assuaged, but I had partially drained the blister of my resentment.

We checked the message boards carefully on the way up; heartened by the absence of any new posts, we found Villette in her rooms studying as promised, and just as studiously ignoring Mossa, who slid out of the doorway after opening it for us. "Steam well?" Villette asked, and then looked up and saw me. "Stars, Pleiti, are you well? I didn't realize you were caught up in that brawl! I have to assure you, that is not in the least usual here."

"Oh, er, not at all." I felt the blood pumping to my damaged face. "In fact—as it happens—well, I was less caught up in it than . . . well, the cause of it."

Petanj spat out a laugh on her way across the room to the tea service. "I see we didn't get through *all* the chisme in the sauna."

I turned from grinning at Petanj to discover Mossa immediately beside me with an expression that instantly spaced any giggles. "The *cause*? Did someone attack you? Or—" She hesitated, and I hastened to shear off whatever scenarios she was hatching.

"Nothing of the sort! I should have said, toch, the instigator." I took a breath for strength, and realized they were all three gaping at me. "Yes, well, I may have been affected by . . ." I took another breath. "What happened is that I bumped into Wojo." Petanj instantly frowned, while Villette looked worried, and I hurried on. "She . . . I don't remember well, but yes, I'm quite sure she said something objectionable, but—"

"That squib!" Petanj burst out. "Pleiti, I'm truly sorry, she's been needling you since we arrived and I should have said something to her about it sooner . . ."

"She may have been baiting you," Mossa muttered intensely at the same moment, "finding an excuse to attack you—"

"No—really, it was not—" I had thought all my tears were cried out already that morning, but I found I had to blink hard. "The truth is, I was distressed by the news from Earth. I think that, more than anything else, put me in a bad way, and . . ." I couldn't find a way to end the sentence, and Petanj patted my arm; from behind me, Mossa put her hand on my shoulder.

"The news from Earth?" Villette asked.

It was Mossa who responded, without inflection, that life had been detected.

"But that's—wonderful! Isn't it? Or at least promising?" Villette looked from face to face.

"We're not Classicists, cousin," Petanj said, although she too sounded unsure. "You must remember how complex this endeavor is. I suppose this is a result of that unsanctioned rocket?" I managed a nod. "So, there is some, er . . . doubt? And to hear the news so suddenly, of course it's . . . well, I was going to say *upsetting*, and I suppose that's right, but more in the upheaval sense than the awful sense. That is, it might be awful . . ."

"But it might not be," I acknowledged. "It might not mean anything at all. Or it might be wonderful." I had to stop there.

"And that would mean you were wrong."

Petanj stared at Mossa, appalled. "What kind of a thing is that to say? It's hardly a personal failing of Pleiti's if, against all expectations and scholarship, the Earth is ready to be reseeded again."

"I tried to stop him," I said, against my tight throat. "We almost did."

In the quiet that followed, I could hear the patter of precipitation against the window.

"Evidently," Petanj spoke at last, "there was more to the story than the chisme circulating in Valdegeld."

"I should hope so," I said with feeling. "It would be horrible if it was all known to be commented on."

Petanj sighed exaggeratedly. "Well, I for one would love to comment on it, when you're ready, even if it takes half a day in the sauna to get it all out." I chortled unexpectedly, and she flashed me a grin. "Chismes, heat, and hydration, it'll be gezellig. But in the meantime, and without knowing all the details . . ." She shook her head. "You can't hold yourself responsible for not knowing better than the entire academy of Classics."

"You underestimate me," I responded drily.

"Well then, consider this: that man was the rector of the most important and respected university on this planet. If he had good reason to believe it was time to launch an experiment like that on Earth, do you really think he couldn't have gotten it done with due process and proper vetting and inclusion?"

I wanted to agree; I almost could. But I could not forget the rector's words sketching the complacency of Classicists; I thought about the accumulated weight of the Classical faculty in Valdegeld and their colleagues around Giant, and I doubted. "Perhaps I was wrong in my trust in the acadème."

Petanj snorted. "Given everything happening to my cousin, I'm not going to argue with that." Villette made a distressed noise. "But again, hardly a personal failing."

"It's true, Pleiti," Villette said, after swatting at her cousin. "We are all trying here, but we each only see a part of it."

Mossa did not speak, but her hand had remained on my shoulder, and even, I thought, tightened a little.

As they fluttered and cushioned about me, I felt again that insistently strong urge to flee; not, now, to Mossa, but away from everyone. At least, away from everyone who had understood my failing: I had a desperate desire to be alone with my self-dissatisfaction. The solicitous queries gradually quieted. Villette ordered some tea, Petanj was saying something about cling-rail. The impulse to escape faded, and in the shadowed relief it left I had to admit to myself, grumpily, that it gave me a certain perspective on Mossa's actions.

She hadn't fled—indeed, it had never occurred to me that she would; even as I upbraided her furiously, I could not have imagined her abandoning this juncture of circumstances.

Even now she was moving around to crouch beside me, her face showing signs of concern.

"I'm perfectly well, Mossa," I said automatically.

"Mm," she responded, in a way that made me think she was not convinced. "Be that as it may, I wanted to ask you—Villette wishes to attend her laboratory, and I myself would like to examine that setting." As well, I assumed automatically, as ensuring Villette came to no harm. "Are you well enough on your own for a while? Or—"

"I'm quite well," I said, rather annoyed. "In fact, I'll accompany you, at least as far as the laboratory building; I had a few inquiries I wanted to make myself."

"Not until we've eaten, you won't," Petanj said. "We'll catch you two up." Seeing me hesitate, she reminded me that walking to the lab might be more painful than it had been the day before, and filling my panza would allow me to take a pain-dampener.

I also used the time to pen a missive to Dean Mars—ta, at least, had written to me, I should respect that courtesy with a reply. That task accomplished, food and dampener consumed, we set off. Petanj chattered as we walked, but I barely heard her. The sympathy I had felt for Mossa when she was before me, taut with emotion, was evaporating; and I was angry about that, too, that I had to feel sorry for *her*.

We stopped at the couriers, my face heating at the thought of all the helpless visits I had made over the past few days. I could not look at the attendant, who had known, him or another, when I asked about connections to Sembla that my telegram wouldn't leave the platform. By the time we reached the lab my fury was simmering briskly. How *dare* she?

I hadn't been planning on going into the lab; I told myself that I changed my idea because Petanj hadn't been able to tell me where Hoghly's wife worked, while Villette would know, but truly I went in to see Mossa: to scan her face for signs of remorse, or anguish, or longing; perhaps to show in some way that I didn't care, that I had my own agenda.

We were made to wait quite some time before the receptionist—the same scrawny fellow as before—deigned to call an escort: a different gradudent this time, close-lipped and pálido, with whom even Petanj did not have a pleasantry to share.

When we arrived I understood the reason for his sullenness or fear: the entire lab was a moonscape of shards and shatters.

- - - - - - - - -

Chapter 21

I stood in the door of the lab, agape, while the gradudent observed my shock with gloomy satisfaction. The lab walls were
scratched and defaced with splatters of paint or other chemicals; tables overturned, instruments scattered; the floor was
covered in acute edges of glass, laminates, book canisters,
ceramics. My glance skated over the confusion and homed
unerringly onto Mossa's face, and I had to suck in air at the
familiarity of her close-whetted focus, an expression that I had
learned to love even though it excluded me. Now it just hurt.

Petanj had already crossed the lab to join her cousin, and I
hastened to join her. Villette, wearing heavy gloves and a sorry
expression, was picking over debris; around the large space,
other scholars were doing the same. "Villette . . ." I said, and
then, for lack of words, embraced her for support.

"I can't understand," she whispered over and over again.
"Why? It's so . . . wanton, so thoughtless and cruel."

"Perhaps it was random, or aimed at one of the other scholars here," I offered, more as a temporary sop to her feelings
than because I believed it.

Villette gestured around at the walls and floor, apparently
too verklempt to speak. "The blast pattern," Mossa commented
quietly, "clearly originates from Villette's counter."

I looked again, parsing the damage as an explosion rather
than random destructiveness, and immediately saw it. "But—
you haven't been here, right? When did this happen?"

"We swung by last night after the karaoke," Petanj said, voice tight and angry. "It was clean then, and no one else was here."

Unintentionally, I met Mossa's gaze, and knew we were thinking the same: a clearer opportunity gap than any the perpetrator had left us so far, and in the lab, where access was at least somewhat controlled.

There was a shift by the door and I looked over to see the lab director gaping. "What," ta enunciated in a way that carried through the entire space, "happened here?" Nobody spoke, nobody that I saw even looked at Villette, but it didn't take the director long to draw ta's own conclusions. "Villette! Again?"

"It wasn't me!" Villette sounded on the edge of tears. "I— we can look at the logs, I didn't even do any experiments last night, I was just picking up some notes—"

The lab director was rubbing the bridge of ta's nose. "Stop, stop. I don't know what happened, we can try to figure it out later, but first we have to take this to the dean." Villette looked down at her feet. "Come on, you know how he is, we have to let him know before he hears it anywhere else. After that we can try to sort through it, vale?"

"I'm going with you," Petanj stated, and Villette grasped her hand.

I met Mossa's glance again, but we didn't speak until the director had led the cousins from the lab. "I will investigate here," she said, low enough that no one could have heard. I only nodded and left her. Not explaining myself was a tiny satisfaction.

I was fortunate to come across Kenore in the corridors of the lab building before anyone noticed me wandering around unescorted (and before Mossa had commandeered her expertise). She greeted me with concern over my injuries, which I brushed aside; between the pain-dampener and the shock in the lab, I had all but forgotten the bruises. She was, naturally, able to direct me to where Vao worked, and even tell me that she should be there on an Earthday. It was not until I had already bid her farewell that it occurred to me that perhaps it was not luck that I had met her; perhaps she had been waiting for me, in order to direct my investigation? I retraced my steps, but the gradudent was already disappearing around a far corner, in the direction of Villette's lab, and in any case I had asked about the shop, she hadn't suggested it. I shook it off and followed her directions towards the station.

Vao's shop was in a cylindrical building resting on its curve, a design evoking the modular components of spaceships, often reused on platforms, although this building was clearly newer. The sign proclaimed it MUST MUTS, illustrated by a rather uneven and undoglike dog head adorned with a wool cap, so I was expecting headwear, and indeed they sold a variety of hats and hoods, but when I stepped inside to the welcome warmth I was startled to a halt: the overwhelming preponderance of their stock was atmoscarfs.

I was considering this as a motive for slander and harassment when Vao stepped forward from behind some rack draped with technology. "Good e— Oh! Oh, sorry, were you looking for something, er"—she danced a hand in the vicinity of her face—"concealing?"

I gaped, caught up in the memory of Mossa's concealing facial prosthesis and wondering how this woman knew I was investigating and trying to hide it.

Her face changed. "Sorry—I assumed—because of your eye—" I had forgotten the shiner. "Wait, don't I know you?"

Trying to recover, I forced a titter. "Not *know* as such, but we did meet the other night—"

"At Villette's party! That's right, you're her friend, isn't it?" Another shift in expression. "I suppose you won't be wanting an atmoscarf then? You'll probably have one of those things soon enough."

She said it as if it were a blague but it didn't quite come out right, although I couldn't tell whether she resented the lost income or was envious about early access to the device; regardless, my newly discovered fabrication instincts took over. "What, that nose thing?" I gave a shudder that was only partly feigned. "Not me sticking bits of filter up my nose, no!" She smiled sympathetically and I kept chattering: as she knew I was visiting briefly—for the donship, yes, but I wanted to enjoy Stortellen, I hadn't been in years, and atmoscarfs made such good souvenirs, didn't they? I certainly hadn't seen any quite like these in Valdegeld!

Vao liked hearing that last bit well enough, and I spent some minutes being hung with various exemplars of the filter-weaver's craft (most of them, to my eye, indistinguishable from those available on any other platform) while I wondered how to elicit her thoughts on Villette. Confide, that's what I needed to do. "I'm worried about her," I said, meeting her eyes while she fussed with the tail of an undyed but intricately woven specimen. "She's awfully wrought up about the donship, nerves at the flower of her skin."

"It's the academic emotional tendency." Her tone said this was filler conversation while she removed the atmoscarf and brought out another one, the sort of statement that she could make without thinking about it, without worrying about unnerving a potential customer, because everyone agreed with it. I made an affirmative noise, but I needn't have bothered; she was still talking. "I see it with my husband all the time. They just can't help getting all worked up about these things. It's probably *why* they got into academia in the first place." I managed to open my eyes wide instead of rolling them. "Just look at the way they talk! *Publish much lately?* It's no wonder they all get complexes about it." Had Hoghly fed her this pseudo-emotionalist theory? I had heard of it before, but never from anyone who took it seriously.

"Villette is certainly . . ." I tried to remember the jargon. "Dedicated?"

"Yes! Reviewer-crazy, so overdone. They are so trained to believe that their only worth comes from their research that they see threats to it everywhere! Or, of course, there's the other kind who will do anything to prove themselves." *Ugh.* I wondered which kind she thought Hoghly was.

"Well," I said, as she draped me with the next atmoscarf (a rather fetching malachite shade), "in this case Villette's got cause to be worried, given those allegations . . ." I hoped I wouldn't have to say more, but no, Vao had been there when Wojo was being so unforgivably indiscreet about it.

She leaned forward. "Hoghly doesn't think there were any accusations at all. She probably made it up for the attention."

Unable to find an answer I could countenance, I crossed the atmoscarf over my face and examined the effect. Perhaps I could get Vao to talk about her impressions of the other possible suspects; she might not know Vertri, but she had been at the party with Wojo and Evna . . .

"So what happened there? If you don't mind my asking." I came back to myself to see Vao indicating the left side of my face.

"Oh! That. Err . . ." I wondered what chisme was saying about the dustup at the karaoke slam. Or perhaps Hoghly had been there? I hadn't seen him, that I remembered, but . . . "You weren't at the karaoke last night?"

"No, indeed." She smiled contentedly. "Hoghly and I were on Quanne." My confusion must have been clear. "Oh, I forgot you don't live here. It's the next platform along on the oh-ninety-eight." The 0'98°. "Lovely dancing, clubs, theater. It's less than an hour away; we often go for a diurnal or two."

My head gave a throb: the pain-dampener was wearing off. "You were away all night?"

"Oh yes. We have a club there, you see. *So* beneficial to have a change of platform every now and again."

Did that mean that Hoghly couldn't have planted the explosion on Villette's counter?

I walked back elated by the idea that I might have discovered a clue. Specifically, I was elated that I had discovered it before Mossa. It was not certain at all, there were too many unknowns: I wasn't even sure of the exact duration when the lab had been otherwise unoccupied. Still, just the prospect of a usable fact that might even eliminate one of our stubbornly nebulous suspect pool was immensely cheering, and I burst into the rooms ready to share the information (and wondering if Mossa would notice my new atmoscarf).

I found only Petanj. "Off checking locations for security or something," she said when I asked. "Villette needed the distraction."

"Oh?" At her nod of agreement I put in an order for tea, and added dumplings as well. "Didn't go well with the dean?"

Petanj sighed expansively. "Not so much, no. You noticed how the lab director doesn't really care? Doesn't dislike Villette, but also just doesn't care enough to believe in anything but the simplest explanation? Well . . . the dean dislikes Villette. He actually threatened to postpone the donfense again."

"What? But their own investigation said there was no substance to the accusations . . ."

"This time it was Carelessness in Experimentation and Damage to University Equipment."

"But Villette didn't do it!"

"He would rather believe she had." Petanj stood from where she had been curled on the cushions and stretched. "I had to get very sharp before he would accept my statement that I had been with her the whole time—in truth I think it was more the ridiculousness of a *second* postponement that convinced him to let the donfense go ahead."

We were silent but for the whoosh of the fire for a few moments. "I have to wonder," I said at last, "whether even becoming a don will resolve this for Villette."

"I am starting to doubt it," Petanj agreed, and then at the ding went to collect the food and tea. "We have to figure out who is doing this."

"Tell me, do you know exactly when it would have been possible to set the explosion?" I told her what I had learned from Vao, and we spent an agreeable hour with the dumplings and tea discussing the worth and possibilities of the information. Could Hoghly have returned from Quanne—less than an hour away— without Vao knowing? Could Vao be lying to protect him?

We were still deep in the conversation when Mossa and Villette arrived, which made it easy for me to act as though I hadn't noticed Mossa at all. Petanj asked Villette about Quanne, the distance and frequency of railcars, and whether people really went there on dates or overnight excursions. Villette was a bit subdued at first, but soon became animated; I suspected that out of all the possible suspects, Hoghly would be the least painful option for her. She was of the opinion that it would be easy enough, if risky, to sneak back from Quanne while Vao was asleep in hopes of returning before she woke, but added that if they *had* stayed at a club, the attendants would probably be able to confirm his movements. She also thought that while Vao *might* lie to give Hoghly an alibi, it wouldn't be entirely surprising if she made up the trip for her own reasons, "Just to make us all admire how happy and glamorous she and Hoghly are."

I accidentally glanced over at Mossa to see if she had noticed Villette! being snide! and also what she made of the character assessment—had she met any of these people? How could she possibly investigate without observing their personalities?—but she was gone.

I barely had time to feel emptied—what if she *hadn't* noticed I was ignoring her?—when she slipped back in the door, nodding at us. I turned away again, but the discussion had paled for me, and I excused myself to the washroom, and stopped on the way back for a drink of water. When I returned, Villette was absent and the door to her recamera closed; Petanj was reclining on the daybed with a book; and Mossa was sidling close to me, her face showing signs of concern.

"I'm perfectly well, Mossa," I said once again, then kicked myself for treating her with such normalcy.

"So you keep saying. I wanted to ask you something else, however." Her voice was low, and she leaned in; I felt a sudden unplanned acceleration of anticipation, but the sequel was not of an intimate nature. "Given that Villette insists on participating in another social event"—her tone suggested that there had been some discussion on this point—"it would be most effective for me to disguise myself again, but would that perturb you?"

"No, of course not, Mossa," I answered at normal volume and with some show of reasonable exasperation. "It is only when you don't *tell* me that you're— What social event?"

"Weren't you listening?" Petanj answered from the daybed. "There's a rather important cling-rail match tonight; naturally we're going." She contorted one side of her face in a way that I took as a repeat of her earlier *Villette needs distraction*.

"Between Stortellen and Valdegeld," Petanj continued, ignoring my involuntary and rather rude exclamation. "You don't have to go, of course, if you don't feel up to it."

I glanced at Mossa and rallied myself to offer an only slightly ironic version of the traditional cheer: "Vaya Valdegeld, vaya!"

Chapter 22

Like all serious cling-rail venues, the Stortellen arena was designed with walls that leaned outward, allowing for more spectators higher around the orb, where the game-winning points occurred. Naturally, many fans preferred to be closer to the early action near the base, often considered more strategic and complex. Spiraling ramps connected the intermediate levels, of which I counted at least five, though I might have missed a mezzanine or two; Villette and Petanj glanced into the varied sections circling each floor until, at the penultimate deck, one of Villette's Modernist cronies waved their presence.

They had eschewed the comfortable but constraining banked seating for a more convivial mingling area; unfortunate for me, as that meant I would have to mingle. Conscious of my marked face, I skirted in behind the cousins (Mossa had arrived separately to embed herself as some sort of gradudent server; that, it seemed, was part of what she and Villette had been up to earlier in the diurnal). I looked for Wojo, and found her dressed exclusively in the Stortellen colors of night sky and stone, as if anyone doubted her inclination. I had thought I should perhaps apologize to her, had even imagined and discarded explaining to her why I had been prone to violence in that moment; but though she must have been aware that we had entered, her face was turned decisively away. I watched her laugh in a very fabricada way and decided I was absolved of the apology, if not of the guilt.

That didn't stop other members of the group from idling up to one or the other of the cousins and burbling inconsequentially while giving me long, weighted looks. I gave my attention to the space around us instead, pretending to myself that I was examining the room for any threats to Villette or her reputation—some tiny, unnoticed graffiti slander, perhaps.

The viewing windows curved away from us along the upper arc of the orb, and I could look down at the clingers as they hoisted themselves into the antapex and found their starting positions. Across the orb, through the windows of the lounge opposite ours, I noticed Haxi and Akash, and some of the others from the picnic; when Haxi's gaze met mine, I offered a small wave, wondering if the Classicists and Modernists always separated into these two specific lounges and whether I dared join them, and got a large one in return. To my surprise, I saw Professor Vertri sitting not far from them, in a row with a few other erai-looking elders; he wasn't talking to anyone, though, was rather staring at our enclosure fixedly, though not directly at me; I hoped uncomfortably that he hadn't seen my wave and taken it as directed towards him? Or perhaps—I cringed at the thought—someone had told him that I was not, in fact, seeking nominees for a prestigious award. I turned quickly away from the windows.

The surrounding walls were lined with shelves holding heavy cling-rail balls in an array of bright colors—decorative, and undoubtedly storage overflow, but also a reminder that very occasionally the ball in play could be knocked entirely off the rings of the orb. In those insólitos cases a spectator at this level would be invited to roll in a new ball through a circular atmoshielded gap in the windows, a proceeding that led inevitably to hilarity and occasionally to notoriety as well. In the opposite corner a curving counter sectioned off the area around a gleaming service shaft, presumably leading up from the kitchens, but I avoided looking too long in that direction as I assumed Mossa was plying her disguise in that area.

The lights flickered as per tradition, the orb's magnetism was switched on with a liminal hum, and the match began, uniting the disparate clatter of conversations into a single roar. The sound of fandom subsided somewhat as the play went on and some people divided their attention, but remained dominant, climbing to a rumble at every événement of the game. I was a little surprised at the degree of enthusiasm expressed for even the smallest gain, and was at first tempted to call it a displacement of academic achievement, but I curbed that thought repentantly. I was not a particular fan of cling-rail, and had not been to a match at Valdegeld since my student days, but from what I recalled of those occasions the spectators had been at least as urgent in their afición.

I had hoped that the zeal would diminish as the match continued, but unfortunately—for my team, as well as for any hopes of tranquility—Stortellen succeeded in an early and graceful manœuvre taking the ball above the equator, and my surroundings erupted in whoops and olés. I ducked away from the viewing windows, hoping I was not making myself conspicuous by my failure to screech and grateful that I was wearing nothing in Valdegeld colors; lacking, as noted, in any particular fealty to the team, I naturally hadn't bothered to bring anything. Petanj, who had come well prepared in Valdean pride, was being jostled and barbed, and she was laughing and seemed to be returning in kind.

The temptation to walk out of the room and circle around to the Classicist's lounge was powerful—they would still be rooting for Stortellen, to be sure, but I presumed they would be more graceful in their rivalry, and at least more friendly to me—but I shuddered remembering Professor Vertri's expression. Besides,

I reminded myself, the goal was not my enjoyment or comfort, but Villette's safety. On that thought I realized I had unthinkingly edged closer to the bar area, perhaps subconsciously hoping to encounter Mossa. Even in disguise, even when I was angry at her, I craved her aura of competence and comfort. Castigating myself, I turned back towards where Villette stood by the viewing windows, and almost slammed into Wojo. Again.

She jerked back, though not as much as I did: she had been approaching me, even if she didn't expect me to turn so suddenly. Recovering, she twitched her lips to the side in scorn. "No Geldan pride?" Without further preamble she swung into my space, grin stretched wide. "Or are you too *Classical* to care about cling-rail?"

It was amazing how much I wanted to defend myself from these meaningless taunts. I felt a chill of unease: Was Mossa right? Was she trying to provoke me into violence? I pretended to glance abstractedly at the bar, hoping to be reassured that Mossa was attent. "I didn't bring the appropriate, I'm afraid. Hadn't noticed there would be a match while I was here."

"Concentrated on something else, were you?" Surprised by the venom in her voice, I turned to look at her, but she had quit leering at me and was gazing over the spectator balcony instead. I could make out a faint discoloration along her cheek; I wondered if I merited the obscure satisfaction that brought me.

"I was thinking more along the sartorial requirements of the donship ceremony, yes," I said mildly. At least I hoped it sounded mild, and not like I was furious that she should dare to question my attire or my priorities.

I should subdue my own feelings, I told myself, use the opportunity to assess her character, find out where she was during the gas leak, the damage to the lab, the placement of the handbills, the secretion of the scorpion; to see how she spoke about Villette. But I was afraid I would punch her (again, and sober this time). "Excuse me," I said, "I was just going to get a gummy." My ears were buzzing and my neck prickling as I walked along the bar. *If she gets in my face again,* I thought, and made myself take slow breaths staring at the metal surface of the bar, imprinted with tiny cling-rail orb motifs.

When I looked up, I did not see Mossa, or at least did not recognize her among the three gradudents in intricate dance behind the counter. Perhaps she had found a way to be closer to Villette. I turned, very cazh, to lean my elbows on the bar and look back at the room, but I didn't see her. I was still trembling: leftover adrenaline from the confrontation. Someone shifted into the space beside me and I looked over. I was determined not to show surprise if it was Mossa, and so managed not to when I recognized the tall woman I had met among Villette's friends.

She waited barely the minimum for recognition and then said, "Benoz," as though she had no expectation I'd remember her name.

"The ethnographer," I replied, inclining my head. "Plezier to see you again." It was, too, or at least a relief; compared to Wojo or the rest of the cheering Modernists she seemed inoffensive.

"Mm. You all right?" She gestured at her own eye while nodding at mine.

I waggled my head to express that it wasn't worth worrying about.

"Bit surprised to see you chatting with her just now, after last night."

At least this woman was direct. "She keeps poking at me," I complained. "I don't know why."

"Don't you?"

"No."

She didn't respond, and I watched the cluster around Villette: Wojo was there, and also Evna, with that iridescent atmoscarf sprawled gracefully over her shoulders, and another person from that first night, name started with *M*, I thought, and two or three others, their attention turned away from the game now, all on whatever they were talking about. No Vao and no Hoghly, but I remembered they had been late the night of the drinks as well, and I wondered how often they hung around with this group.

"I've been thinking about what you said," Benoz commented, "about being surprised that there are Modernist ethnographers."

I tried to keep my cringe invisible. "The different universities," I temporized, "have naturally different divisions of . . ."

"Valdegeld has an ethnography department in the Modernist faculty. I presented there five months ago."

I tried a disarming smile, wondering what Mossa would say in this situation. "I'm afraid the faculties do not confer nearly enough." I looked back across the room, and caught Wojo's eyes flicking away from me.

"Indeed. But what I wondered was, why do you think we are less worthy of study than our ancestors?"

I went entirely blank, my attention snapping back to Benoz as though yanked. I opened my mouth, with no idea what would emerge from it—her painful suggestion, or analysis, entangled in my head with the rector's accusations against Classicists, and I was almost choked with outrage and unexpected emotion. I was saved by a multivocal roar rising around us. It was a chagrined one, I realized, peering towards the orb with pretended interest in the proceedings. The balance had shifted suddenly, as it does in cling-rail: one of Valdegeld's strategies had come to fruition in a flurry of speed-skating that took several of their players upside down along the rails arcing above, and a simultaneous struggle over two of the markers had resulted in both of them turning gold and green, almost at once.

"Oh, well done," I murmured, as though I had no greater concern, and was wondering if I could drift away from this uncomfortable conversation on the strength of that alone when the lights went out.

Chapter 23

In the sudden obscurity I lanced myself across the room towards where I had last seen Villette.

It was not a considered response. I had no reason to believe that Villette specifically was in danger, or really that there was any threat at all, but I believed it anyway. I reached the clutter of people glomming towards the viewing windows, silhouetted against their dim glow: the blackout was only in our lounge, or perhaps on our floor; indeed, as I wove through the spectators, I caught the green-and-gold winking of one of the Valdegeld-claimed markers on the orb. Then those extinguished too, and over the renewed yelling I heard a ruidous tumult of reverberations, thuds, and a disturbingly loud crash: the players and the ball crashing down the orb. The magnetism had failed.

There was still some faint light, and I wriggled my way through the bodies around me, looking for Villette. Something grabbed my attention, a waver—I saw the rack of weighty balls by the window wobble. I yelled something incoherent as a warning, instantly swallowed up in the noise, thrust towards the weighty case and shoved it back—a heavy ball slipped past my fingers and I jumped my foot up, heard the ball thud into the floor, pushed again at the rack—it swung back to upright, wobbling, and I leaned against it, arms outstretched, waiting to feel the balls roll their weight into me, but the other railings held.

There was a whoosh and another horrid crash: something

heavy hitting the windows. I was in the wrong place. I swung around, struggled back towards where I had last seen Villette.

Through the screams (I myself was, I realized, yelling *Mossa*, with no regard for secrecy or rationality) someone was suddenly propelled into me. I caught at their arms, and in the dim light I saw it was Villette. "Get her out of here!" Mossa's voice said, by my ear, and I reversed my course and started tugging Villette towards the door. It wasn't until we had pushed free of the crowd that I realized Petanj was clinging to her cousin's shoulders.

We got out the door of the lounge and, freed from the crowd, sped up, dragging both cousins down the darkened spiraling ramp towards the exit.

"What is it?" Villette asked, sounding breathless; the first anyone had spoken since we had found each other.

"I don't know," I replied, "but best be far away from it."

That was all Petanj needed to hear; she powered forward, pulling us both into a trot. Even so, the spiraling ramps felt interminable, and empty. Apparently no one else at the match had yet thought it necessary to leave, which should have been comforting, but instead the shadows and echoes of the rampway seemed eerie and unstable. I tried to parse what I had seen. "What was it that hit the window?"

"One of the spare cling-rail balls." Petanj was panting slightly.

I shuddered. "It didn't hit anyone?"

"Mossa pushed us out of the way," Villette said. "I think . . . I think it was aimed at me? And then someone pushed me—"

Then one of the shadows detached and leaned towards us, and I juddered and sprang away, tugging at Villette's arm. On her other side, Petanj was leaning in at the aggressor, though she let out a breath of air that had probably been intended for a scream. "Everyone all right?" the voice boomed out of the shadows, the tall frame of Hoghly Katak looming in the dimness.

"Hoghly!" Villette sounded relieved; Petanj was still rapidly turning her head to look from corner to corner. "Were you upstairs? Do you know what happened?"

"I was in one of the lower lounges." *Was he?* I wondered. Vao's alibi for him seemed a lot less convincing now that we were alone with him in a shadowy tunnel. "The power to the orb went off; probably a short or something. I was just trying to find someone to ask if they were going to restart."

There was a roar from above and I jumped again; impossible to know whether those were spectators cheering the relaunched match or cries of fear as the crisis unfolded.

"Were any of the players hurt?" I asked, trying to distract from my reaction: I was reliving the moment a few months earlier, when the heavy façade of a building had fallen scant handbreadths from where I was sitting in a courtyard in front of it.

"Of course, you're right, some of them probably were banged up," Hoghly agreed; a little too readily, to my ear. "No point in sticking around in that case. Shall we go for a drink?"

He could have gotten down here before us—or maybe, maybe the ball flying off the stand really had been an accident and *this* was the ploy: shutting off the power to drive us out and then waiting in the gloaming . . .

"Not tonight, Hoghly," Petanj said, her voice edged with tension.

"Come, it's early yet! What about you, Villette?"

Before she could answer, there was a thudding from above, as of many feet stomping in place; again I cringed. "We should get out of here, anycase," Hoghly offered, as though whether Villette spoke mattered not at all to him, and I doubted again. I glanced over my shoulder, hoping to see Mossa appearing to explain all, but the ramp was still empty.

Hoghly set off decisively downwards. We could either follow him or turn back towards the fracas above. Petanj rolled her eyes and Villette looked at me uncertainly and I tried to hide my queasiness and we all followed. I stared at Hoghly, walking ahead of us, until my eyes burned, but he didn't swing a wrench or reveal a knife or turn around at all. Perhaps he didn't need to, perhaps there was someone waiting just ahead, or along the walls . . . My nape prickled, and I compulsively looked back, then forward again.

We came around a corner, and the darkness receded, light coming in through the entranceway just ahead of us, and I almost relaxed.

Villette stopped suddenly, pulling Petanj and myself to a halt.

"What is it?" Petanj swept back to her. "Villette?"

"I'm bleeding," Villette whispered, holding up scarlet-stained fingers. "Someone, someone bumped me, and I thought—but then it felt wet, and—"

Petanj was already scrabbling at her sleeve, and I let out the breath I was holding: even in the dimness, I could see that the blood was a trickle, smearing from a long thin cut on her arm.

"What . . . ?" Hoghly had turned around and was staring at us, at Villette's arm. "What happened?"

"I don't know," Villette said, dazed. "I think . . . someone cut me?"

"Stop looking at it if it bothers you so much," Petanj said

harshly—not to her cousin, of course, but to Hoghly, who was still staring at the blood and seemed on the point of swooning.

"Oh," he said, still not looking away. "Yeah, always takes me this way."

"We should get to the clinic," I said, wrapping the end of my new atmoscarf around Villette's arm. I glanced at Hoghly to see if he would try to suade us into some snare-laden alternative, but he was backing away.

"I don't know what happened here," he said, shaking his head. "I'm going to go back up. Maybe someone else is hurt."

Petanj and I exchanged incredulous glances, but we didn't have time to question it, and he disappeared back up the ramp as we helped Villette out into the night.

Chapter 24

When we left the cling-rail arena it was still well before dawn; night was falling again before Mossa returned to the lodgings. Unsure where she was sleeping, and doubting that she would knock on my door at that ridiculous hour, I was waiting for her in the entrance hall. Indeed, I had begun to doubt that she was staying in that building at all, and then nearly missed her arrival; it was only because I was so hoping to see her, and there were so few people of either diurnal arriving at that time, that I looked more carefully at the bulky person of average height who entered swathed in atmoshawls and a neat hat. I might not even have dared to speak, so different did she appear, but when I stood she saw me instantly.

"Pleiti." She gave a little sigh but not, I hoped, indicating that she was unhappy to see me; rather, pure exhaustion. "You're up late."

"No more than you," I retorted, falling into step beside her. "Are you well?"

"Well enough, I suppose." Once we were in the stairwell she unwound the three separate atmoscarfs and 'shawls; her face was made up again, but differently than before, which was fairly disturbing. "How is—" She stopped and followed me to my room. Only after I had closed the door—rather slumping against it as I turned back to her—did she return to her question.

"How is Villette?"

I mueca'd. "Distraught. Do you need tea?" I went over to

press the order without waiting for an answer. "She has finally accepted that someone is trying to hurt her, and she is both sorrowful and terrified. Petanj says that this is why she was resisting it so hard, because once she faces something she can't—look away, soften it for herself." I stumbled a little at the end of the explanation; the words seemed to take on another meaning, and I couldn't quite look at Mossa.

She responded with her usual impassivity, saying only, "Indeed." After a moment which felt achingly long to me, she started. "Villette was injured? Not seriously, or you would have said so . . ."

I reflected that Mossa must be very tired—or dispirited?—for her leap of logic to have taken so much longer than usual. "She was stabbed, well, slashed rather, but not seriously indeed. The clinic told us we could have dealt with it at home, but, well, we all needed the reassurance." I hesitated. "Mossa . . . you were there, beside her, when she was cut?"

Mossa sat abruptly in one of the rather silly chairs this lodging provided, rubbing her face with her hands. "Yes, I was there." She stopped and looked at her palms, perhaps realizing that some of her disguise had blurred into them, then resumed. "It was dark, and very crowded. I cannot identify who struck her; I only barely managed to deflect it." Lower, she added, "I thought I had bumped her completely out of its path."

I felt she would brush off any direct assertion that preventing grievous harm under such circumstances was already a significant accomplishment; instead I commented, with a mildness aided by exhaustion, "Was that *after* getting her out of the way of the cling-rail ball?"

Mossa shook her head in apparent disgust. "*That!* I certainly should have seen that coming."

"Oh yes, perfectly obvious since yesterday," I snapped

with the weightiest sarcasm I could muster while I went to retrieve the tea from the dumbwaiter slot. I set it down and prepared two cups; when I handed Mossa hers she was looking at me interrogatively.

"I'm surprised you didn't go to sleep."

"I tried." I sipped at my tea before time, and had to suck in air around the stinging heat. "I was worried about you."

Mossa looked down at her own cup. "You needn't have been. I am past that phase of melancholy. I can't call it an aberration, as such episodes have been a constant, if unpredictably sporadic, element of my experience and I don't see any reason to hope that will change, but for the moment you need not—"

"Mossa! I was worried about you being *injured*. Tonight, you know, when I left you at the scene of a crowded and chaotic event where violence had been attempted."

She blinked. "Oh. That. But I was fine, Pleiti, I was in no danger."

"That is *evidently* not true, Mossa, if you deflected a knife attack with your body, and moreover *how was I to know*? You told us to get Villette away, quite correctly I'm sure, some many hours ago, and we've had no word, and *you didn't come*."

It had been embarrassing: lying awake once Villette had finally dropped off and Petanj pushed me out of the room, I had told myself over and again that Mossa was competent, trained, prepared; that she did not need me to fear for her, that I could stop worrying and sleep. Impossible.

It had not occurred to me until that moment, when I had already made a fool of myself, that she might not *want* me worrying about her. "You were there a long time," I said, hoping it sounded like an explanation of my actions rather than a whinge about hers.

She took a swig of tea as though she needed bracing. "I was

hoping to find some evidence, but I failed. That is, there was plenty of evidence, but nothing conclusive about the culprit. The process resulted in my being compelled to reveal my affiliation as an Investigator to the local bureau, and that was . . . tiresome." I looked questioningly at her, and she swallowed the rest of her tea and stood. "There's not much night left, and tomorrow we will be busy. Villette's donfense is the day after tomorrow. We need to try to identify and evidence the perpetrator, and if we fail to do so, make a plan to ensure her safety."

"Yes, of course." I stood too. She was right, I was made dust by exhaustion; it was long past time to go to bed.

"Until tomorrow, then," Mossa said, and hesitated for just a moment. "Thank you for your concern," she murmured at the last, and left.

I stared at the closed door: somehow, after all that, it hadn't occurred to me that she wouldn't stay.

Chapter 25

I was only barely awake the next morning when there was a klop at my door. I felt my pulse speed as I wended my bleary way over, and even attempted to flatten my pillow-puffed hair before I cracked it, but it was not Mossa after all, but Petanj, who came in with an armful of packages.

"Morning, Pleiti, have you breakfasted? Well, you have a bit of time yet, but you should get along. Mossa has decreed that we shouldn't do the Investigator stuff in our room, because we don't want Villette seeing any of the detritus while she's trying to prepare herself for the donfense, so it's got to be here. Sorry. But I've brought some decently strong tea to bolster us for it."

By the time she returned I had consumed a cardamom swirl (rather stodgy compared to the ones at home, in my estimation) and set a pot of smoky tea from the Tiester cultivations—known for their potency—to steep. Petanj and I were chatting over the first cup when Mossa knocked and then, at my call, slipped inside. The sight of her woke me like a douse of chill water, because she was *Mossa* again, her face unmodified and her form undisguised. Not only that, but as she came across the room I saw something that I hadn't realized was missing (or purpose-fully changed?): her walk, her movement, her confidence and grace. I wished fervently that Petanj weren't there; I had to bite my lip against saying—I don't know what, something joyful and risueño, or maybe simply kissing her.

But would she welcome that? She didn't show any awareness of me; as she began arranging her storyboard cards on a blank stretch of wall between the windows, I could have been any other old school acquaintance. I thought back to our quarrel; though I had been too upset to think much of it at the time, Mossa had dashed out with easy abandon the kinds of endearments I always craved more of. Since then, however, she had been more aloof than ever. Was she angry at me for my harsh words to her? Or attempting to respect some unexpressed wish she assigned me, or avoiding my anger? Or perhaps—I ached—still too ashamed to think of me?

"I've chosen to focus on the most proximate suspects," she said without preamble, bringing the two of us to attention. "As based on my own observations and Pleiti's." She nodded at me, and I schooled my face and my too-ready pleasure at her notice. "To wit: Villette's former tutor Professor Vertri; her coauthor, Hoghly Katak; and two colleagues or rivals, Evna Pima and Wojo K'tuvi; as a fainter possibility, there is also Hoghly's wife, Vao, but I don't believe—"

"What about the gradudent Kenore?" I interrupted. I still had only a partial memory of the aftermath of the karaoke brawl, but Kenore's presence there, at the laboratory after the explosion, constantly hanging around these lodgings, seemed too suspicious to be ignored. "She really seems to be everywhere."

"Wait." Petanj was staring at the storyboard. "*Wojo* is a suspect?"

"Of course she is." I wondered if she had missed every single interaction we'd had with the unpleasant Modernist. "Do you not agree?"

Petanj shook her head. "I can't see it," she said flatly. "I know,

Pleiti, that you and she had that altercation, but you yourself admitted you were the instigator."

"Even if I did push first, the incident shows she's ready with violence, but never mind that. She's relentless around Villette, constantly sniping and finding ways to undermine her . . ." I looked to Mossa for confirmation.

"I have barely seen them together, certainly not when I was close enough to hear their conversation."

Petanj had started laughing quietly.

"What?" I asked her, somewhat exasperated.

"Wojo has been crushing on Villette for years. She's not— that's just how she interacts with her. I think she can't trust herself to be too nice with her, or maybe it's some rhythm they fell into."

I paused to reevaluate my memories. "Does Villette know?"

Petanj's smile ombréd into a sigh. "I don't know. *I* don't see how she can miss it, but we always have blind spots behind our eyes, you know? Or it may be that she knows but isn't interested and practiced ignorance is her way of not facing the awkwardness, or not putting Wojo through it." She shrugged, taking one of the choclo arepas I had ordered to power our cogitations. "That's why she's so rude to you," she added indistinctly around it.

"What? Villette hasn't been ru— Oh, you mean Wojo? Why?" I was staring at the cards, trying to rearrange my mental calculations around this new insight.

"She thinks you're here to woo Villette."

I turned, shocked again. *"What?"*

Petanj giggled and reached for the teapot. "You didn't notice this at all? Hija, how?" Tea poured, she counted on her fingers. "You came *all this way* for Villette's donship. You, a

Classicist, with no real interest in her work! You've been following her around and even moved into her lodging house. You're a scholar at Valdegeld, which, as you *may* have noticed, immediately triggers insecurities in everyone here."

"Yes, I have noticed," I said aridly. "It's probably that more than anything else."

"Oh no. I believe she suspects an entire epistolary affair, probably with me as the celestina."

"Well." I could not look at Mossa. "Perhaps we should disabuse her of that."

"Going to be difficult without telling her why you're really here."

"Is it really *that* strange to take the opportunity to travel to a friend's promotion? Anycase," I went on, moosishly, "I don't think we can take her off the list."

Petanj raised an eyebrow with admirable control. "I told you. She adores Villette. She wouldn't hurt her like this."

"*Unrequitedly* adores, at least so far," I retorted.

"You just don't like her because she's been so rude to you."

True, but so was what I had to say: "It would hardly be the first time that someone tried to wither the interests, the *accomplishments*, of the object of their affection, requited or no. Not wanting her to get ahead, trying to shake her fixation on work, shaking her self-esteem, hoping she will turn to her one true friend for solace . . ."

Reluctantly, Petanj nodded. "I still don't see it, not from Wojo. But I can recognize that it is not impossible." She shook her head, as if to rid herself of the ugly reminder. "I still can't believe you didn't see how devoted she is. Ah! She's been that way since university, you mean you didn't notice it then?"

I thought I hid my shock better that time, but Mossa at least saw it, because she breached the conversation for the first time. "Remind me, where did she live when we were in school? I remember seeing her at a few of your parties, but . . ."

I fossicked through my memories of uni, scrabbling for any recollection of Wojo's wide-eyed expressions or desperate attention grabbing—but maybe she hadn't been like that then? Surely I hadn't been so dismissive of Modernists as to completely forget her, or ignore her in the moment? Or perhaps it was simply that she wasn't Mossa, who had taken up rather a lot of my attention and affective capacity in school; I had other friends, yes, but perhaps I didn't pay friends of friends as much mind as I might have. And now, of course Wojo had realized I didn't remember her—or maybe, worse, thought I was pretending not to—either way adding frost to the snow of her suspicions. I face-planted into my palms while the other two shared reminiscences around me.

Naturally Mossa did not let that continue over-long; however, at that point Petanj asked about other possibilities, like the atmoscarf producers. I hardly listened as Mossa explained the rationale that the attacks were mostly academic in approach, distracted instead at first by my own self-recriminations and then, gradually, by Mossa's presence.

It was unfair how easy it was, watching her, to forget my anger and resentment; unfair that I was off-balance and spinning while she was perfectly composed; *so* unfair that after desperately wanting her near, now that we were in the same room I was still desperately wanting. The need to touch her, smell her, taste her was like the worst bouts of homesickness: utterly irrational; impossible to ignore; undermining everything else in its capacious hollowness.

"Pleiti?" Mossa wasn't looking at me, had not deigned to address me during that entire conversation—or perhaps in kindness she had avoided drawing attention to my stupor—and was fiddling with the storyboard cards while Petanj touched my arm. "Are you well?"

"Just wool-gathering, I'm sorry." I offered an apologetic moue. "Thinking through Wojo's situation, now that I know how badly I misunderstood it. But I still think she's dangerous."

"Do you think she did it?" Petanj turned to include Mossa. "Shouldn't we be deciding—or deducing, or what have you—who is responsible?"

"It might be more than one person," I pointed out. "In fact, I'm not sure whether the attack last night could have been carried out by one person alone."

"Oh, you mean turning off the magnets?"

"And then arriving in time to attack during the confusion. Unless of course the electricity outage was chance and the attacks were opportunistic . . ."

Mossa coughed gently. "I believe it was planned. A henchperson or partnership would certainly have made it easier, however I was able to demonstrate last night that it would not have been impossible for a single actor to carry it out. If you recall, the lights went out in our lounge before the magnets were cut, allowing a certain amount of movement by a daring saboteur, and there is an emergency button in each of the viewing rooms to cut power from the magnets. Difficult, however. With the choice I would prefer to do it with an accomplice."

"So either alone or not," Petanj responded glumly. "And who do you think did it?"

I turned to Mossa expectantly, but she remained impassive. "You both know the suspects better than I do."

I tried to scoff, even if the same thing had occurred to me. "You're telling me that in all your surreptitious time here you haven't engineered an encounter with any of them?"

She doubtless heard the staticky anger that still under-pinned my tone, but she met my gaze with equanimity. "I've observed, but only barely interacted. More importantly, I am interested in your impressions."

I resentfully considered. I didn't care to wager even a shred of my reputed acumen on my analysis of these characters, so I fell back on logistical constraints instead. "Professor Vertri was in the lounge across from us last night. Could he have made it over to ours? Did anyone see him in ours?"

"He could have come around, easily," Mossa replied (show-ing no surprise either that he had been there or that I had no-ticed him). "Shortly before the lights went out I saw him leave his seat, but he went in the direction of the serving counter in his lounge; I didn't see whether he left the room entirely."

"A lot of people must have been moving then," Petanj agreed thoughtfully. "The gameplay was rising up the orb, and then there was that Valdegeld play . . ."

"In addition," Mossa went on, "from where Vertri was seated on the opposite side of the arena, he could have easily seen Villette in the viewing window, and would have known where to look for her in our lounge, even in the dark."

"Ugh." I ran through the other candidates. "Hoghly was acting very oddly last night," I offered at last.

"He was," Petanj agreed thoughtfully. "We need to check on that alibi Vao gave him." She sighed and stretched. "You know, I would have said he's too useless to plan something this per-sistent."

"Wojo would be persistent," I suggested tentatively. "I still don't know Evna that well."

"Hm. I don't know her very well either, but I certainly think she could plan something and follow through. I just don't un-derstand *why* she would do this."

"I do not believe we have enough information yet to be certain of any of them." Mossa spoke with resignation. "I suggest that at this point we turn our focus to protecting Villette at the donfense tomorrow."

Chapter 26

I had hoped, in a very vague way that allowed me not to think about whether it was a good idea, to find a way to talk to Mossa alone after our discussion, but she evanesced almost immediately, not even staying for the sunset meal, saying that she was going to preview the hall scheduled for the donfense the next day. It was Petanj who lingered. "Are you quite well, Pleiti?"

I chose the less painful explication. "I somehow believed that once Mossa arrived the mystery would be solved."

Petanj looked down to pick dispiritedly at her crumbs. "I had certainly hoped that this would be resolved before the donfense. Villette's in a right state. Sad *and* terrified about something totally unrelated, not a good mix for an oral examination."

"I can't blame her," I said with feeling. "Petanj." I'm not sure why I hesitated, since I knew I would not be able to resist asking. "Do you know where Mossa is lodging?"

She studied me briefly, but answered without comment. "She told me that when she arrived she somehow managed to sneak one of the empty rooms, and has been illicitly staying there so as to be close all the time and keep an eye on Villette. I suspect she got the gradudents to help, though I can't imagine how she managed that. After last night, though, she showed her Investigator credentials to the lodgings management and convinced them to let her have a room—the room she was staying in before, I suspect."

"Down the hall?" I guessed.

"Second door after Villette's." Petanj sighed and wiped her hands down her thighs. "Well. I must go and bolster Villette's courage, so I'll leave you to it."

I did not immediately go to Mossa's rooms; there was little point, as she was reconning the hall, and in any case I had no idea what I would say to her. I wasn't in the mood for a meal, either, but I peeled and ate a few snakefruit that I had left over from the day before. I tried to work, then gave it up as a bad job, took up my atmoscarf, and left the room. I didn't know at first where I was going; I made my way downstairs, again bemoaning the lack of decent public spaces, and then, on a whim, turned towards the university. I had a laminate map of the institution in my satchel, and in the persistent mizzle I plotted a route for the library. Mossa might learn about people from conversations and character intuition; I would see if I could get a better sense for our suspects from their publications.

The Stortellen Modern Library turned out to be a brightly multicolored building, an attempt at whimsy that I thought evidenced a bit too much effort, but the reflections from the multi-tinted windows, surely an echo of those streetlights, were appealing, and the seats not uncomfortable. I collected whatever I could find from any of our suspects, at first selecting the nearest to hand and later attempting a triage for possible intersection with Villette's work.

I might have made a tactical error, in that I started by reading some of Villette's more recent publications, on the basis that understanding what she was working on would help me see points where her antagonist might feel resentful, overlooked, or even more ideologically annoyed. I expected a struggle to keep my focus on technical details of the chemical composition of atmospheres and filter parameters; while there were certainly a few sections like that, most of those details were in annexes or footnotes, and I was riveted by Villette's narrative: how she had imagined a particular question and why she chose to pursue it; how she approached the answer, or an answer, and what it meant; how other scholars reacted and what that meant. Though I never felt that she was hyping her own intellect, I was certain from the contextualization that her insights both derived from an unusual perspective and were skillfully delved for useful learning. After a few articles I was no longer surprised that Villette was being honored with a donfense so early in her career. But I was not there to review her oeuvre. With some reluctance I put aside Villette's work and started in on the suspects'.

I first picked up a monograph by Hoghly (on the variations of mesh in filtration systems) hoping for insight: he had been entirely indifferent when I found the scorpion, jittery at the cling-rail match, absent from the karaoke slam. Everyone admitted his resentment of Villette, yet he was also said to be too indolent to plan and execute the attacks.

Sadly, his monograph told me little more about his responsibility for slander and sabotage than it did about filtration systems. His writing, or perhaps more accurately his thinking, was tangled and inchoate, so much so that I eventually flipped to the appendices to see if I could glean more from those despised skeins of numbers. A headache later, I leaned towards the conclusion that his experiment had been worthwhile, but I wasn't entirely confident of that.

I stood, stretched, collected some tea from the refreshment station, and returned to my pile of literature, which was looking insurmountable. I was feeling less sure about the merits of this approach, but returning to the empty lodgings also held little appeal, and I determinedly opened a book by Vertri. It was a chonky tome, but easier going than Hoghly's, and I glided

through as well as I could, with the strange sensation of reading not for content retention but for an oblique understanding
of the author's personality. That, however, grew increasingly
distasteful. Vertri could communicate in a way that Hoghly,
apparently, could not; he even evinced a certain amount of
charm, with occasional anecdote and very occasional humor.
But the longer I read, the more that smoothness felt false: the
stories were nearly all self-serving, the analysis thin, the col-
loquialisms a bit desperate, while the glimpses I got of actions
and principles ranged from disagreeable to wrong.

I threw down the book at a considerable time after midnight,
too annoyed and repulsed to keep reading. It was not working.
Both Hoghly and Vertri were awful, in different ways; I had no
further insight as to the perpetrator but was angry that Villette had to interact with these people at all; and my headache
had worsened. Suddenly unable to abide the cheeriness of the
library's design a moment longer, I stowed the bloc I'd been
annotating, packed up the suspect publications I hadn't read,
and darted out the first egress I could find.

The precipitation had relented and it was quite cold; not unpleasant though, especially with the moons glowing above. I
looked around, getting my bearings, and noticing a dark bulk
nearby I made for it with quick certainty: the hill where I had
picnicked with the Classicists seemed the ideal spot for a little
perspective. The hike up the side warmed me, and the view
at night was as charming as I remembered, the city lit up in
different colors around me. After a few admiring revolutions,
though, I found myself a bit at a loss. I hadn't brought a blanket, and it was too cold to give up my coat. I bent and patted
the grass: slightly spongy, and chilly indeed. I lowered myself
and settled with a grimace at the oddity as much as at the cold.
Still, my ancestors had done this all the time, hadn't they? It

was hardly unnatural. With that thought I slowly leaned back until I was nestled into the matted vegetation.

Hmm. Truly not ideal. Surely my ancestors must have favored the warmer seasons and climes for this sort of thing? But I let my eyes focus on the spangled darkness above me, and gradually relaxed enough for my mind to sort through the information I had consumed, the meeting that morning, the persistent wriggle of discomfort I felt because I was not at ease with Mossa.

After some time, feeling somewhat more settled but also exceedingly chilled and rather in need of a lavatory, I rose, brushed myself off, and descended. On the way back to the lodgings I ate a quick meal of fried lotus root, the mustard not quite as piquant as I would have liked, and then went back to my rooms. I had expected some message from Mossa, perhaps another meeting, but there was no note, and as the night crept towards dawn no knock on my door, so I supposed our earlier plans stood. Bed, then. It was after dawn and there was no chance of Mossa coming back.

I took a bath. I put on my pyjamas. I looked at my bed.

Then I tied on a robe, slid out my door, and walked silently down the hall.

Just to confirm that there was no update. Just to see. Just to see her. Just to see what would happen.

I shouldn't knock, I thought. *It's late, I'll wake her, and to-morrow we all need to be alert.* I didn't know why I was standing in front of that door, why I wanted to go in. It seemed at least as likely that it would only lead to more conflict and confusion. And yet, I softly knocked.

She opened it promptly, so she hadn't been asleep, but she was wearing a nightshirt. "Pleiti." Her eyebrows lifted in surprise, but she stepped back to allow me access. "Did something happen? Are you well?"

I opened my mouth to offer the very convincing story about confirming our plans for the next day, or perhaps mention my hypothesis, then didn't. "Are *you* well?"

Her expression blanked. "Pleiti. I told you, I do not plan to succumb immediately to another bout. You need not *supervise* me."

"I'm *not!*" I turned away in frustration. "Pues, Mossa, if asking about your well-being is now forbidden, let me tell you about mine. I miss you!" I spun back around as I said it and so caught the moment when her face was unguardedly shocked. It didn't last more than a second, but it gave me confidence that I had found the right rail. "Do you think I wanted to come here tonight? Do you imagine I thought it was a good, sensible, well-considered idea to approach you at this hour? No, of course not, Mossa. I'm not here to insult you, or to coddle you, or to pick a fight, even if that's what I seem to be doing. I'm here because I could not stay away." I shook my head at myself, heaving a breath in. "I don't understand it, Mossa! What is this ungovernable impulse that sends me to you?"

She took a step towards me. "As well ask, Pleiti," she whispered, "what pushed me to travel partway around the world to be close to you."

"Ask it then." I, or whatever it was that ruled me where she was concerned, took a step closer. "You're close to me now, and yet you feel just as far away as though you were still on Sembla."

Mossa shivered. "I—Pleiti, I—can't—"

I reached out, ran my palm down the softness of her hair. "I know you're afraid, Mossa." I spoke softly too. "You've been through a tough time."

She shook her head in mute denial.

"I know. And I was angry with you. But—" I stopped, in desperation, in frustration. She was so close, her hitched breath on my wrist, and I did not know if I could find the right words.

Her eyes were low, her voice was low. "I hurt you."

"Yes, but you didn't want to."

"But I couldn't stop myself."

I wanted to throw my hands up in frustration, but I couldn't, they were still stroking her hair and I had to be so gentle, keep the rhythm. "And I hurt you too. And—Mossa, I still trust you." Her eyes rose at that, and I leaned helplessly into her gaze. "Trust me?"

A long moment, and then, her smallest smile. "Always."

Burn through me, Pleiti, she whispered later that night. *Obliterate me, please, please.*

I tried my best.

Chapter 27

Waiting in the hall the next morning I felt as self-conscious as though it had been my first tryst, as though Petanj would be amused or Villette shocked or the entire university scandalized, as though everyone could see it from my face. Perhaps that last was not entirely unsupported: Petanj looked at me, then at Mossa, then back at me, and smirked. I offered a helpless half smile back, then glanced involuntarily at Mossa, and realized that I was truly unconcerned about what the cousins, or the university, or anyone, might think: it was of myself, and Mossa, that I felt unsure.

Had I forgiven her? She looked decidedly morose; was she unhappy that we had both given in to the physical impulse?

There was no way to enter into the topic at that moment: Villette emerged from her rooms looking somewhat tremulous but determined, and we walked together to the hall where the donfense would take place, arranging our disposition to allow each of us to keep lookout in a different direction. Mossa had scoped the site the day before, but she went in ahead to observe it again while the three of us waited in the entrance arch. The tension was truly noxious; I did not envy Villette the responsibility of defending her research career in this mood. Mossa reappeared in the window above to motion us in.

The hall was not so large, but even so it was not nearly filled. I saw and nodded to Haxi, the Classicist who had collaborated with Villette; Benoz was there, and some of the other Modernists from Villette's clique. Hoghly was absent; perhaps he couldn't bear to watch her success, but as her coauthor his lack seemed more egregious than that of Professor Vertri, also not in attendance. I also didn't see Kenore, but perhaps she was unable to get away from some gradudent duty or other. Evna and Wojo, in contrast, sat next to each other in the front row, to all appearances full of well-wishing and support. Wojo, in particular, watched with her hands clasped and eyes fixed on Villette with the intensity of devout prayer, and I wondered how I could have failed to notice her devotion.

I had planned to sit far from Mossa, so as not to distract her; I needn't have worried, as she stood propped against the doorframe for the entire donfense. Rather, I should have guarded against distraction myself; my eyes kept straying towards the door, pulling my glance back over my shoulder; thus can I confirm her steadfastness, and that *her* focus, while not on the donfense, was not on me either, but rather roamed continuously about the room for signs of danger. Only once did our gazes catch on each other, and I elicited the tiniest hint of rue before she returned to her scanning.

Gradually the drama of the donfense enganched my attention. I was pleased that I had spent the time reading Villette's articles the evening before; I had a far better understanding of the nuances of the examination, and could tell who on the committee was an admirer; who was a skeptic; and who had only skimmed her work and was therefore, perhaps unintentionally, offering her the gentlest of rail curves to follow. By the end, my eyes were swimming with the vicarious tears of pride that so tritely accompany such a ceremony in the popular imagination, and I found my fingers tightly clasped not in fear of an attack, but as if I could hold the candidate up physically myself.

The donship is not considered finalized until the committee has deliberated for several days and presented the result in a plaque; however, it is not unusual for committee members to offer verbal congratulations at the event, and so they did in this case. Villette stepped down from the dais looking adrenaline-flushed and happy (I was by then so wrapped up as to imagine myself, someday, perhaps, in that place), although when her friends encouraged her to join them in a celebration she demurred gracefully, letting Petanj take the more forceful role in putting them off, and the cousins made their way back to the lodgings with Mossa and me following alertly behind.

"A happy outcome," I sighed, once we were within the building and I felt I could relax my vigilance enough to speak. Donships always made me sentimental.

Mossa seemed unaffected by the momentous occasion. "I don't like it, Pleiti. That is," she added hastily, seeing Petanj turn back to glare at her from ahead, "Villette did indeed present herself well, but—I am disturbed that there was not so much as an attempt, not a disturbance, not even a whisper. It seems uncharacteristic. But perhaps—"

We had reached our floor, and Mossa broke off, hurrying ahead of the cousins to enter their room with a decisive caution which was, I thought, quite dashing. She returned muttering discontentedly, and blocked my entrance into our room to do the same there. "Really," I said, almost laughing once she allowed me in and closed the door behind us, "do you think the perpetrator would attack me instead of Villette? I told you that the incident at the karaoke was a misunderstanding." I was removing the tokens of finery I had worn and was just about to put in the order for tea when she rounded on me.

"No, Pleiti, it won't do. If the attack was not on the donship directly, and not on the rooms here while we were out, then it must be somewhere else."

"But where?"

"Where indeed?" She pondered, continuing absently, "And don't think you're exempt, Pleiti! The scorpion might well have been intended for you rather than for Villette."

"Maybe they really did give up once the donship was settled. Although," I added, my thoughts catching up to me, "I see what you mean. Whoever is doing this . . . yes, I think they wanted to prevent the donship if they could. But it's not the main thing."

"Go on."

I looked up to find Mossa staring at me with an intensity that I would have welcomed under other circumstances; in the face of that fierce scrutiny of my character-assessment skills, however, I atmoshielded a bit. "I am just agreeing with you. You said before that whoever it is hates Villette, and that . . . that seems right. After all, the attack at the cling-rail match . . ." I trailed off, thinking.

When I finally looked up, Mossa watched me with unmistakable approval. "You're not just agreeing with me. You have a sense for this person now."

"Maybe . . ." I hesitated, and my glance strayed to the pile of scholarly material I had brought from the library. I wanted to start reading immediately; I did not, however, want to explain to Mossa why. It seemed so tenuous a method for sussing out a criminal, and after all, my first essays in using it had not been entirely successful. Perhaps thinking about the suspects through their published writings had given me a clearer sense of what I was looking for, but since all the ones I had read so far had been equivalently horrid, it had not yet led me to any conclusions. Then again, the entire project of Classicism had been ongoing for centuries, and we hadn't come to any conclusions on that yet, either.

Following the rail of my own thoughts I said, "One of those Modernists said something to me the other night—" I stopped, but of course Mossa waited. "She's an anthropologist, you see, and she said—" I still couldn't get through it. "There may be some sense in these Modernists after all."

"I would imagine so," Mossa agreed mildly.

That was oddly encouraging. "As to your question . . ." It hadn't been a question, had it? "Your observation, that is . . ." I might not have identified the culprit through my readings, but I thought back to that evening lying on the hill, thinking about what I'd been looking for.

"Come now, Pleiti," Mossa said encouragingly, and it sounded so familiar and safe that I opened my mouth and then had to pause to figure out what I was going to say: *Welcome back* (relieved) or *Welcome back* (snarky)? *Well you see, I had an idea . . .* ? Or—

I heard the thumping footsteps down the hall, the quick klop beating on our door. I got it open before Petanj could call our names, and she almost fell into the room.

"Is Villette—" But Villette was just behind her cousin, and almost as wild-eyed.

"Are you harmed?" Mossa asked with severe competence.

"No," Villette gasped. "No, but—" She held a laminate out to us with shaking fingers. "It's Hoghly!"

"Hoghly after all?" I asked, relieved that I had not tried to guess the perpetrator in those few moments. I reached for the laminate, imagining he had done away with himself in remorse or some such archaism.

But Petanj was shaking her head. "No, no. Hoghly's been kidnapped!"

Chapter 28

Mossa grabbed the laminate, and Villette sat down, or collapsed, onto the cushions, face in hands. I felt a sudden, urgent moment of fury that she had enjoyed so little of this triumphant day. Then I angled to read the note over Mossa's shoulder. A glance convinced me that it came from the same hand, the same hate-wracked mind as the postings and the previous anonymous letters. The content was a mash-up of ransom notes from various telenovelas and pulp novels: IF YOU WANT TO SEE YOUR COAUTHOR ALIVE AGAIN HAND OVER YOUR LATEST RESEARCH AT MIDNIGHT ON YOUR OFF-DIURNAL IN SUB-LAB D. DO NOT TELL THE UNIVERSITY, THE INVESTIGATORS, OR YOUR NEW PARAMOUR.

My cheeks scalded. "Does that last bit refer to *me*?"

"Cutting quite a swathe, Pleiti," Mossa said mildly.

Petanj was practically snorting with impatience. "If you're *quite* finished, you are missing the salient bit of information!"

I squinched doubtfully. "That it's a ransom demand? We have grasped that."

"My latest research," Villette moaned from behind her hands. "It's—it's experimental, on harvesting water from the atmosphere."

Mossa and I looked at each other. "That's . . . good, right?" I hazarded. "Helps people? Lucrative, no doubt? Loads of academic glory?" Water was no longer the desperate need it had been in early settlement, but it was still a resource we were careful of.

Villette dropped her hands and glared up at us. "*Good,*" she spat. "How like a Classicist. Normative to the core. It's not *good* or *bad*. It's a complex technological process that I'm not sure should ever be applied at all and if it is, then with extreme care and calculation in which *lucre* should have no part. Handing that research over to someone so demonstrably scrupleless would be irresponsible in the extreme!"

"Still. Missing. The point." Petanj tapped her foot in emphasis.

"What's the point?" Mossa asked.

Petanj switched to tapping the laminate instead. "Sub-lab D."

"What's that?"

Petanj looked down at Villette, who looked away, so she looked back at us. "The off-platform detonation lab." She turned back to Villette. "You can't go. I don't care how responsible you feel for that useless excuse for a scholar—"

"I *don't*—"

"There's only one way in or out—"

"That's not strictly true—"

"It's completely isolated if no one's booked it, and for all you know *they might be planning to blow it up!*" She glared at her cousin. "Odds are they don't even have Hoghly, or won't bring him there. They probably won't even show up themselves, they'll just lure you there and then figure out how to trigger the release and—" Petanj slapped her hands expressively.

"Well, *that* wouldn't work," Villette said. "The room has a human counter, so that people on the outside know if it's in use, or, well, in the case of an emergency, how many people they have to worry about. I suppose in theory they could hack it, but . . ." She chewed her lip.

"Pleiti," Mossa said. "I believe you have come to some degree of understanding of this person's character? I urge you to interrupt or correct me, then, if you don't agree with my analysis at any point." She refocused on Villette. "You have, in my estimation, two viable options: you may ignore this missive, which I do not counsel, because apart from any responsibility or lack thereof towards the missing scholar, the person who did this will certainly have considered that possibility and will have a contingency in place; or we can ready ourselves immediately and move now."

"What?" Villette looked from Mossa to me and back. "But it's hours yet till midnight! I would need time to gather my research, and Hoghly may not even *be* there yet if the handoff is later, and—"

I found I was shaking my head emphatically. "Mossa's right. She knew there was going to be an attack of some kind tied to the donfense, and she understands this kind of action. And if we look at what's happened so far it's clear: this person does not care about your research. They only want to hurt you. The purpose of their plan is not"—I hesitated, because I had been on the point of saying *not to hurt Hoghly,* but a scenario had just occurred to me in which hurting Hoghly would indeed be a goal, if a secondary one—"not to access your research, but to discredit you or to physically harm you, or both."

Villette looked back at the note, still dubious, and I could understand: a ransom was a familiar idea, and made sense to her in a way that irrational viciousness did not. "My research . . ." She trailed off, surely also disliking the idea of handing over her work.

"Your research may be valuable, and it may be dangerous," Mossa replied, her tone ever more urgent. "But throughout this saga this person has used your research only as a bludgeon against you, or, at most, its success as a measure of resentment. You have accomplished, virtually, your donship; they will now attack you as desperately as they can, and your best option is to defy them by doing the unexpected."

"The best option is to walk into the trap, only earlier?" Petanj said, with a skepticism bordering on anger.

"The safest option in terms of physical harm is certainly to ignore this message." Mossa was speaking deliberately, choosing her phrasing carefully. "But I cannot believe that the person responsible for this campaign has not designed repercussions for that path."

"Do you think Hoghly is in real danger?" Villette asked, her eyes shadowy with exhaustion and worry.

"Or is it a trick that he came up with?" Petanj snapped.

Mossa and I exchanged a speaking glance. "I am starting to believe—" I began, and then deferred to Mossa, who at the same time responded, "I think he is in danger, yes. Unless he is already beyond danger." She raised her hands in the face of Villette's startlement, Petanj's doubt. "I cannot be sure that moving now will save him. But I doubt that following the instructions on this missive will be of any use to him."

Villette nodded. "We should go now then."

"This is not your fault," Petanj said furiously to her cousin. "You owe Hoghly nothing!"

Villette shook her head slowly. "I'm not doing this for *Hoghly*. I mean, if I didn't do it and he—well, I would feel terrible, but because of myself, not because of him. But I have to do something, or this will never stop. I can't let this person keep attacking me and my scholarly reputation and everyone associated with me just because I'm too scared of confrontation." Petanj reached for her, murmuring something comforting, but Villette wasn't done. "I'm doing this because I'm *furious.*"

"Espectacular." Mossa tapped her gently on the shoulder in a rare gesture of physical approval. "Now, and quickly, tell us about this other way in and out of the detonation lab."

Chapter 29

The detonation lab was attached to the platform proper by a long corridor extending out from an access point in a university building near the edge of the platform. Designed to allow for the manipulation of volatile chemicals, and on occasion for intentional detonations as part of experiments, the lab was blast-shielded in all the usual ways; it was also supposed to automatically detach from Stortellen if the force of an explosion overwhelmed the shielding and threatened the integrity of the platform, a fact that Petanj had mentioned repeatedly during our brief tactics session, primarily conducted at tongue-twisting pace and low voices while we walked. According to Villette, that precarious corridor arched slightly along its almost three-kilometer length, and, particularly in the stretches farther from the platform, bobbled noticeably underfoot in response to the gusts of Jovian weather surrounding it. A nightmare, evidently. And yet I envied Villette and Petanj, who were at that moment traversing it towards an uncertain and probably dangerous situation.

Because Mossa and I were in the alternate access option.

"Oh," Villette had said, when Mossa asked her about it. "Well. There's a kind of—a kind of horizontal dumbwaiter. It's mainly supposed to be used to transport either bulky or hazardous materials to the lab."

"It's atmoshielded?" Petanj had asked with reasonable skepticism.

"Oh yes. Minimally atmoshielded—it gets very cold—but it's certainly sufficient to human survival for the short journey." That sounded extremely confident. "I, er, believe it is rated as an emergency exit as well." Villette was avoiding our eyes, and after a pause, adorned with a rather pointed look from Petanj, added: "Every few terms some student or other uses it for a prank, or a dare . . ."

Petanj snorted. "And what did you do?"

Villette grinned. "Installed a music player that was set to play a pigeon coo at random intervals. Kept the professor looking for it through the entire class. A bit tame, I know," she added, "but of course it being the detonation lab with all sorts of protocols and so on, we couldn't do anything that would cause explosive reactions or frighten people."

I wouldn't have pegged Villette as the type to pull daring pranks. Although that innocent, retiring countenance probably shielded her from suspicion—"Wait a moment! Were you the one who sent Professor Lyufin all those fried termites in our last term?"

"Everyone underestimates her." Petanj's voice was brimming with pride.

"I wonder if they have in this case," Mossa had murmured.

And so we sat side by side in a box too small for us to fully extend our legs or stand without crouching, hooked (one imagined) to a wire or two stretched between the platform and the off-site, as the chill thickened and the trailing curls of tempest tossed us from side to side. *Like a boat,* I told myself, trying to use this as a way to better imagine that Classical experience. A particularly fierce ráfaga jostled us, and I forgot the comparisons and concentrated on breathing. A moment later I felt a warmth around my shoulders.

"Is that . . . helpful?" Mossa asked. I could not speak for a moment, and she went on, still hesitant. "I recall that when we traveled to Io, you had a similar physical reaction to the motion of the shuttle, and my explanations of the safety of the technology did not seem to help. I thought physical comfort might be useful for you in such circumstances, but if you prefer not to be touched while under these conditions I will not be offended, you know."

I leaned my weight against her gratefully as the cargo box continued to sway. The sway was still distractingly strong, and it took a moment for me to realize her arm was still tense: she was still waiting for my reply. Well, it stood to reason: if her instinct was intellectual comfort, then she probably needed me to verbalize my answer. "It *does* help," I said emphatically. "It does not, in the spirit of honesty, *fully* negate the disturbing effects of this situation, but it feels wonderful and that makes it better." Mossa relaxed and offered a few tentative pats on my arm. "Does all this tossing truly not bother you?" I pursued, curious.

She reflected before answering. "The movement is not comfortable, per se, but I have every confidence that we are well within the safety parameters of this, so to speak, vehicle, so it does not worry me."

I sighed against her. "I know my fears are not rational," I said with apology, "but feel them nonetheless."

"Rationality," Mossa said, "is a tool; and, like any other, it is fallible, and only of use in some circumstances." While I sat discombobulated by that statement, she went on. "Would distraction help? Because I must admit I am far more disturbed by the idea of what we are moving towards than by the way we are getting there."

"Do you think the person responsible for all this will be waiting for us?" That thought was almost as nauseating as the jouncing of the cargo box.

"I hope not." Mossa hesitated, either to prepare her thoughts or to decide how much to tell me, and I imagined Vertri's leer, or Wojo cackling, or Evna looking coolly superior. Or could it yet be Kenore, using her extensive knowledge of the university to prepare this complex scenario? "I do not believe whoever it is will have expected us to move so quickly, and I don't think they would be waiting there for the hours until midnight, if they would even attend the supposed handover. And they would not want to be caught entering or leaving the lab. No, I believe that if we find anyone there it will be Hoghly, and whether he will be in a state allowing *waiting* or not, I am not at all certain." Another hesitation. "I am more concerned that they may have snared the lab."

My skin prickled uncomfortably; the possibility had already occurred to me—given that we were heading for a laboratory filled with explosive materials, how could it not?—but that Mossa was concerned enough to give voice to it made the possibility seem far more real. "Then why are we even here?"

Mossa sighed and minimally adjusted our mutual lean. "I don't *think* they will have expected us to come this early. I don't *think* they will expect us to use, or even know about, this approach, although given the pranks Villette mentioned, it is very possible they do know it. I also don't believe they will be trying to kill Villette—yet. It is a risk, however."

I was still digesting that—and finding that, on the whole, I was inclined to believe her, that this comemierda would want to visit extensive humiliation and disgrace on Villette before getting around to murder—when Mossa glanced at her timepiece. "Forty-seven seconds." The whole trajectory only lasted a little over seven minutes, although since the box was not intended for sentient travelers there was no timer on the inside. Mossa took the emergency interior handle from its slot and fitted it to the octagonal hole in the door. I wondered if Villette and Petanj had arrived yet, and what—who—they had found. The air warmed noticeably as we passed through the stronger atmoshield keeping the lab at platform standards, and the creaking sound of our winch, faded into the background over the journey, took on a new echo. There was a grinding sound as we docked; Mossa waited for the safety light to ignite, then yanked the crank around. The lock thunked; we pushed the door in concert, and it opened onto chaos.

Chapter 30

The room beyond was thick with brume that pressed dense and slow into our cargo box (which suddenly seemed a haven of safety) even as the door opened. I pulled my atmoscarf up automatically, which helped a little with the breathing, but not enough. Naturally (I thought, coughing and wishing passionately that I had one of Villette's horrid nose-inserts), it was not planetary fog, but smoke, its noxiousness underpinned by some unknown and unpleasant tang. Various alarms were shrieking in concert, and even as I peered into the murky room there was a thudding sound that vibrated through me and another plume of smoke billowed from somewhere ahead of me. I dropped, reaching for Mossa, but she was already gone; when I stared around in a sudden sharp press of panic (*Why had we not prepared for this contingency? Connected ourselves with cord, held hands?*) I saw her to my right, where a dim figure—Petanj?—was struggling with something in the wall. I thought to follow, then hesitated, considering it would be better to stay by the cargo box, and then I heard Villette's voice calling for help from somewhere towards the middle of the room. Without further twijfels, I plunged towards the sound.

Villette was only a few meters away from me—the lab was not so very large, although in those frenzied moments it felt like an enormous havoc-ridden space—and I found her doubled over coughing. I caught her shoulder and by gestures—for the alarms were making it hard to think, let alone speak—I offered her one end of my long atmoscarf, which she pressed to her face with one hand while pointing at the ground with the other: Hoghly—or his corpse? I couldn't tell if he was breathing, but when I matched Villette's movement to lift him, his wrist was warm; or perhaps it was my hands that were frigid with fear.

We got his upper body off the ground, an arm around our respective shoulders, and dragged his long legs behind us as we pushed towards the cargo box. In the confusion and the smoke, I had gotten slightly turned, so we met the wall a little farther along its curve, but Petanj was there immediately to grab Hoghly's arm from Villette and harry us both to the exit. Mossa was waiting; we heaved Hoghly onto the floor of the box without ceremony, and as soon as Villette had crouched uncomfortably in with us, Mossa squeezed herself in and pulled the door shut.

The piercing noise of the alarms was immediately dampened, leaving our gasping breaths the only sound. Mossa threw the lock. "Everyone well?" Apparently our silence, or the rapid glance she passed over us in the lantern light, satisfied her, because she hit the disengage, then, as the box rattled down its shaft, found the button for ventilation. It wasn't quick, and the new air that filtered in was bitter cold, but presently the atmosphere in the box cleared a little.

"It was a trap," Petanj gasped, and then turned a glare on Mossa. "*Unsurprisingly.*"

"What happened?" Mossa asked, impassive.

"The door from the corridor shut behind us and locked, or jammed with something. I was trying to open it when Villette saw Hoghly and ran towards him, and that's when the explosions started."

By this time I had found the wherewithal to put my fingertips to Hoghly's neck; finding a pulse, I lurched awkwardly to the first aid kit strapped to the wall and pulled it down.

Villette had found a way to flatten her back on the floor, legs propped up along the wall, and gradually her coughing had eased. "Of course it was a trap," she said wearily. "But Mossa was right. Hoghly was already unconscious before the explosions. If we had come later it might have been too late."

"Might have," Petanj grumbled as she helped me administer a stasis pill and check for any obvious injuries. "Or maybe it's some harmless anesthetic he administered to himself to trap you."

Villette made a dismissive motion. "There was no shrapnel— the explosions were for chemical release. And I can't be sure what all of them were"—the idea of what toxins could have been suspended in that murky atmosphere sent a cold wash of fear through my whole body, but I recovered enough to unfold the shock blanket onto Hoghly's necessarily crumpled form— "but I don't think they were intended to kill us."

"No, more likely to delay you," Mossa said. "It was a trap intended to show you as culpable for whatever has been done to Hoghly, not to mention the lab. You would have arrived just in time to be blamed, with no evidence that anyone else was involved."

"He's sweating and clammy," I reported. "I don't think it was just an anesthetic."

"More important," Mossa went on, "is what we do once we arrive at the other end of this hawser. We cannot assume any grace period beyond the"—a glance at her timepiece—"five and a half minutes that remain in our trajectory. We must be prepared to move."

"Hoghly's going to have to get to the clinic," Petanj said, with noticeably less ire; she seemed to have calmed, as well as coming to the conclusion that his life was indeed in danger. "And maybe my cousin as well."

"I'm fine," Villette managed. "But I'll go along with Hoghly, to make sure he's all right."

"I believe that would be ill-advised," Mossa said slowly. "The trap may not have sprung at its optimal point, but it has still sprung. Consider that this event has caused a commotion that will have been noticed at the university. Those alarms that were triggered surely connect with alerts on the platform, yes?"

"Oh stars, she's right," Petanj sighed. "We'll have to go see the dean again."

Chapter 31

I wanted to accompany Mossa to the clinic, if only to assist with the transportation of the inert Hoghly, but she insisted on going alone. After a few blank refusals, she stopped herself abruptly mid–*no really Pleiti* and then explained. "I hope to get some intel about his condition, and that may be easier if I am there openly as an Investigator, and without less-official witnesses. In addition"—lowering her voice, although the cousins were at that moment intent on a similarly murmured discussion—"I suspect they may benefit from your support."

And so I found myself accompanying the cousins to the office of the dean of the Modern faculty of Stortellen, feeling only slightly out of place. It was, it seemed, the dean's off-diurnal, but he had already been called from his rest to be informed about the alerts sounding from the detonation lab. I could understand that putting him de mala leche; I had some hope that our arrival, to provide further details about that disturbing circumstance, might be welcome, but no: he was quite choleric when, after a not-insubstantial wait, we were invited into his office.

"Well?" he barked. "You again, hey? I had thought you would stop causing trouble when we allowed your donfense"—Petanj and I bristled simultaneously at the implication that Villette's donship hadn't been fairly earned; the all-but-don herself twisted her hands in her lap—"but no, you had to go and destroy our detonation lab anyway. For the greater glory of, is it? Do you have any idea how much it will cost to replace that equipment?"

He was shouting in a quite unsanitary way by that point, and I could feel Villette shaking beside me. "Sir," I began.

"And who're you?"

"Pleiti Weihal, scholar in Classics of Valdegeld, and as a witness to—"

"When I want your *Geldan* opinion I'll ask for it! In the meantime there's only one person here with any standing in the matter, as far as I can see." He glared at Villette.

"I didn't destroy the detonation lab," she said. I could see, though hopefully the dean couldn't, that Petanj was clutching her hand. "I only went there because Hoghly was in danger, and then the explosions were already set to go off—"

"You and your coauthor trying something dangerous, were you? Avoiding procedures, trying to keep it secret, hey? Very, ah, *technobro,* quoi?" I had to bite my lip to keep from correcting the solecism.

"No," Villette said, patience starting to fray, "I wasn't doing any experiment there at all. When I arrived, the explosions were already *set.*"

"Is that so? I have here"—thumping a laminate on his desk—"the records of the lab authorizations for the past twelve hours, and you are the only one who has signed out a key!"

I turned to look at Villette; beyond her, Petanj seemed to be silently demanding patience of the ceiling.

"Because I follow procedure," Villette retorted, with a sudden access of fire. "Even in an emergency. Apparently someone else didn't."

It was at that interesting juncture that there was a knock on the door, and Mossa entered and introduced herself as an Investigator. "I've been following the case," she explained, stepping to position herself just behind Villette's shoulder.

"Case?" The dean had damped his yell in the face of an Investigator, but he still sounded suspicious and ornery. "What case? Why do I not know about this?" His pointy gaze swept back to Villette.

"I have reported," Villette said steadily, "the threats, the— Just last week I was here to report to you the damage to my lab."

"And no evidence," the dean answered, volume rising again, "that you didn't manufacture all of it yourself!"

"I can attest," Mossa began, "as indeed we all can, that Villette was only in the lab for scant minutes—indeed, given that she returned to her rooms after the donfense, it is difficult to see how she would have had time to set up the detonations involved in the destruction there."

"We don't know yet how the destruction was engineered! You said the explosions were preset; that could have been from before her donfense even! Perhaps a contingency in case it didn't go well? I know the tricks you scholars get up to!"

I was beginning to grasp why Villette had been so reluctant to appeal to the university for assistance; indeed, why her antagonizer had felt free to harass her for so long.

Mossa ignored him. "I can also confirm that this is considered an element in a series of escalating incidents, which Investigators have been aware of—"

"Oh, *truly*? Because I have here," recurring again to the rather insolitamente useful surface of his desk, "a message from the Investigators' Bureau of Stortellen, avowing that they know entirely *nothing* about such an investigation, and have not deployed any of their Investigators to it."

"Quite," Mossa agreed. "I am from the Sembla bureau, and while I have been coordinating with the bureau here—"

"Is that where you're *from*?" I had been looking at my hands in an effort not to look at Mossa's face—*had she not coordinated with the Investigators here? Did her bureau*—deeply worrying thought—*even know she was here?*—but at the emphasis in his voice I glanced up sharply. "Awfully *far* for you to come, when we have Investigators on our own platform."

"It was felt," Mossa replied, without specifying by whom, "that some experience in academic affairs would be helpful—"

"Are you suggesting that the *Stortellen* Investigators do not have experience with academic affairs? We might have more urb to our platform than Valdegeld does, but I assure you, they deal very reliably with our académe, and they, like myself, see little need for *outsiders*."

I flinched. After his previous emphasis on *from,* I was almost certain that "outsiders" meant *Ionians*; but it would be easy enough for him to explain that word away as meaning *not from Stortellen,* and I hesitated while he went on. "In fact, we're a little doubtful that you're an Investigator at all."

Silently, Mossa withdrew her textile badge from a pocket and displayed it. The dean flicked his fingers impatiently. "Perhaps. We have a 'gram out to your supposed bureau in any case, making sure that you do work there and that you are assigned to this case. Surely they will be pleased to explain why it was so urgent to supplant our local Investigators."

I couldn't keep myself from looking to Mossa at that, even knowing that she would show nothing.

"Can't understand why they would have someone like you on the Investigators at all," he muttered, "but they certainly shouldn't be sending you to platforms you're not accustomed to. Cultural differences alone . . ."

I did not react quickly enough. Even after all the time I had spent with Mossa, all the many occasions on which I had heard or seen someone slight her because of her lunar origin, I still found myself briefly, appallingly flustered.

Petanj had no such difficulty. She sallied in immediately with welcome belligerence: "What exactly does that mean?"

"You." The dean snorted. "I know you visit a lot, but I don't believe you are associated with our university. Another *Geldan*. Don't try your Valdegeld snobbery here, we have no rail for it. *Oldest, first, best,* indeed! And your own rector went off in a rocket without telling anyone, that's what comes from your unhealthy obsession with Classics!"

"Do you believe everyone to be the merest triteness of where they're from?" I asked, finally exasperated into speech.

"No. For example, I have never heard that Geldans were brawlers, particularly, but I believe you to be one."

I had entirely forgotten about my shiner, which the passing of days had only made more lurid; the surprise muted me again.

Petanj stood up. "What an embarrassment." For a horrible second I thought she meant me and my bar fight, but that was my own shame; she was quite clearly aiming at the dean. "Villette, you don't owe this person or this university anything. Let's walk out of here right now, be home in a few days, and we'll have you set up at Valdegeld in a fortnight." I had some private qualms about that—positions at Valdegeld were not so easily found, even for someone of Villette's calibre, or she would doubtless already be there—but at the moment solidarity was the game, so I nodded sharply as if it was all entirely expected.

"Quite," Villette replied, startling me with her decisiveness; even aside from the loyalty she must feel to the university, the connection to her colleagues and students, I didn't expect such sternness from her personality. "I cannot countenance institutional power callously wielding insults about inherent characteristics. Let's go." She stood; I followed her lead. Mossa, already standing, did not move even as Villette brushed by her in turning.

The dean sighed extravagantly. "Come, come. No one's going anywhere; Valdegeld doesn't have openings come up with the regularity of railcars; and, if it's really necessary, I apologize for whatever you *think* I meant. Fine? Now can we deal with the problem at hand?"

Villette paused, without looking like it was a hesitation, at the door. Petanj looked back. "How do you propose to deal with it?"

"A full investigation." The dean sounded much more reasonable, even amenable. Perhaps he was tickled to have irked his scholar to the point where she was ready to leave, or perhaps venting his spleen on people who were not at fault had made him feel better about his lost sleep and the waiting administrative mess. Certainly he was one of those people who thought bullying others for his own emotional comfort was a fair trade. "I'll appoint two or three departmental scholars to look into it. Transparent. They can loop in the *Stortellen* Investigators if you like, although it will only make it more cumbersome."

There was a silence. Neither Villette nor Petanj spoke.

"Naturally," the dean said, as if it were an unimportant afterthought that had just occurred to him, "we'll have to postpone the donship confirmation until that is complete."

"Oh *stars*," Petanj said, in a tone of complete annoyance. I saw Villette shake her head slightly and look down at her hands.

"I don't suppose I could convince you," Mossa said quietly, "that the safest thing for the university and its reputation would be to formalize the donship as quickly and quietly as possible?"

The dean stared at her for some time, as if attempting to slowly work through her logic. I rather hoped he was; I hoped he was not the person who all this time had been trying to keep Villette from getting her donship. Satisfying as it would have been to eject him from his position on those grounds, it would also, as I knew to my regret, have consequential complications; and in this case, most of them were sadly likely to reverberate onto Villette. "I cannot," he said finally, "let such considerations outweigh the proper procedures in a case like this."

"Well then," Petanj snapped, "I suppose there's nothing more to say." And she left, Villette close on her heels, Mossa and I following behind, with only the thin satisfaction of the last word.

Chapter 32

The dean's office was on the top floor of a domed ovoid building, each quadrant's floor level at a quarter-story offset to the next, so we had a longish gradual ramp to descend in silence. I cannot speak for the others, but while I was not unaware of the grimness of Villette's situation, my thoughts orbited rather around the crudeness of the insults to Mossa, and my poor reaction time. I had just gotten to the point of wondering what, exactly, was the situation with the Investigators when we reached the ground level, and Petanj halted abruptly before the exit door. "Listen, Vil. I know that was gritty, but let's not show it to everyone out there, sabes?"

I turned to see Villette, tear tracks glimmering on her cheeks, sniff and nod and blink rapidly. "Maybe an atmoscarf?" I suggested, having used that dispositif more than once in similar situations.

"But everyone knows she doesn't usually wear one," Petanj argued, dabbing at Villette's face with her sleeve.

"You're right!" Mossa said from behind us, with rather more enthusiasm than I would have expected from her in such a cause. She glanced upwards, but there was no way to know if anyone had entered the ramp at a higher level. "We must confound this person," she went on, leaning close to us and lowering her voice. "The best, perhaps the only way at this point is to feign that all is well—better than well, formidable in fact."

Petanj was staring at her with open skepticism; Villette was not showing any signs of being able to act happy. "She's right," I put in. "Villette, your antagonist wants you unhappy. Let's show the opposite."

"Won't they just try harder then?" Petanj asked.

Mossa glanced arriba again. "Can we pretend to be celebratory until we arrive at our lodgings and then discuss further?"

Petanj grumbled something, but Villette nudged her. "I'll try. I think at this point I'd rather cosplay happiness than feel like this." Petanj put her arm around her shoulders, dabbed again at her face, and then we sauntered forth with as much swagger as we could manage.

Though the interlude in and around the off-site lab had seemed hours, it had in fact been brief, and even with the time waiting for the dean's dubious attentions, it was still full night, the weather finally clear, the variegated hues of the streetlights rivaling the moons with their glows, and the streets were crowded with merrymakers. Mossa kept up a steady stream of bright commentary which was the most improbable yet convincing disguise I had seen her in yet—and that was droll and discomfiting in unequal measures. Petanj, for all her doubts, could not resist fully joining in once committed, and she told Villette jokes and reminded her of funny stories from their youth, laughing raucously herself and studding her commentary with loud *Did you hear*s and *Can you believe*s as though it were all new gossip. I tried to help the effort by telling Villette how much I admired her scholarship, how thoroughly she deserved all the accolades; her effortful smile wobbled towards tears, and from then on I constrained myself to nodding and laughing along, and to attempting a subtle surveillance of the crowds around us. I didn't catch sight of any of our suspects, or indeed anyone else in Villette's circle, but they could have been anywhere among the chatting, mingling, wandeling, eating, drinking, and dancing students and scholars around us.

At last we all piled into Villette's rooms, lapsing into an exhausted silence by common consent. Filled with her cushions and colors, the apartment was far more inviting than the impersonal suite I was kipping in, and I felt a sudden longing for my own rooms. Villette went to wash her face while Petanj ordered tea; Mossa examined some laminates that had been left for Villette, presumably checking their potential for physical or psychological harm; and soon we were all reclining around the fire in relative comfort, if some not entirely at ease in our minds.

"I'm in awe of your fortitude in front of that awful man, Villette," I said at last. "From the way you spoke in there I would have thought you didn't care two pigeons about leaving."

"Oh, that's just our Strategem," Petanj said, with Capitalization.

"We have an agreement," Villette explained. "If we're in any kind of difficulty together—of course that doesn't happen much these days, but when we were children, well." They shared a smile. "Anyway, whichever of us sets the tone of how to respond, the other follows wholeheartedly. We don't divide in front of others."

I was, if anything, even more astonished. "But—but what if you don't agree? Petanj doesn't know how you feel about leaving!"

"Well, I *do*," Petanj drawled. "But that's not the point. In that moment, I just *knew* we couldn't bow to that petty fascist. Show a man like that any weakness and he will never let go of it. I had the distance not to be as worried about it, you see. But if later we came back here, and—say it had gone differently, or even now as it went—" Villette made a dismissive gesture. "Well, in any case if she disagreed, we would discuss it, and she could always go back alone and apologize, say that I overwhelmed her into following my lead."

Villette made a face. "In this case, as usual, you're quite right though. Recanting on this to the dean would be—well, wrong, but also tactically foolish. But in any case I *could*. And if I take the lead when we're together, Petanj can always go and say she felt sorry for me and was just trying not to cause a problem or something like that. It doesn't mean we never disagree or that the person who speaks first always gets their way. But in effect"—she looked at her cousin for confirmation—"we've very rarely chosen to change direction, in cases like these."

Petanj nodded. "Usually the person who feels clearly how to respond—and it's not always me, I promise you!—is quite correct."

"You certainly were this time," Villette said sorrowfully. "I mean, he backed off, so there's that. But you were also right! How dare he treat people that way? I really think I may have to leave anyway. You know"—turning to Mossa and myself—"I was always able to just—just study, and experiment, and write, and I could ignore how terrible he was, and not just him, but—" She covered her face again.

Hesitantly, I reached out to rub her shoulder. "I know," I said. "When our rector—" I had to swallow hard. "I had no idea that someone in that position would do something like that. It never occurred to me. Since then I've been seeing quite a lot of things—and people, and institutions—very differently."

Villette smiled at me through her tears. I was glad that Wojo couldn't see us; it would have looked terribly romantic.

"It's an admirable strategy," Mossa said, breaking her quiet. "And enviable to have someone you trust so deeply."

It hit me like a blow, so hard that I didn't hear or register the undoubtedly deprecating response. I *knew* Mossa wasn't aiming for me—she didn't employ veiled allusions or oblique attacks, and the case did not fit. I *knew* she was speaking of her feelings, not of our relationship. But I *wanted*—I wanted in that moment to throw myself at her feet, declaring vividly that she could trust me to the bone, to the marrow, to the atom, to the spinning core. Not that there was any use to it; declaring oneself trustworthy was about the worst possible way to convince another of one's fidelity.

"Thing is," Petanj was saying irascibly, "it's marvelous and all that she can trust me, her closest family, but she should be able to trust her university as well! At least to the point of not undermining her at the first opportunity. Maybe it's the dean himself who's doing all this! Or maybe at least he's in league with whoever is."

"If the dean wanted Villette removed from the university, there would be easier ways for him to accomplish that," Mossa opined. "Also I have to imagine that if he did want to approach it with this level of clandestinidad, he would try to avoid costly damage to university facilities."

"Why? It's not that he has to pay for it himself." Petanj threw her hands up. "Bien. Suppose it's not him. She's being driven out of the university anyway. What do we *do*?"

Mossa, as though she had been waiting for that very question (indeed, she probably had been) handed over the laminates that she had been checking earlier. They were both from Wojo; the first asked if Villette was planning a donship party and the second offered to invite her out for a quieter celebration. If Wojo *was* the malefactor, she was exceedingly chill in her machinations; if this was flirting, considerably less chill.

"Is it another trap?" Petanj asked wearily.

Villette raised her head at that but didn't find the energy to protest.

"No, I don't think so . . ." I began.

Mossa leaped to her feet. "Oh, but it is!"

I stared. She caught my eye, and her minimalist smile widened just a bit, and she shook her head at me. "A perfect trap. But *ours,* not theirs."

"Another plaaaaaan," Petanj groaned. "The last one almost got us killed and"—she turned a glare on Mossa—"did *not* keep my cousin out of trouble, either."

I couldn't let that pass. "Have you thought about what would have happened if we *hadn't* gone immediately? Our best chance at exculpation is the fact that there wasn't *time* for Villette to set all that up. Did you notice all those irradiated laminates that confounded dean kept picking up off his desk, so conveniently waiting right at hand with exactly the information that would put us in the worst appearance? If we had gone later, it would seem far more plausible that Villette was involved, they probably would have even more evidence against her, and Hoghly—" I stopped, suddenly, remembering that we didn't know if we had saved him. My mood plummeted from indignant to glum. "How is he?"

Mossa held out a level palm. "When I left, his prognosis was yet uncertain, although the clinic staff did not seem completely without hope. They did tell me he had ingested some sort of poison—fungal in origin, they suspect—and he had bruises to his neck indicative of strangulation." She looked at Villette. "They don't know if they can save him," she repeated, "but further delay would certainly have worsened his condition."

There was a somber silence.

Villette stirred at last and turned to Mossa. "So what do we do?"

Mossa held up Wojo's laminates. "We throw a party."

Chapter 33

Mossa insisted that we hold the celebration during the very next diurnal. "The aim is to push this person into such a fury that they make a mistake, a public mistake, so that the defamation campaign becomes obvious to everyone. To do this we need to present them with a vision of Villette celebratory and triumphant, demonstrating that the plan has failed: that the university does not blame Villette, that her donship is assured. Perhaps we could even put it about that the university is acclaiming her a hero for rescuing Hoghly." Villette looked physically ill at that suggestion. "The longer we wait, the more likely that the malefactor hears about the true circumstances."

"Won't the dean just tell them?" Petanj asked. "I mean, they are apparently collaborating, given all that information he had about Mossa and Villette."

"I'm sure it was shared anonymously," I said. "Or possibly planted for others to collect."

Mossa nodded agreement. "I doubt the dean is consciously, actively collaborating with the perpetrator against Villette. I don't think"—in the detached tone that demonstrated her disgust—"he cares enough about either of them to do so. But I also doubt that he will refrain from chismoseando about this to *somebody*; it's only a matter of time and connections before it gets around to our target."

And so we settled on the following evening. The venue for the party was the next problem. Villette didn't want to sully her preferred taverns with the memory of a fake celebration, and it was too late to book most of them anyway, but even when Petanj suggested some more anodyne options Mossa vetoed them. "There will be too much chaos at any of these pubs, especially the outdoor settings. Too much liminal space, overlapping with passersby and vicinitous shops. Easy for the perpetrator to make their escape, or attack Villette in a way that's not obvious to all the witnesses. Perhaps we could use a room in one of the university buildings?"

Villette gave a dissatisfied expression; Petanj started in again about the danger of someone attacking Villette and why we would even leave that possibility open. It was some minutes before I was able to make my suggestion that we hold the party on top of Stortellen's hill.

The cousins, at first surprised, agreed almost immediately; Mossa demanded detailed descriptions of the topography and finally swept out to examine it herself. Petanj began to work on Villette, trying to get her to agree to take up Wojo's offer of assistance with the party preparations; I cast her a skeptical glance but she glared right back at me and I decided to stay out of that particular dynamic.

But I couldn't silence the querulous internal voice suggesting that Wojo still *might* be the enemy, that letting her into the party planning was the worst possible move, even if we didn't tell her it was a provocation. Well, maybe there was something I could do to either quiet that voice or validate it. I slipped back to my rooms, dug into the pile of materials I had brought from the library until I found something by Wojo, and started reading.

I read the monograph by Wojo, then one by Evna, then the article and research note that were all I could find by Kenore. When I heard a tap at the door I had gone back to Vertri; in the middle of a chapter, I pressed the release without looking up from my reading. Mossa hissed at me. "Haven't I impressed on you by now the need to be cautious?" I made some noise or comment and went on reading; she stood there for a while then left quietly at some indeterminate moment. I thought I could discount Hoghly at that point but . . . well, maybe just one. To be sure.

I read Hoghly. I went back and read through everything I had by Wojo, by Evna, by Vertri. By the time Mossa crouched in front of me, I was staring into space as much as reading, though I still had a monograph open on my lap. I blinked at her. "What is it?" I was sure she had left earlier, and indeed when I thought about it I found a memory of the door opening and her saying something about food. I looked around and saw the table set with a bowl and mugs.

"It's late, or early," Mossa said, when she saw that my cognition was more or less present again. "Nearly dawn. You should eat. And then, if you can, try to sleep a few hours. We should be at the hill by sunset."

I opened my mouth, closed it again, blinked a few times. I had things to say, but I wasn't sure I should say them, and the scent of spices had made me aware that I was hungry. I nodded, transferred myself to the table, and started spooning laksa into my mouth.

Mossa hadn't asked me what I had been doing, or berated me for not assisting with the preparations. I swallowed the last of the soup and she leaned over to pour the tea for me, and I tried to hold that moment, that feeling that she was completely with me without needing to understand me.

"Mossa." I almost said something sentimental, but I didn't think she would welcome it in that moment, when she still felt fragile and was probably already half in hyper-focus on the coming gambit. "Tell me. Do you know who we're looking for?"

She stood and started pacing, as though it were a difficult question, and indeed when she spoke her voice betrayed frustration. "I am not sure how to answer that, Pleiti. I have suspicions, and in the past you have suggested that my suspicions are more like knowledge, more certain than I am willing to rate them, in any case—"

"How certain do you rate this one?"

She gestured frustration. "Not nearly certain enough! With this kind of motive—hate instead of gain—it is harder to triangulate from circumstances, and worst of all I have barely so much as *spoken* to any of the likely suspects! My entire rationale hinges on a single anomaly that you found; it could be less of an anomaly than it appears, or there could be other, more pertinent oddities among the other suspects that simply have not been brought to our attention!" She turned suddenly to me. "How certain are you of your suspicions, Pleiti? Oh, don't look so surprised. You were clearly asking for a reason, and you've been holed up here all day doing something, not your work, something to help Villette. What have you found?"

I wriggled. "It's not a very . . . usual method."

"Have my methods ever prized usualness?" Mossa rolled her eyes; despite myself, I could not help smiling to see her confidence in action again.

"No, but, well, I am not—trained, as you are." I almost said *talented*, but that would have started another argument. "I *have* spoken with all of them, and, Mossa, this job of yours is the very void. I didn't know if they were lying to me; I started to suspect everyone. I hated it."

"Yes, yes, and then?"

Deep breath. "I thought about my usual media for evaluating theories and, well, I went to the library."

"You researched the suspects?"

"No." I could feel my face heating: that would have made more sense. "I read them. Their work, I mean." *Worthy of study.*

"Ah." Mossa loosed a tiny smile. "And?"

"And, yes. I have a suspicion. And I feel very sure, but also, I have been mistaken before in my suspicions on this investigation. *Multiple* times, Mossa."

"Mm, but those weren't based on this unusual method of yours, which seems quite solid to me."

"I'd feel much more certain if we suspected the same person."

We did.

"Mossa," I asked, while she was still folding my impressions from my reading into her character analysis, "should we tell the cousins?"

"What reasons not to?"

"Well, for one, we still could be wrong, and if they are only focused on the one person they might not be sufficiently on guard against the others. And then, if Petanj believes me—which she might not, she saw how I was wrong before—she'll be angry, and she might not be able to hide it during the party."

"Practically," Mossa replied, "I believe we can trust both of them to understand that there is doubt; and while it's true that Petanj does not place a high value on concealing her emotions"—I snorted in agreement—"she is also skilled at taking on a persona, when she has committed to one, and I believe in this case she has accepted our approach."

I was reflecting on that, and thinking about how I had taken on a role as I questioned the suspects, when Mossa went on. "As for the principle of it, you have generally objected when I secluded information from you during an investigation."

I opened my mouth to say *It's different*—Mossa and I were in a *relation of affection,* after all, and in any case I hadn't been personally implicated in the investigations—then stopped, wondering if any of those differences really mattered. Mossa slid her arm around my waist, kissed my temple, leaned me towards the daybed. "Sleep a whiles," she whispered, and curled in beside me, as though that—or the suspense—were in any way conducive to slumber.

And indeed, though Mossa's breathing evened out into soft snores almost immediately, I lay awake as the light sneaking around the curtains brightened and then mellowed. Scenarios played out in my speculative organ, possible causes and consequences, bits of violence or painful confrontation following one after another as I drifted in a semidoze. The last was a reimagining of the moment when the dean obliquely insulted Mossa and I was too stunned to respond; the horrified shiver of that woke me completely, and I sat up and stretched, ordered tea, woke Mossa. Half an hour later we met the cousins in their rooms.

"So you're saying you know who it is now?" Petanj radiated skepticism, which was a good thing, I reminded myself.

"We have a strong suspicion," Mossa replied, "and it is particularly strong since we came to the conclusion in different ways."

"What ways?" Villette looked as though she hadn't slept at all either.

"For me," Mossa began (she never minded explaining her methods, once she was convinced that the listener was truly interested), "the suspicions stem from a small anomaly: Pleiti reported on chisme that Evna"—Petanj's skepticism intensified; Villette raised an eyebrow—"is *unhinged* about Villette; but Villette said she was unaware of any particular obsession."

"That could just be a misunderstanding," Villette said, while Petanj looked at me.

"Evna, now? First Wojo—"

"You thought it was *Wojo*?" Villette sputtered a laugh. "No way."

"Then you thought it was Kenore—"

"She seems to be everywhere, always around when something is going on, so . . ."

"And now," Petanj repeated, "you say Evna. Truly?"

"Pues I—I went to the library and read their publications." Mossa was smiling, only slightly but enough for me to catch the hint of proud approval, and I scrunched my nose at her as though I didn't love it. The cousins were still waiting, and I shrugged at them. "That's it. I read their work. And . . . well, several of them are *awful* people, to be sure, but Evna was the only one of them who seemed to me like the kind of person who would do *this*. The way she writes is so . . . mean-spirited? Self-important? You can *tell*, even when it's an article about something you don't know anything about, because it's not the content, it's the way it's written, the sentences, the asides, the way other scholars are referenced . . ." I looked at them helplessly, but Petanj was nodding, and Villette had a thoughtful expression.

"I've never seen her act that way," she said, but more as though considering it than as an argument. "She's always been nice to me. Or at least . . . collegial. She's a bit . . . well, I think she navigates socially in a way that I don't know how to do, so perhaps I missed something."

"Have you ever read her work?" I asked.

"No," Villette admitted, with a little laugh of embarrassment. "I think she even sent me one of her book chapters once, but—you know, there's so much to keep up with just in my field! And she wasn't asking for a critique or anything, it was already published."

"I wish you had," I muttered. "I would like a second opinion. But you should know," I added, remembering, "she's read all of yours."

"What?"

"Most of them, at least. She cites you."

"In astronomy papers?"

"Yes. I mean, there are often atmospheric concerns . . . but you're the only one in that field she ever cites. Of course, that could be simply—" What had she called it? "Collegiality."

"Creepiness, more like," Petanj muttered. "Still—are you . . . ?" She mimed shuffling a saucepan, student cant for *certain.*

"No," I admitted. Petanj threw up her hands, and I imagined a half-fried egg flying against the wall with a wet slap. "I'm no expert in character and motivation."

"But you're the expert in textual analysis," Mossa interjected.

"Anyhap, I'm *glad* you don't fully believe me," I told Petanj, "because in case we're wrong I want you to be cautious of *everyone.*"

"But extra cautious of Evna," Villette said. I wondered if she was remembering some cues or hints that made her more ready to believe it.

"I still think it's that crank Vertri," Petanj said, "but fine, I will be cautious of everyone. Shall we go?"

"Remember, though," Mossa admonished us as we donned our jackets and (except for Villette) our atmoscarfs, "you must not look like you're being cautious! This should be a celebration, or it won't work."

"I'm happy," Villette muttered through almost sealed lips. "I'm happy."

Wojo had, as promised, prepped the party. When the four of us arrived at the hill, flush with many more last-minute reminders of enforced cheer and suggestions for useful provocations, we found the lanterns strung, the blankets spread, and the hampers ready. I was somewhat anxious that, after so much over-hasty preparation, not enough people would join us, but I needn't have worried. Villette was well-known for her research and far better integrated into the university than I had understood during this brief, odd visit; more than that, based on the conversations I overheard during the festje more than half of them liked her at least half as much as she deserved, which was heartening indeed—and at the same time bittersweet, if after all this she was compelled to leave for another platform.

It was, however, less ideal from the perspective of safety and clarity. Petanj, Mossa, and I were all circulating around Villette; I couldn't help scanning the faces around us for our suspects as well. Wojo was there, of course, as laughing and obnoxious as if she hadn't helped at all. Kenore seemed relaxed for once, sipping at something with a group of gradudents under a tree. I caught my first glimpse of Evna chatting with Haxi, although Haxi's expression suggested she was seeking an escape route. I wanted to keep an eye on her but was too nervous about giving our suspicions away, and looked in the other direction, where I saw Vertri's Classical face, bereft of the last few hundred years of evolutionary selection, frozen in a nonexpression as he listened stonily to a disquisition by Zan, the dean of Classics.

Despite her obvious exhaustion, Villette was playing her

part excellently, glowing with happiness as though she were in fact celebrating her donship, instead of forked on uncertainty and a terrible ethical decision. I glanced around again, nervous; something had to happen soon, and if it didn't, I didn't know what we would try next—leaving the platform in disgrace and lack of closure, probably—and if it *did*—well, I just hoped everyone would survive it. I felt a tug on my arm and looked around to see Vao.

"Is it true?" she whispered. She looked a bit out of breath and flustered, as if she had just walked up the hill to the party without any planning or suitable pauses during the ascent. I braced myself for bad news, but she only asked, "Do you know who did that to Hoghly?"

I looked around, baffled at who might have told her. Petanj was talking to the tall ethnographer, the sight of whom hit me with a vague pang of guilt at my missteps; Villette was talking animatedly with Haxi, Starshka, and Wojo, while Mossa— who would not, in any case, have discussed such a thing with anyone—was hovering alertly nearby. I turned back to Vao, trying to decide between disavowing all knowledge with a lie and hedging the truth in a way that might lead to more entanglement when I needed to be aware and detached.

I was spared the dilemma by an arm catching around my neck and the scrape of something sharp along my bicep.

The trap had been sprung.

Chapter 34

Vao recoiled away from whatever she saw over my shoulder, and the motion spread through the crowd like ruffling feathers as people turned, saw, stepped back. I saw Villette's eyes widen as she took in the situation, and that's when my captor spoke.

"Villette!" I wouldn't have recognized Evna's voice if I hadn't been expecting it: contempt and ugly triumph harshened it. "I have your namourade here, and I'll stick her with the same toxin I used on Hoghly unless you renounce your donship, your research, your—"

"You've been misinformed, I'm afraid," I said, as loudly as I could. "I'm not Villette's lover. I'm here for another reason." I paused to take a breath, as the last one had fallen rather short, and also for dramatic effect, because I had just had an idea. "She's in love with *you*."

By chance, my gaze traced over Wojo's face as I spoke, and I saw the devastation there with a twist of scruples, but at that moment everything was secondary to tracking Evna's attention. I didn't know whether she was thrilled or horrified at the idea that Villette loved her, but it surprised her enough that I felt the pulse of distraction diluting the intensity of her grip. I pulled away, but gently, steadily, not wanting to jerk her into a sudden reaction that might put the needle into my arm sinquerer. As I pulled I felt a gentle brush against my arm, as I might imagine the antenna of a giant moth, and I looked down to see the end of Mossa's whip-lasso curling around Evna's wrist, which was reassuring; it also let me see the syringe, which was not, being huge, pointed, and glistening with its toxic burden.

"Sembla Investigators Bureau," came Mossa's voice like a clarion, "holding you to account—"

"For what?" Evna laughed with distressing abandon. "For letting people know the truth about what a fraud she is? *She's the one you should be holding to account.* She is a fraud as a scholar, she has tricked everyone, thefted my renown—"

"—for destruction of property, harassment, slander, and attempted physical injury."

"Slander!" Her voice reached shriek level. "Slander is what *you're* doing right now! And I must question your authority, because what is an Investigator from Sembla doing here? *You* should be held account for your lies! Any *true* Investigator would be investigating what *Villette* has done, with her research, her anti-university selfishness, her *pretend* friendship . . ."

Evna seemed likely to go on for some time—much as she had, I recalled, when I first met her—and I was still tugging my arm away from hers and Mossa pulling steadily at her wrist, but her forearm was unforgivingly tight across my neck and at any moment she could crush my body towards the hand Mossa had lassoed, with its wicked point. And all along, I was peripherally prickling with awareness of the mood around us. Would these people believe Evna, against the evidence of every experience they'd had with Villette? I could already see some scholars looking askance at Mossa; but then, she was a stranger.

A howl of anguish: "Why are you doing this?" Villette, stepping forward from the stunned, wavering group. "I've always tried to be nice to you! I liked you! Why are you so—so absolutely determined to hurt me?"

"*Liked* me? *Nice?*" Evna was screeching now, her arm against my throat vibrating, and I knew that Villette's cry of anguish

.was real and also that she was trying to distract Evna from me, but the escalation was unnervingly unpredictable. "Liked me as a foil for your perfection, I suppose. Nice? Mealy-mouthed, more like it. The first time we had a disagreement, on a small point of theoretical chemistry, I wrote to you, offering my position. And instead of a vigorous defense, a rigorous debate, something that *would actually contribute to scholarship,* you apologized and offered to look again and praised my work and then somehow without ever saying I was wrong continued to claim you were right. How can I win with someone like that? How can I defeat you? Too nice, if it really is niceness. But it's not. It's just a pretense!"

I cut my eyes in Mossa's direction, but I couldn't quite see her without turning my head. Something needed to happen, because I was feeling my effort at calm slide out of my grip. My arm itched with panicky phantom scritches, and I wanted to rub at it, make sure the needle hadn't broken the skin. I wished with desperate invention that I had a metal plate over my bicep to protect it. Or that I had anything, really, to block and blunt the syringe. Anything hard, that I could slide into that gap . . .

And I did. Of course I did. Didn't I? I moved my leg slightly, and was immensely relieved to feel the slight form in my pocket: a laminate or two, forgotten as usual.

"You're not even a proper scholar," Evna was shouting by my ear as I eased my left hand into my pocket. "You're only doing things to help yourself, small mean *practical* things that don't tell us anything new." My fingertips clasped the laminates, at least two and I'd bring them both up; the more I had between me and the toxin-laden needle the happier I'd be. "Clever fiddling jiggery-pokery! Merchandising of the most mercantile sort! And then she pretends she is so disinterested, that she's giving it away out of higher feeling! And you all fall for it!" She panted for a moment, and I adjusted my grip on the laminates, now out of my pocket and folded against my palm.

"What," I said into that brief gap, "about the people that her work is going to help?"

That paused her for a moment, because she hadn't thought for a second about Villette's work as a real thing that had effects on other people. For her it was only a measuring stick or prize ribbon, and *other people* might as well not exist at all.

And in that moment I slid the laminates, small enough squares of safety that she could easily go around, between my arm and the needle.

And in the next moment, Mossa yanked.

It took Evna off balance, and she did jerk back in a way that could have been highly unhealthy for me, but the laminates held in front of that wicked point, my hand trembling with terror lest it bobble off and jam into my fingers, but no, I caught it squarely in the plastic. The syringe didn't stick into the laminates quite as conclusively as I had hoped, but it did judder on them, not sliding smoothly off into my skin, and Evna had loosened her grip on my neck. I was able to throw myself away from her, jostling into several people and immediately, without thinking really, brushing my arm, dropping the laminates back into my pocket so I could feel along my sleeve for any puncture, any telltale wetness of welling blood or poison.

As I looked back up, somewhat relieved and additionally comforted by the solicitous murmurs around me, Mossa flicked the whip-lasso off of Evna's wrist, no doubt hoping to catch her more securely with both arms pinioned to her body. Evna lunged, the syringe raised, directly at me—no, not me, past me, towards Villette. The whip-lasso whistled through the air, but Vao was in the way, railcarring right into Evna and pummeling her, furious sobs tearing through her as she did. Evna stumbled, then pushed herself away again and danced back, somehow a few steps ahead of Vao, who was probably blinded by her tears. Evna still had the syringe in hand, and she laughed, and Petanj was advancing now too, yelling something extremely irate. Vao lunged again, and Evna dodged, and stumbled, and laughed again, breathlessly, as she struggled for her footing, and then—I could see it about to happen, but I couldn't think of what to yell in warning or if I even wanted to—then, she tried to step where there was nothing to step on and fell off the hilltop.

- - - - - - - -

Chapter 35

It was a not-uncommon plot device in Classical narratives of a fairly wide vintage to have antagonists fatally disappear over the side of a cliff (or occasionally into a flooding river, or under a coincidentally falling boulder, etc.), a way of restoring the supposed balance of a supposedly just universe without requiring that the supposed heroes act in any way punitively.

The idea that nature would save us the trouble of doing away with evil people largely went out of fashion when evil people destroyed nature, and the Stortellen hill, however steep, was not a cliff, nor the platform's edge, which really would have been definitive, so that was not the end of Evna's story.

It did provide a convenient pause, however. The effects of her tumble were sufficient to keep Evna well and distracted until the Investigators—Mossa, and the person from the local Investigator's bureau that we'd invited to the party—were able to descend the hill more cautiously and reach her before she caused anyone further harm. Evna had a broken ankle and wrist, a number of scrapes and bruises, and possibly a cracked rib, but she was conscious, quite vocal, and still thrashing angrily at anyone within reach until they restrained her sufficiently to permit transport to the clinic. She had managed to protect the syringe as she fell—either instinctively or because it truly was more important than her own bones to her—and the contents facilitated Hoghly's treatment to the point where he was expected to live, although the doctors suspected there would be some remainder of damage.

We learned all of this when Mossa joined us in Villette's rooms late that evening. At the hill, we waited only to be sure that Evna had survived and would be prevented from threatening us again before Petanj and I hastily closed the party and helped Villette home. I felt a bit bad deserting everyone we had so ultimately invited, but most of the guests seemed either horrified and quite content to retire, or fizzing with the thrill of it all; I could almost hear the excited chisme branching out from the hill through the colorfully lit neighborhoods of Stortellen as the partygoers retreated.

Villette was shaking with shock and I was, in all honesty, not far better. Petanj bundled us both into the sauna, ordered lemonade and tea and bowl after bowl of dumplings, and once we were back in the rooms ordered more food—bean soup with salty cheese and khachapuri, rich and comforting—and set us down with cushions, blankets, and calming music. I managed to lever myself standing at one point to go to the necessary, and passed Petanj in the bedroom screaming into the inside of her elbow. I waited out of sight until she was done, then offered her a long hug. We were both somewhat teary when we returned to the sala, but Villette was beyond noticing, having already fallen asleep on the floor. That set Petanj and me off in a hail of giggles that ended only when Mossa came through the door, looking absolutely wrung out.

She told us the updates, smashing what was left of our food into her mouth in between words. Then I said good night to Petanj and tugged Mossa out the door and into my rooms.

I had thought she would fall asleep immediately, but once I

had closed the door and stood awkwardly before it, she started pacing instead.

When she had completed five of the constrained laps I asked, cautiously, "Are you well?" I wanted to reach for her, hold her, but perhaps what she needed was to expend energy instead.

"It's—Pleiti, for all the time since we parted by the hill, all the way to the clinic, all the way through triage and primary assistance and the Investigator paperwork, all the time that person was inveighing against Villette, attacking every aspect of her character and work, and for what? For a hatred the origins of which even she cannot fully explain." She shook her head. "And of course, as I'm sure you have guessed, Hoghly helped her. He switched off the lights at the cling-rail game, probably planted the scorpion as well, and it was only when he learned that Evna intended dire physical harm that he lost his nerve, told her to stop, and was nearly killed for his trouble. He was perfectly happy to ruin Villette's reputation, waste her years of work, and deprive people of its applications."

"Nice to know that at least some people can still manage a normal academic grudge," I said, and Mossa snorted a reluctant laugh. "Why does this bother you so much?" She was usually well distanced from human vitriol.

She turned and paced again. "I don't know. I suppose . . ."

I waited, but she didn't continue. I waited longer, and then said what I'd been wanting to tell her. "Mossa, I wish . . ." I had been wanting to say it, true, but that didn't make it any less painful to force out. "I wish I could offer you that trust the cousins hold for each other."

She looked away from me. "Pleiti, my dear, it is kind of you to say that; I am . . . honored that you would, but I know it's not possible." A plosive escaped my mouth, but she held up her hand before I could articulate my objection. "Listening to that person—Pleiti, her hate may be turned outward and mine inward, but if we condemn her for her compulsions, can we really forgive mine?"

"Firstly," I said, and had to stop, because the first was that I could not believe, could not countenance, that even in her lowest moments she hated herself so, but I did not believe that would be a useful tack. "Mossa, we do not condemn her for her compulsions, but for her actions."

"And?" She still held her face turned away; I could see the line where her cheekbone had been broken and reknit, and I wanted so desperately to touch her there. "My actions were human, you said so yourself. I hurt you by them, and I wish I could take them back, or promise that it will never happen again, but I cannot, Pleiti, I cannot."

"Consider," I began, and then wished I had time to do so myself. "Consider, Mossa, we say all the time *That was such a human thing to do* or *The utter humanity of that person, thinking they could do that,* but if you think about where the saying comes from . . . well, yes, it reflects that people have done awful things, but also that, well, it's human to do so." Perhaps etymology was not the comforting approach I had hoped. "That is, perhaps you can forgive yourself for being a person who doesn't *always* rise above her human urges."

She scoffed or perhaps snuffled a little, it was hard to tell without seeing her expression.

"But Mossa, truly, if you would listen—when I said I wished I could offer you that trust, what I meant was not that I wished I could trust you, because I *do*—but that I wish you could trust me enough so that . . . so that when you do feel melancholy, you don't mind my seeing it."

She looked at me at last. "You don't want to see it."

"I don't enjoy seeing you sad, no, but I do want to see you, always." It was odd, feeling like the emotionally contained one in a conversation with Mossa; I was partly thrilled by it but also worried that I might break at any moment.

"But . . . it's awful."

"I know, love," I said, letting my hands slide over her hair. "I'll take it anyway."

"But . . . why?"

"Mossa. I don't know what impulse pushes you into melancholy, but I promise you, it is no stronger than that which pulls me to you."

A whisper of a smile. "It sounds like an affliction."

"Perhaps," I said with a sigh, at last letting myself touch her cheek, the corner of her lips, her shoulder. "A deep-abiding fever, but a welcome one."

"Pleiti." Her voice was low, her eyes were low. "I cannot guarantee—I cannot promise you that I will not again find it impossibly difficult to—to—"

I waited, but she seemed unable to find a conclusion to the sentence, or perhaps she had found it but could not admit to it.

"Mossa, you don't have to promise that."

"I wish I could."

"I know."

Petanj was staying on to help Villette pack her things. "And then perhaps," as she told me in an undertone while Villette spoke to Mossa, "a vacation. Somewhere we've never been, I think, something distracting while we wait to hear from other universities or perhaps a firm, if I can get her to apply to some."

Villette had given me a hug and some incoherent thanks; I

got the sense that she was still largely in shock, and I was glad she could get some time away from everyone, including us, and I told Petanj I thought it was an excellent idea. "And of course," I added, feeling inadequate, "as you know I don't have many contacts in the Modern faculty at Valdegeld, but if there's anything I can do . . ."

"Thank you, Pleiti." Petanj paused. "And I mean that, for everything. I won't forget what you did here—"

"Petanj. I flubbed this investigation in half a dozen different ways—"

She stopped me. "No. You came when I asked, and you told me what you weren't sure you could do and tried to do it anyway when I wouldn't listen, and you stood by us and kept trying, even with everything *you* had going on. You didn't leave, even if you wanted to at the beginning. I won't forget, Pleiti. If you ever need anything I can provide, I hope you'll tell me; and even if you don't, I hope we'll see each other a lot more from now on."

I appreciated the last sentence, both because I thought I would enjoy hanging out with Petanj in Valdegeld and because she was giving me a cue to close off a conversation that otherwise could have devolved into mutual escalating assurances of regard, growing sentiment, and inevitably more tears. "I hope so too," I said, wiping a stray bit of moisture from my eye, and then I joined Mossa in setting off for the station.

Both cousins had urged us not to wait, and I found that I was eager to get back, even though I somewhat dreaded the long ride. That dread was misfounded; I had forgotten that Mossa had the private Investigators' railcar, and so we would return in somewhat greater comfort and, greatest comfort of all, privacy.

"I'm amazed they let you keep it so long," I remarked as we boarded, and when Mossa didn't answer immediately I turned to look at her, only to see a surprising color to her cheeks. "Mossa?"

"They didn't, exactly."

"You *stole* the *Investigators'* railcar?"

"Not *stole*," Mossa repudiated indignantly. "Not at all! I simply . . . Well, they will know when I tell them."

I laughed at first—I couldn't help it—but it did not seem funny at all. "Mossa? Truly, is this a problem?"

She threw herself into the seat with a sigh. "In all likelihood they will let me talk them out of it being a problem, especially given the way things have gone here. This *was* a necessary investigation, even if that wasn't entirely clear at the time when I left. But in truth, Pleiti, I am tired of it."

"Are you." She had said something similar before, so it wasn't entirely a shock, but I was still a bit wary of the idea.

"I was thinking of perhaps leaving the Investigators." Mossa's tone was idle, as though this were barely worth remarking on, but I shot up in my seat; I had not expected her to go so far so quickly.

"What? Why?"

She shifted in the plush seat, rare evidence of discomfort from her. "As I said, I am growing . . . dissatisfied. The Investigators are somewhat limited in the types of problems they can take on, for one; they would not have approved my coming here, though Villette was clearly in need. And they have their reasons, and they generally give me margin, but . . . well, I am tired of having to fight for it. And, and, well . . . I find myself having ethical quandaries as well, at times, that I would prefer to resolve with my own principles only, and not the needs of an organization."

I was silent for a time, considering her words relative to my own situation. My discontent with the acadème had certainly

not been ameliorated by observing Villette's trials and trib-
ulations.

On the other hand, there had been some lovely moments,
like that (first!) hill picnic, and the way I had felt my perspective adjust, like tuning the knob of a microscope, every time I
spoke with that Modern anthropologist.

I sighed, and addressed to her the question I always disem-
barked on myself. "What will you do?"

"I *thought . . .*" I saw her sly quarter-smile, realized she was
enjoying my reaction, and relaxed: whatever this change was,
Mossa was in control of it. "I *thought* I might strike out on my
own."

"A . . . what is it? Private investigator?" I conjectured.

She made a mueca. "Independent investigator, let us say. After all," she added, as if I needed any further suasion, "Petanj
came looking for you because she did not *want* to go to the
Investigators; there may be others who feel the same."

"Well." I subsided back into my seat. "That *is* an idea." I
liked the idea of Mossa disassociating herself from the Investigators, and she had always prized independence, but
what if she didn't find enough scope for her abilities? After
all, Mossa needed, or claimed she needed, her work to stave
off the melancholy. Could we manage it if she was unoccupied for any length of time? Or might we find something else
to occupy her?

"I had hoped"—Mossa peered at me with an expression that
I would once have called *arch,* but now saw was fluted with
hints of uncertainty—"that you might assist me in some of my
investigations. When your studies permit, that is."

That (as she might well have known) immediately distracted
me from my concerns. I wasn't sure how much more permis-
sive my studies could become. But on the other hand, if Mossa

was willing to quit, perhaps I could at least be braver about asking for greater latitude. A sabbatical, even.

"You might even write them up."

"Hmm?"

Mossa smiled, some of her confidence returned. "Our investigations. I think they merit the documentation, and you might enjoy it. Now that you have a greater appreciation for Modern studies, that is."

Did I? Mossa raised an eyebrow, and I remembered telling her without telling her about the anthropology, the question of relative worth.

Perhaps I did, then.

"I suppose so," I replied, trying not to sound too grudging or cautious.

"I imagine the university would be quite interested," Mossa went on. "Perhaps nonacademics as well. And you have a sadly underused talent for narrative, Pleiti, you know."

I took a moment to disentangle the idea from the warmth of her praise and found it surprisingly appealing.

"Not a bad thought, Mossa," I agreed, settling in for the long ride home. "Not a bad thought at all."

Acknowledgments

Enormous thanks to my editor, Brent Lambert, who pushed me to make this book better and better with clear-eyed direction about what needed improvement. Thanks also to everyone at Tordotcom and Tor who has worked to bring this book out in the world with a gorgeous and evocative cover, marketing and publicity so that people know about it, copy edits, proofing, design, editorial direction, and managing the whole complex process:

Assistant Editors: Eli Goldman and Matt Rusin

Copy Editor: Christina MacDonald

Proofreader: Jaime Herbeck

Cold Reader: Melanie Sanders

Jacket Designer: Christine Foltzer

Interior Designer: Greg Collins

Managing Editor: Rafal Gibek

Production Editor: Dakota Griffin

Marketing: Sam Friedlander

Publicist: Jocelyn Bright

Editorial Directors: Claire Eddy and Will Hinton

Thank you to all the friends that supported me, in person or virtually, directly or indirectly, through the writing of this book. You are too many to mention but if we had a conversation or WhatsApp chat or Slack conversation or Zoom call in 2023 or 2024, I probably mean you. Thank you to my family, Amari, Daniel, Britt, Dora, Marc, Azul, Paz, Calyx, Lou.

About the Author

Allana Taranto/Ars Magna

MALKA OLDER is a writer, aid worker, and sociologist. She is the executive director of Global Voices, a community of writers, editors, and translators providing community journalism from all over the world and advocating for indigenous and minority languages, media literacy, digital rights, and online freedom of expression. Her science-fiction political thriller *Infomocracy* was named among the best books of 2016 by *Kirkus Reviews*, *The Washington Post*, and *Book Riot*; with sequels, it was a finalist for a Hugo Award. *The Mimicking of Known Successes*, a murder mystery set on Jupiter, was on four best-of lists in 2023 and was a finalist for the Nebula, Hugo, Locus, and Ignyte Awards for Best Novella. She is a faculty associate at Arizona State University, where she teaches on predictive fictions and hosts the Science Fiction Sparkle Salon. Her opinions can be found in *The New York Times*, *The Nation*, and *Foreign Policy*, among other places.